THE
UNMADE
BED

THE UNMADE BED

Sensual Writing on Married Love

Edited by

LAURA CHESTER

HarperCollins*Publishers*

With special thanks to Pancho and Stella Elliston.

Copyright acknowledgments will be found at the end of this book.

HarperCollins books may be purchased for educational, business, or sales promotional use. For information, please call or write: Special Markets Department, HarperCollins Publishers, Inc., 10 East 53rd Street, New York, NY 10022. Telephone: (212) 207-7528; Fax: (212) 207-7222.

FIRST EDITION

Designed by Alma Orenstein

Library of Congress Cataloging-in-Publication Data

The Unmade bed : sensual writing on married love / edited by Laura Chester.—
1st ed.
    p. cm.
  ISBN 0-06-016609-6 (cloth)
   1. Erotic literature, American. 2. Marriage—Literary collections.
3. American literature—20th century. 4. Love stories, American.
5. Love poetry, American. I. Chester, Laura.
PS509.E7U56 1992
810.8′03538—dc20   91-50461

92 93 94 95 96 CG/HC 10 9 8 7 6 5 4 3 2 1

For Mason Rose

two by two in the ark of
the ache of it

—DENISE LEVERTOV

Contents

Part II THE HOT BED

Part III THE MARRIAGE BED

Part IV   THE BOVARY BED

Part V   THE BROKEN BED

Part VI   THE FOREVER BED

Foreword

The image of the well-loved, unmade bed satisfies the soul somehow. The senses respond to this picture of pleasure, with its mess of pillows and feather comforters. A sumptuous disarray of sheets reminds us that the best of all conjugal comforts is rarely nice and neat. So this anthology of contemporary American writing is a literary loosening of the linens, replacing enmity with intimacy, drudgery with enjoyment.

I realize that there are many committed relationships that are not legally bound. Nonetheless, I wanted to explore what was particular to the marriage bed, from the early thrills of "The Newlywed Bed" to the more mature response of husband and wife as they continue to please each other. The themes of long-lasting love and sensuality intertwine throughout this book with many complications, for modern marriage is never static or easy.

Indeed it can almost be frightening when a marriage partner gets up and goes to sleep elsewhere. The bedroom turns from haven to horror, and one can't help but remember Big Mama in *Cat on a Hot Tin Roof*, pointing at the bed and yelling, "When a marriage goes on the rocks, the rocks are *there*, right there!"

Soon enough the question is always asked—how to keep that marriage simmering. I have included a section of particularly erotic writing, "The Hot Bed," where married passion is explored. A loosened familiarity and strengthened trust can give a couple access to a special sensual freedom, a place where fantasy and experiment often play their part.

But the heat of attraction can also turn to disillusionment. We can no longer remain naive about marriage. It is simply not all going to be white roses and doves fluttering about the couple on the cake. On the other hand, commitment is no longer the dirty word it used to be, and monogamy is clearly back in favor.

It also seems to me that the best marriages occur when a couple shares a sense of humor. The poets and prose writers included here bring a mature and yet often humorous perspective found lacking in more sentimental publications that focus on the lifting of the veil.

In this day devoid of ceremony, the wedding itself is one of the few events where we are encouraged to let ritual nourish us, but this anthology focuses more on what follows. What happens when a couple faces the decision—to have or not to have children. "The Marriage Bed" is the smallest of stage sets, where so much of life is enacted, but it can become an even bigger arena when a couple becomes a family.

Up to this point there has been a certain amount of sensual availability, and when husband and wife begin to focus on procreation a new dimension of stress can arise. With an infant in the foreground, it can be more difficult for a married couple to retain their initial ardor. A new kind of love fills the bed, and the bond is both tested and inevitably deepened.

Many American writers reflect the idealistic cultural belief that we should be able to find it all in one person. Either this can lead to a perennial rediscovery, where what we have sown resumes growing, or it can lead to serial monogamy, where the same mistakes are too often played out again and again. While the expectations for marriage increase, there is less religious and moral support to meet the strain. It can seem so much easier to look for new romance, rather than trying to rejuvenate the same with an all too familiar partner.

Issues of fidelity often arise. As Ginette Paris writes in *Pagan Meditations*, "Truth and honesty are among the highest of human qualities. But these virtues, like love, require reciprocity, without which they conspire in the victimization of the one who is honest." Paris goes on to say, "It is the most natural thing in the world for satisfied lovers to be faithful to one another, and without resentment. True fidelity is not promised, it exists." But why not *pledge one's troth* when it is also quite "natural" for married partners to wander. Why can't we deny ourselves at times? Is the marriage sacrament worth self-sacrifice?

Ever since Flaubert created Madame Bovary, adultery has been a central theme of the modern novel. Certainly the temptation to step outside the restrictions of the marriage bed is something most contemporary couples face, and this conflict between security and infidelity is explored in "The Bovary Bed." Here we are offered intense pictures of passionate love while we are also asked to reflect upon the substance of long-held relationships.

John Hawkes in his novel, *The Blood Oranges*, comes closest to describing corporeal pleasures with an almost Continental sensibility not typical of the American mind. Personally, I read him with relief, for his vision seems so nonjudgmental, and his main character, Cyril, is entirely ready to receive the blessings of Eros while continuing to cherish his most desirable wife.

Aphrodite, the goddess of love, often seems to be at odds with the head of the heavenly household, Hera, who rules over marriage, but Ginette Paris relates how both matrons and young married women would go to Aphrodite's temple in order to revive their husbands' ardor. "For sexuality to recover its color and magic," she writes, "it must be associated not with sin and darkness, but with pink and golden beauty, and with Aphrodite's civilizing power . . . Aphrodite assures the reciprocal pleasure of spouses that keeps them together, and without her the marriage remains cold and sterile."

The desire to secure and maintain true sensual love persists today; in fact this urge to find and keep a partner seems universally compelling, but because the idealized merging can never be fully realized, the impulse toward fusion often takes the form of an affair. Too often an inner sense of unity has not been found before it is sought in some outer way, and then the illusion is bound to fail.

This violation of the vows, so sweet at first, can suddenly sour in "The Broken Bed." The delusion of new love replacing the old shifts when the haze of projection wears off and harsh reality sets in. John Updike shows this most masterfully, displaying the heartbreak and disruption when there are children involved. Laurie Colwin writes, "Of all the terrible things in life, living with a divided heart is the most terrible for an honorable person."

There is a darker aspect reflected in the title to this anthology, for when the marriage itself is being unmade, torn apart, when love is no longer there—"Chaos is come again." And yet it seems that we must meet the challenge of these most difficult times, to encounter our deepest selves, our own inner marriage. Even children can no longer be protected from the painful shifts parents thrust upon them as their lives go through upheaval. When a marriage is broken and divorce ensues, it is often likened to major surgery for both parties involved. We limp and lunge through recovery, wondering at times: If marriages are made in heaven, can they be undone here on earth?

Maybe even after divorce the connection continues, but in a different way. Some say this is such a compressed time in history it is not surprising we often experience more than one marriage partner. Or perhaps life has become so speeded up that our desire for change simply mirrors a cultural franticness. Still, second marriages made in the more mature years have less to do with impulse and hormones, and more to do with true companionship.

What propels two people to come together, to stay together, or to make a new marriage for the second time? Hope can triumph over experience, as it does in the final section of this anthology, "The Forever Bed." Here love songs and stories rise to meet the optimism we all need to carry with us. Sometimes the simplicity of mature love can be disarming. Sharon Olds writes that "we are bound to each other with the huge invisible threads of sex, though our sexes themselves are muted, dark and exhausted and delicately crushed . . ." and in Raymond Carver's story, "What We Talk About When We Talk About Love," an old man who has been in a serious automobile accident is miserable because he can't see his wife through the eyeholes of his cast: "Can you imagine? I'm telling you, the man's heart was breaking because he couldn't turn his goddamn head and *see* his goddamn wife." It can make you wonder, in what unseeable ways a husband and wife are truly one.

With practice, the marriage bed can be wonderfully and wantonly unmade, over and over again, but it can be delicious when those white cotton linens are remade too. There is nothing quite so luxurious as the cool smell of wind-dried sheets, sinking into the plush of comforters and pillows, while awaiting the perfect partner.

—LAURA CHESTER

PART I

⚜

THE NEWLYWED BED

A SHORT HISTORY OF SEX

Gary Soto

"Hijo, this is the light switch. No pay you bill, no light, and you make babies with no light." This was Grandmother telling me about sex, or hinting about how sex works. If you don't pay up to the PG&E, then all there is to do at night is lie in bed and make love. This was my first introduction to cause and effect, how one thing leads to another. I was eleven, eating a peach from her tree and watching her water the lawn that was so green it was turning blue. Grandma turned the hose on me, said "Now you be a good boy and play." She squirted me as I ran around the yard with my jaw gripping the peach and my hands covering my eyes.

It was different with my mother, who broke the news about sex while folding clothes in the garage. "You get a girl pregnant, and I'll kill you." No logic there, just a plain simple Soto threat. I felt embarrassed because we had never talked about sex in the family. I didn't know what to do except to stare at the wall and an old calendar of an Aztec warrior eyeballing his girlfriend's breasts. I left the garage, got on my bike, and did wheelies up and down the street, trying my best to get run over because earlier in the week Sue Zimm and I had done things in Mrs. Hancock's shed. It was better, I thought, that I should die on my own than by my mother's hand.

But nothing happened. Sue only got fat from eating and I got skinny from worrying about the Russians invading the United States. I thought very little about girls. I played baseball, looked for work with a rake and poor-boy's grin, and read books about Roman and Greek gods.

During the summer when I was thirteen I joined the YMCA, which was a mistake—grown men swam nude there and stood around with their hands on their hips. It was an abominable exhibition, and I would have asked for my money back but was too shy to approach the person at the desk. Instead, I gave up swimming and jumped on the trampoline, played basketball by myself, and joined the Y "combatives" team, which was really six or seven guys who got together at noon to beat up one another. I was gypped there too. I could have got beaten up for free on my street; instead, I rode my bike three miles to let people I didn't even know do it to me.

But sex kept coming back in little hints. I saw my mother's bra on the bedpost. I heard watery sounds come from the bathroom, and it wasn't water draining from the tub. At lunchtime at school I heard someone say, "It feels like the inside of your mouth." What feels like that? I wanted to ask, but instead ate my sandwich, drank my milk, kicked the soccer ball against the backstop, then went to history, where I studied maps, noting that Russia was really closer than anyone ever suspected. It was there, just next to Alaska, and if we weren't careful they could cross over to America. It would be easy for them to disguise themselves as Eskimos and no one would know the difference, right?

In high school I didn't date. I wrestled for school, the Roosevelt Rough Riders, which was just young guys humping one another on mats. I read books, ate the same lunch day after day, and watched for Mrs. Tuttle's inner thighs above her miniskirt, thinking, "It's like the inside of your mouth." I watched her mouth; her back teeth were blue with shadows, and her tongue was like any other tongue, sort of pink. By then I wanted a girl very badly. Once almost had a girlfriend except she moved away, leaving me to mope around the school campus eating Spam sandwiches with the ugly boys.

My mother's bra on the bedpost, my sister now with breasts that I could almost see beneath her flannel nightgown. One night my brother bragged that he knew for sure it felt like a mouth and in fact was drippy like a marble coated with motor oil. In the dark I scrunched up my face as I remembered cross-eyed Johnny's sock of sweaty marbles, for which I had traded three bottles of red stuff from a chemistry kit.

I had to have a girl. I was desperate. I stuffed Kleenex in my pants pocket and went around with no shirt. I thought of Sue Zimm. But she was now lifting weights and looking more like a guy than a girl, which confused me. I was even more confused when George from George's Barber rubbed my neck and asked me how it felt. I told him it felt OK. He asked if I was going steady, and I told him that I sort of was, except my girl had moved away. He said that it was better that way because sometimes they carried disease you couldn't see for a long time until it was too late. This scared me. I recalled touching Sue when I was thirteen, and wasn't it true that she coughed a lot? Maybe something rubbed onto me. Biting a fingernail, I walked home very slowly, with a picture of a scolding priest playing inside my head. At home I noticed Mom coughing as she stirred a pot of beans. Fear ran its icy fingers up and down my back. I gave my mom the disease, I said to myself, and went to hide in my room and talk to God about becoming a priest.

Years passed without my ever touching a girl. My brother seemed to get them all, especially when we roomed together in college and he would bring them home. I was studying history then, things like, "In 1940 Britain invaded Tibet; in 1911 the first Chinese revolution began; about that time, people began to live longer because they had learned to wash their hands before eating." I would hover over a big book with few pictures while my brother and his girl went at it, howling so loudly that our cat would stir from sleep and saunter to the bedroom door and holler some meows herself.

I was twenty, the only guy left who went around eating Spam sandwiches in college, when I had my first girlfriend who didn't move away. I was a virgin with the girl whom I would marry. In bed I entered her with a sigh, rejoiced "Holy, holy" to my guardian angel, and entered her again with the picture of a tsk-tsking priest playing inside my head.

Twenty years, I thought. It's nothing like cross-eyed Johnny's sock of sweaty marbles. And I couldn't believe what it looked like. While my girl slept, I lowered myself onto an elbow and studied this peach mouth, squeeze thing, little hill with no Christian flag. Pussy was what they called it: a cat that meowed and carried on when you played with it very lightly.

LOVERS OUT OF THIS WORLD

Michael Benedikt

While these two otherwise really quite ordinary people who have just met are talking with one another, what are their eyes doing? These two otherwise really quite ordinary people are leaning forward and looking at each other with such intensity that it's somehow as if their eyes are doing almost all the listening! They speak, as we can already see, with a certain "Luminously Intense Fascination." Already, they are both almost "Out of This World." Already, their conversations seem mostly to consist of preparing vast, immensely intense, temptingly empty spaces, which the other person might just want to fill with something to say. So, increasingly, they both become what we might conventionally call "Mutually Involved." And somehow they both sense how their deepening feelings—which even at the very outset began with such wonderfully easy ecstasies—are continuing to grow and develop. Now, as they move closer, they are leaving this world as we know it! Now they look a whole lot more, even, as they listen—now their ears are doing almost all the talking. . . .

ESTHETIC NUPTIALS

I invited our favorite famous writer, who happens also to be a very close friend, to our wedding. To celebrate, he gets high and cuts up the manuscript of one of his most famous love poems, using a pair of scissors and a paper punch; then he throws it all over us in our hotel room, like confetti! And everybody considers us just one more nice, normal, average couple when I tell them that we spent the first night of our love in a hotel room, crawling around on our hands and knees.

THE ANSWER

Laura Chester

He couldn't decide if he should marry. He was already in his 40's and he'd never been married. People said that he'd be the perfect partner except for this flaw. Being a bachelor had become a stigma. But for the last couple of years he'd had this idea that he wanted to get married. He even spoke of it the first time we met, though he wasn't referring specifically to us.

"What do you think you want?" he asked.

I said I'd be happy with a committed weekend relationship. "I'm not saying I'm against marriage. I just don't believe in divorce."

But he thought he wanted a baby. Everybody else had a baby.

"Even if a child were conceived," I said, "we still wouldn't have to get married."

"Not with me, kid." He believed one got married first.

I began to wonder if he only wanted to get married because he thought that he should. Or if he did get married, would he only be trying it on to see how it felt? Maybe he had doubts about me—if I was the right woman.

He admitted to friends that he wasn't sure. One friend admitted to me this admission. That friend said that I should sit him down and ask *him* to get married.

"No way, José," I answered.

Still, one night I confronted him. "Do you think we'll ever get married?"

"I don't know," he said.

"What don't you know. If I'm the right one?"

"I don't know," he said.

"Well then, why don't you go ask God," I suggested.

He looked at me oddly. He was more likely to ask the cigarette he was smoking.

"Really," I smiled. "Just try it. Go on. Go in the other room and ask."

He got up slowly, then put out the cigarette and left the room.

I sat on the bed, thinking about what God would say to him. I imagined God would say, "Do you think you'll find anyone better? Of course not. So go ahead." I had to believe in that answer.

Suddenly he returned. He was also smiling.

"What did He say?" I asked.

"He said no."

"That's funny." I must have looked disappointed. "That's not what He told me."

"What did He say to you?"

"I guess I didn't really ask," I admitted. "I was only trying to overhear your conversation."

"But," he paused, "I still want to marry you."

I looked at him blankly.

"What do you say?" he asked.

"How can I say yes, if God said no?" I responded.

"He didn't really say No. I just made that up."

"So you didn't really ask?"

"I felt stupid," he admitted.

"That's all right. That's how you're supposed to feel. We *are* stupid."

"*I'm* not," he responded. And then he stood up. I thought he was going to leave. Maybe he had his answer and it was over.

"Where are you going?" I asked.

"In the other room."

"What are you going to do?"

He walked to the door and then looked at me. "I'm going to see if He changed His mind," he said.

AIR

Tom Clark

The sweet peas, pale diapers
Of pink and powder blue, are flags
Of a water color republic.
The soft bed, turned back,
Is a dish to bathe in them.
This early in the morning
We are small birds, sweetly lying
In it. We have soft eyes,
Too soft to separate the parts
Of flowers from the water, or
The angels from their garments.

BIOLOGICAL SUPREMACY

Biology still reigns supreme
In this zone around your hips
Where perception guides me
To perform what is no more than
The expected function after all
But let one thing be understood
I'd be dead if it wasn't for
The inspiration provided by your body
By which I don't mean information
For there are some things one can't know

They are of course the only things worth knowing
And it is the pursuit of these
On an everyday basis no less
Which makes life almost worth living

From: DURING THE REIGN OF THE QUEEN OF PERSIA

JOAN CHASE

She didn't think much of it at first, his still wanting to see her in the evenings, now riding out from the town, but she figured if it was worth it for him to travel that distance to sit and watch the fire, there wasn't any harm in it. He never did have much talk in him, even as a young man. He was out of the plain people, maybe shunned for something, folks suspected, though no one ever knew his past for sure. But Lil was seventeen and the mystery of Jacob's past was part of what intrigued her—she liked the different way he dressed, in shirts of home-dyed indigo and suspenders, and she liked his quaint old-fashioned manners, so at odds with his rough hard look. Tall and lean, he had straight dark hair falling to frame both sides of his face, and the little habit he had of tossing his hair back showed the strong bones clearly and his slanted, long-lashed eyes; and she began to want him in the way you want something you think will occupy you until Doomsday. The wanting felt like enough. There was no mother to warn her, and the other girls she knew were thrilled with Jacob too and envied her, though there was not a father or mother who would have sanctioned his attentions to their daughter. Lil did not desire the children that would come in a marriage; already she knew their demands well enough. But neither did she fancy the endless monotony of cooking for twenty farmhands every day while guarding herself against the teasing, fresh-mouthed married ones who, sensing her loneliness, determined to break her off and make use of her. Better that she should have her own man and the life he would bring her.

She did not deny it—Jacob drew her. He would sit with no words for her before the wood stove, watching her continually with his dark, dark eyes, and she began to feel his hunger, so that often she would get up to put more wood in the stove or busy herself at the sink, just to avoid his eyes and hide her trembling. Every night his eyes were watching, wanting her and letting her see it in him; but he wouldn't touch her, not so much as to let a hand graze hers, though when she would pass close beside him she would hear his breathing, harsh and quick. It nearly drove her wild and her mind came to dwell on him nearly every second. Sometimes, when she lifted up the handle of the stove to stir the wood, the glutted, ashy coals crumbled at the slight touch and something inside her seemed to fragment in the same way.

Lil would plot to forget him. During the day, going about her work, she would plan how she would be gone in the evening when he came. But she never was, and again she'd open the door to him, to his silent and steady need. It got so peculiar between them that neither of them said a word to the other through whole evenings. Lil would back against the wall when he entered and feel the exact dimensions of his body, the insistent presence of his nature. He would pass close to her, nearly touching her, his eyes locking on her, where they would stay fastened through whole evenings. Eons. She forgot time.

It took Hebbard Watson coming to court to change things, or else, Lil thought, they might have jumped together off a cliff to end it, both of them stubborn beyond belief. But Hebbard tied his horse by the gate a time or two, and although Jacob didn't even come to the door, his feelings were plain enough on his face as he stood outside and glared as if he wanted to strangle the horse. Then he took away in the direction of town without a further glance, though Lil was certain he'd known she watched from behind the parlor curtain. After a third evening of that, Lil was in the kitchen in the morning, peeling through a pail of early yellow apples, thinking about Jacob and his silent withholding, when she heard a commotion on the road. She went to the door and then out in the yard, wearing her flowered apron, her braids frayed with curl. Coming along was a wagon team of six horses driven by Jacob, who was so intent on managing things he didn't even glance up to see her, though they both knew she was there, the same as when they sat beside each other at the fire. The piano from her sister's house was strapped onto the wagon bed, swaddled with quilting and roped down to keep it steady. She watched it pass, slow and resounding, the wagon out of sight but the raised dust keeping its memory a little longer, almost like a song resonating, and Lil knew they would be married. It was the only semblance of a proposal that passed between them.

Married, they moved into rooms up over a store on the town's one street and in the secret dark Jacob touched her and moved himself in her, and though she got accustomed to it, a part of her was more aggravated by his touch than satisfied, and then it came to seem more invasion than touch, his need something he took care of, quick and by dark, by daylight no trace left, as though it had never happened between them. Lil felt resentment rising in her; his tacit denial shamed her, convinced her that he felt he stole something from her, was taking without asking. Every night, nearly, he turned to her and held her against him while, rapid and brutish, he moved in her. She began to be sick to her stomach nearly all day long. Afraid that it was a baby coming, dreading it, she lay under his heaviness, which blocked out any trace of light, and thought: Soon I'll be dead.

Then Jacob became more active in his cattle business. He left her alone, stayed away for days at a time, and Lil began going out to the church for prayer services or hymn sings, a little society one way to distract her mind from continual hating and grieving. Jacob didn't like going to church. He'd left his own religion but some of the teaching stayed with him, that fancy music mixed with religion was an abomination. Though he didn't try to stop her, a few times she'd seen him standing outside the church window staring in. Sometimes she was harmonizing with the schoolteacher and she felt it served Jacob right to see her with another man, for she had come to hate him for his neglect.

One night Lil watched him standing outside the church window for a long time. She trembled, knowing something was changing. When she got to their rooms, she felt certain of it, smelled the strong drink in the air though he stayed hidden and didn't answer when she called, "Jacob." She built up the fire because of her shivering, though that wouldn't touch the part that came from fear. She felt him watching her again. Waiting. Wanting her and still hiding it like a thief. She would give him something to want, and she began to remove her clothes, with the fire hot and dancing over the walls, shattering the shadowy places. Lil excited, knowing she was beautiful and that he had never seen her and that it would be a power over him and would cause something between them to change. The thought of it made her fumble over the layered items of winter clothing and her nipples stood erect, chafed by the fabric. It came into her mind that she would take his head in her two hands and place it against her breasts, each one in turn, press his mouth to suck on her, his tongue to lick her nipples. Wanting that all through her, she turned, fully naked, toward the doorway, where she heard his step.

By firelight all his need was finally visible in his face, what she'd longed to see. But there was such anger in it too that she tried to cover herself. When she saw the kindling hatchet raised in his hand, she thought that would be the end of it and part of her was glad, fire staining the blade red before blood. She couldn't get her breath even to scream. He brought the hatchet down then, on the piano, and twice more he struck, to leave it then, anchored in the wood, the piano vibrating as though it shrieked out and held to its voice long afterwards, as though it were her voice. Still she seemed to hear it, after he'd gripped her to bring her hard against him and then carried her to the bed. She couldn't take breath but repeated wordlessly: why didn't you, why didn't you?

THE MARRIAGE MADE IN HEAVEN

Sherril Jaffe

Ann dressed herself all in white. She had attended to the animals and the garden, and now she could head down to Abraham's. The moon was just rising as she reached the highway. It was clear to her that she and Abraham couldn't go on the way they had been going—although it had only been for two weeks. It was too clumsy to have two houses.

She loved her house and had thought that she would die there. She loved the peace and privacy of living in the country. She loved the pure sweet air, she loved to pick her fruit from the trees, and she loved to watch the sequence of flowers appear and disappear each year. Her house was more than a house. It had watched her life unfold. She was finally living in that house the way it wanted to be lived in and the heart of the house had opened. That house had become the world to her.

Now, Ann saw, it was nothing. She would gladly give it up and go to live with Abraham, even in the city.

She parked the car in front of his gate and quickly walked up the path to his cottage. Suddenly she was inside and his arms were around her. Some music was playing. Angels seemed to be singing.

Then he told her what he had been thinking. The separation was too painful.

"Yes," Ann said. She had been thinking the same. She would move to the city.

"I want you to marry me," Abraham said.

"Yes," Ann said. Although she had sworn many times she would never marry again. But this would be different. This would be a marriage made in heaven. And the angels sang.

ABRAHAM TELLS ANN HE LOVES HER

Many times a day Abraham would take Ann in his arms and hug her and kiss her and tell her he loved her. If he left the house for even a few minutes he would kiss her and tell her he loved her. He didn't need to tell her. She knew that he loved her. But the telling was a pleasure. And every day, also, he told her she was beautiful, and when he did she would go and sit in his lap and he would kiss her and tell her he loved her, and she told him she loved him again and again, for her love for him was always welling up and overflowing, and it was a pleasure to be able always to tell him, without embarrassment, how she loved him, without restraint, she loved him, without fear that her love wouldn't be returned. It *was* returned, over and over, and she never got tired of hearing it.

THE GLASS IS BROKEN

The wedding guests began to arrive. Friends and relations. The dead and dying. The cynical. The beaten. The lost. Those who lusted after power. Those who lusted after success. Those whose love had dried to dust. And they gathered from far and near. Even though the storm had begun to roar. The storm which was their lives began to toss. And it blew all about the house. And torrents of rain poured forth while inside all was aglow. All was aglow in the flickering firelight. Under the marriage canopy all was at peace. There Ann and Abraham joined hands, their little dog at their feet. Then William handed Abraham the ring, and Ann and Abraham promised to love each other forever and ever. Everyone looked on, but they just saw each other. And the glass was broken.

THE RECEPTION

Deborah Harding

Friends still say how lovely it was, the candlelight,
the sun setting over the Pacific, it's all
   a blur to me   I never saw the beauty—
Mom's whining about where to sit, didn't I make place cards,
did I know Steven's parents are ignoring her
   she never lets up— I'm at the head table now
some horseshoe type thing arranged so you can't
talk to anyone except whoever's on your right or left—
   When I look up, she's bombing towards me
across the dance floor while the photographer is taking
a picture of Steven and me kissing, the sun going down
   behind us over the golf course—
Anyway, she slaps both hands down on the table, says she
wants coffee, did I forget to tell the hostess, do they
   have decaf— I trudge back towards the kitchen
I think my train unhitches itself two or three times and I
keep tripping over the hem, which is dirty as hell by now—
   When I get there, the ladies are already wheeling out
carts with two hundred cups of coffee on them
so I go back to the table   try eating a crab puff
and here she comes again— how will she get all those
gifts to the car, do I think they have a dolly somewhere?
   We hadn't even cut the big mousse cake yet—
I thought the party was just starting and she's worried
about leaving— The band is playing so loud I can't hear anybody
not that one person comes up to congratulate us
   like we were royalty or something   like it wasn't OK
to cross over to our side of the dance floor—
   I was so lonely, Steven off mingling like we were supposed
to— I could see him out there getting kissed by relatives,

shaking hands with the men— I'm waiting for my Dad
or even his Dad to come for me,
   I guess mostly I wanted my Dad
so I keep waiting, the best man's telling me something
about his first cadaver at med school   then a couple I don't
   even know moves onto the floor— I want to tell them
go back, not yet you idiots, me and Steven
are supposed to have the first dance—
   the singer's wailing "Stand by Your Man"   I can hardly
swallow, but now it is time for the bride and groom dance
   so we go out there   Steven's cousin glaring at us,
   the one who tried to get me in bed that time when he
was away— she's out there doing voodoo on me . . .
   I'm staring into Steven's eyes, it's almost romantic
then he says his Mom has diarrhea, Grandad's pissed
'cuz nobody took a picture of him— Godfather Jimmy
cuts in, holds me so tight I swear I feel a hard-on pressing
into my thigh— Drum roll   time to cut the cake
Steven feeds me, I feed him, chunks of mousse plop on my gown
His uncle makes a toast   who knows what he said   things are
winding down now, just family, no one to throw my garter to
   so I slide it off   geez I'm not even on a balcony
or anything— fling it to Steven's little brother, big deal—
   Almost time to leave, here comes the cousin again
says how glad she is I'm finally part of the family—
it's all I can do to make it to the car, not in the mood now,
   dark out, as Steven gathers up my train like
something I should cherish.

THE SONG OF LOVE

Janet Hamill

Magnificent angel. in your white convulsive arms
I'm a delicate green bird of song
singing in praise of her cage. my ankles
lend themselves willingly to your slave bracelets

I'm a succulent pink dessert. the edible fruit
of a jungle flower. begging to be eaten
in your white convulsive arms
magnificent angel. I'm a dancing flame

clinging to your eyes of blue mirrored glass
my desire renews itself endlessly
in waves breaking over my anchored waist
waves that smell of fish and sweat

the intimate odors of a summer night
wrap around me. in your white convulsive arms
magnificent angel. I'm lifted up with moonlight bleaching my skin
to the measureless ocean in the stars

MARRIAGE

Amy Gerstler

Romance is a world, tiny and curved, reflected in a spoon. Perilous as a clean sheet of paper. Why begin? Why sully and crumple a perfectly good surface? Lots of reasons. Sensuality, need for relief, curiosity. Or it's your mission. You could blame the mating instinct: a squat little god carved from shit-colored wood. NO NO NO. It's not dirty. The plight of desire, a longing to consort, to dally, bend over, lose yourself . . . be rubbed till you're shiny as a new-minted utensil. A monogrammed butterknife, modern pattern or heirloom? It's a time of plagues and lapses, rips in the ozone layer's bridal veil. One must take comfort in whatever lap one can. He wanted her to bite him, lightly. She wanted to drink a quart of water and get to bed early. Now that's what I call an exciting date. In the Voudoun religion, believers can marry their gods. Some nuns wed Jesus, but they have to cut off all their hair first. He's afraid he'll tangle in it, trip and fall. Be laid low. Get lost. Your face: lovely and rough as a gravestone. I kiss it. I do.

In a more pragmatic age many brides' veils later served as their burying shrouds. After they'd paid their dues to Mother Nature, they commanded last respects. Wreaths, incense, and satin in crypts. In India, marriage of children is common. An army of those who died young marches through your studio this afternoon to rebuke you for closing your eyes to the fullness of the world. But when they get close enough to read what's written on your forehead, they realize you only did what was necessary. They hurriedly skip outside to bless your car, your mangy lawn, and the silver floss tree which bows down in your front yard.

His waiting room is full of pious heathens and the pastor calls them into his office for counseling, two by two. Once you caressed me in a restaurant by poking me with a fork. In those days, any embrace was a strain. In the picture in this encyclopedia, the Oriental bride's headdress looks like a paper boat. The caption says: "Marriage in Japan is a formal, solemn ceremony." O bride, fed and bedded down on a sea of Dexatrim, tea, rice, and quinine, can you guide me? Is the current swift? Is there a bridge? What does this old fraction add up to: you over me? Mr. Numerator on top of Miss Denominator? The two of us divided by a line from a psalm, a differing line of thinking, the thin bloodless line of your lips pressed together. At the end of the service, guests often toss rice or old shoes. You had a close shave, handsome. Almost knocked unconscious by a flying army boot, while your friends continued to converse nonchalantly under a canopy of mosquito netting. You never recognized me, darling, but I knew you right away. I know my fate when I see it. But it's bad luck to lay eyes on each other before the appropriate moment. So look away. Even from this distance, and the chasm is widening (the room grows huge), I kiss your old and new wounds. I kiss you. I do.

THE PREGNANT BRIDE

Larry Woiwode

Chris and Ellen were spending their honeymoon at a lodge in the Michigan woods, and this evening when the meal was finished, he uncovered the furniture in the main room and, under her supervision, began to scoot it back and forth over the board floor, from one corner of the enormous room to the other, arranging and rearranging it to suit her whims. There were several large pieces: three or four stuffed chairs, a plank banquet table, a daybed, a couch. The furniture rumbled and thundered over the floor, and it gave him a strange feeling to make so much noise, with no one present but her, in this big building so far from other human life. At last she was satisfied. He decided to add a touch of his own, and went to the piano and took the bearskin rug off its top. He carried it across the room and placed it where he felt it properly belonged, on the floor in front of the fireplace.

"Oh," she said. "We never put that down."

"Why's that?"

"Grandpa says we'd wear all the hair off. He wants everything preserved the way it was. He's very fastidious."

"Oh."

"Leave it if you want."

"No."

"I like it there," she said.

"No. Better not."

He carried the unwieldy thing back to the piano. She stretched out on the couch in front of the fireplace, turned on a floor lamp, and started leafing through one of the books from the library. He stared at her for a while, juggling the bearskin, then walked back with it and spread it on the floor. She gave him a curious look, and said, "I thought you decided not to put it there."

"I did. But we must, absolutely must, have it down for tonight."

"Why?"

"To use it," he said, and grinned.

She blushed and turned back to her book.

"It's in all the movies," he said.

He went to a wicker hamper next to the fireplace and picked out the thinnest twigs, pencil-size and smaller, snapped them into even lengths, and laid them across the andirons. He broke up more twigs of the same size and placed them in a crosshatch over the first layer. He repeated this procedure once more. He broke up larger, dowel-sized branches and laid them in a row over the little ones, and of these he also made a three-layer crosshatch. He put down a row of larger limbs that were sawed to length. He took up kindling the size of his wrist, nine pieces of it (an odd number being the best for a fire), and laid down five sticks, then laid the remaining four over the gaps he'd left between the first pieces. He took up a scroll of birch bark, tore it into strips, and made a pyramid of the strips on the floor of the fireplace, beneath the wood on the andirons. He lit a piece of newspaper, held it as flat as he could at the top of the fireplace, near the flue, and let it burn down until he had to release it. The orange and black papery ash hovered for a while above the wood, dipping down, winging up, and in a sudden swirl was sucked up the chimney. A good draft. He put a match to the birch bark and when the twigs, the branches, the limbs, and the sticks of kindling were lit and burning, reporting and spouting sparks, and the flames had begun to climb the chimney, he laid on three logs.

He sat on the bearskin rug and watched the flames, feeling his cheeks grow warm and his pants legs heat up over his shins. She rose from the couch and came and sat beside him. He lit a cigarette and smoked it slow, handing it to her for drags, and when it was smoked down he flipped it into the fire. She took him by the arm and they stared at the flames.

"What books did you check out?" he asked.

"The usual ones. Birds. Trees. Plants."

"No others?"

"No. Why?"

"I thought—" He shrugged his shoulders. "Birds, trees, bees"—he made a face and altered his voice to cover his uneasiness—"uh, duh, you know. Babies."

THE NEWLYWED BED

"Oh." She swung her legs around and lay down and put her head on his lap, placing her hands, clasped as in prayer, under her cheek. "I don't think about that."

"Why not? Shouldn't you?"

She lifted her shoulders and snuggled closer; she obviously didn't want to talk about it.

"What did the doctor say?"

"What doctor?"

"What doctor? The one I sent you to."

"Oh, him. Nothing much."

"He didn't give you any instructions?"

"About what?"

"*You* know." He was getting irritated.

"No. Nothing."

"Well, what did he say? He must have said something."

"Just that I should be myself, but go easy. Drink a lot of milk. No horseback riding. And that if nothing came up, I wouldn't have to see another doctor for about two months."

"That's it? It's that simple?"

"He did mention that most women aren't in the shape I'm in. He said I was very muscular."

"What did he mean?"

"Inside."

"Inside!"

"He said I have strong walls."

"He said *that?*"

"Yes."

"The bastard!"

Her mellow self-satisfied laughter matched the play of the flames. He lit another cigarette and smoked it down. He tossed it into the fireplace. He looked at her face and ran his hand over her hair, which was hot from the fire, and drew gold strands of it back from her cheek. He laid the back of his fingertips on her cheek and it seemed more hot (*her* temperature?) than her hair. Then he turned, easing her head onto the rug, and lay beside her. She moved against him. He kissed her, and for the first time he felt that he was married, that he was with a married woman, his wife, and he savored and prolonged each stage to fill himself with the experience, feeling the familiar shape of her mouth, teeth behind lips, the tongue, the curve of her rib cage and firm stomach, her hip, the strength of her legs, the cords in her inner thighs, and then the same curves with no clothes, the closer curves, the aroma of her skin, the feel and texture of it when she was ready, the taste, savoring that, her breasts aroused, one cool and one hot from the fire and both tipped up to him, their texture, tips, stretching out her arms to feel them taut against him, and he would enter for the first time, now, his wife, wet, the strong legs, walls, and then in a blossoming in his upper consciousness knowing she held his child, a life inside her, there, the nudge of muscle, that kiss, the light of the fire over her hair, her eyes, thighs rising, the points of her hair like stars, like Orion, Oh, love, love, Oh, El, Oh, love, "Oh, El."

"Yes, Chris, yes."

Holding him tight inside, she whispered, "That's the first time you've talked to me like that since we've been back together."

HOLD

David Giannini

A shadow
the texture of star moss
and lightly
you slip through
the placket of your dress
its wrinkled sun
on a tom-thumb lawn.
A lake the color of deep fern
and after swimming you shake off
its seed
after your moist strip
your face
like peeled birch
rubbed with oil.

Your breasts without tan
I moisten
your dark inland
open
I feel where the lake brushed
kiss where
the lake washed
the damp walls
around the warming pool
the wet stone
swelling and
hold (Hold) come around me now.

I GO BACK TO MAY 1937

Sharon Olds

I see them standing at the formal gates of their colleges,
I see my father strolling out
under the ochre sandstone arch, the
red tiles glinting like bent
plates of blood behind his head, I
see my mother with a few light books at her hip
standing at the pillar made of tiny bricks with the
wrought-iron gate still open behind her, its
sword-tips black in the May air,
they are about to graduate, they are about to get married,
they are kids, they are dumb, all they know is they are
innocent, they would never hurt anybody.
I want to go up to them and say Stop,
don't do it—she's the wrong woman,
he's the wrong man, you are going to do things
you cannot imagine you would ever do,
you are going to do bad things to children,
you are going to suffer in ways you never heard of,
you are going to want to die. I want to go
up to them there in the late May sunlight and say it,
her hungry pretty blank face turning to me,
her pitiful beautiful untouched body,
his arrogant handsome blind face turning to me,
his pitiful beautiful untouched body,
but I don't do it. I want to live. I
take them up like the male and female
paper dolls and bang them together
at the hips like chips of flint as if to
strike sparks from them, I say
Do what you are going to do, and I will tell about it.

THE NEWLYWED BED
27

THE WEDDING

Joy Williams

Elizabeth always wanted to read fables to her little girl but the child only wanted to hear the story about the little bird who thought a steam shovel was its mother. They would often argue about this. Elizabeth was sick of the story. She particularly disliked the part where the baby bird said, "You are not my mother, you are a *snort*, I want to get out of here!" Elizabeth was thirty and the child was five. At night, at the child's bedtime, Sam would often hear them complaining bitterly to one another. He would preheat the broiler for dinner and freshen his drink and go out and sit on the picnic table. In a little while, the screen door would slam and Elizabeth would come out, shaking her head. The child had frustrated her again. The child would not go to sleep. She was upstairs, wandering around, making "cotton candy" in her bone-china bunny mug. "Cotton candy" was Kleenex sogged in water. Sometimes Elizabeth would tell Sam the story that she had prepared for the child. The people in Elizabeth's fables were always looking for truth or happiness and they were always being given mirrors or lumps of coal. Elizabeth's stories were inhabited by wolves and cart horses and solipsists.

"Please relax," Sam would say.

At eleven o'clock every night, Sam would take a double Scotch on the rocks up to his bedroom.

"Sam," the child called, "have some of my cotton candy. It's delicious."

Elizabeth's child reminded Sam of Hester's little Pearl even though he knew that her father, far from being the "Prince of the Air," was a tax accountant. Elizabeth spoke about him often. He had not shared the 1973 refund with her even though they had filed jointly and half of the year's income had been hers. Apparently the marriage had broken up because she often served hamburgers with baked potatoes instead of french fries. Over the years, astonishment had turned to disapproval and then to true annoyance. The tax accountant told Elizabeth that she didn't know how to do anything right. Elizabeth, in turn, told her accountant that he was always ejaculating prematurely.

"Sam," the child called, "why do you have your hand over your heart?"

"That's my Scotch," Sam said.

Elizabeth was a nervous young woman. She was nervous because she was not married to Sam. This desire to be married again embarrassed her, but she couldn't help it. Sam was married to someone else. Sam was always married to someone.

Sam and Elizabeth met as people usually meet. Suddenly, there was a deceptive light in the darkness. A light that reminded the lonely blackly of the darkness. They met at the wedding dinner of the daughter of a mutual friend. Delicious food was served and many peculiar toasts were given. Sam liked Elizabeth's aura and she liked his too. They danced. Sam had quite a bit to drink. At one point, he thought he saw a red rabbit in the floral centerpiece. It's true, it was Easter week, but he worried about this. They danced again. Sam danced Elizabeth out of the party and into the parking lot. Sam's car was nondescript and tidy except for a bag of melting groceries.

Elizabeth loved the way he kissed. He put his hand on her throat. He lay his tongue deep and quiet inside her mouth. He filled her mouth with the decadent Scotch and cigarette flavor of the tragic middle class. On the other hand, when Sam saw Elizabeth's brightly flowered scanty panties, he thought he'd faint with happiness. He was a sentimentalist.

"I love you," Elizabeth thought she heard him say.

Sam swore that he heard Elizabeth say, "Life is an eccentric privilege."

This worried him but not in time.

They began going out together frequently. Elizabeth promised to always take the babysitter home. At first, Elizabeth and Sam attempted to do vile and imaginative things to one another. This was culminated one afternoon when Sam spooned a mound of pineapple-lime

Jell-O between Elizabeth's legs and began to eat. At first, of course, Elizabeth was nervous. Then she stopped being nervous and began watching Sam's sweating, good-looking shoulders with real apprehension. Simultaneously, they both gave up. This seemed a good sign. The battle is always between the pleasure principle and the reality principle, is it not? Imagination is not what it's cracked up to be. Sam decided to forget the petty, bourgeois rite of eating food out of one another's orifices for a while. He decided to just love Elizabeth instead.

"Did you know that Charles Dickens wanted to marry Little Red Riding Hood?"
"What!" Sam exclaimed, appalled.
"Well, as a child he wanted to marry her," Elizabeth said.
"Oh," Sam said, curiously relieved.

Elizabeth had a house and her little girl. Sam had a house and a car and a Noank sloop. The houses were thirteen hundred miles apart. They spent the winter in Elizabeth's house in the South and they drove up to Sam's house for the summer. The trip took two and one half days. They had done it twice now. It seemed about the same each time. They argued on the Baltimore Beltway. They bought peaches and cigarettes and fireworks and a ham. The child would often sit on the floor in the front seat and talk into the air-conditioning vent.
"Emergency," she'd say. "Come in please."

On the most recent trip, Sam had called his lawyer from a Hot Shoppe on the New Jersey Turnpike. The lawyer told him that Sam's divorce had become final that morning. This had been Sam's third marriage. He and Annie had seemed very compatible. They tended to each other realistically, with affection and common sense. Then Annie decided to go back to school. She became interested in animal behaviorism. Books accumulated. She was never at home. She was always on field trips, in thickets or on beaches, or visiting some ornithologist in Barnstable. She began keeping voluminous notebooks. Sam came across the most alarming things written in her hand.

Mantids are cannibalistic and males often literally lose their heads to the females. The result, as far as successful mating is concerned, is beneficial, since the subesophageal ganglion is frequently removed and with it any inhibition on the copulatory center; the activities of male abdomen are carried out with more vigor than when the body was intact.

"Annie, Annie," Sam had pleaded. "Let's have some people over for drinks. Let's prune the apple tree. Let's bake the orange cake you always made for my birthday."

"I have never made an orange cake in my life," Annie said.

"Annie," Sam said, "don't they have courses in seventeenth-century romantic verse or something?"

"You drink too much," Annie said. "You get quarrelsome every night at nine. Your behavior patterns are severely limited."

Sam clutched his head with his hands.

"Plus you are reducing my ability to respond to meaningful occurrences, Sam."

Sam poured himself another Scotch. He lit a cigarette. He applied a mustache with a piece of picnic charcoal.

"I am Captain Blood," he said. "I want to kiss you."

"When Errol Flynn died, he had the body of a man of ninety," Annie said. "His brain was unrealistic from alcohol."

She had already packed the toast rack and the pewter and rolled up the Oriental rug.

"I am just taking this one Wanda Landowska recording," she said. "That's all I'm taking in the way of records."

Sam, with his charcoal mustache, sat very straight at his end of the table.

"The variations in our life have ceased to be significant," Annie said.

Sam's house was on a hill overlooking a cove. The cove was turning into a saltwater marsh. Sam liked marshes but he thought he had bought property on a deep-water cove where he could take his boat in and out. He wished that he were not involved in the process of his cove turning into a marsh. When he had first bought the place, he was so excited about everything that he had a big dinner party at which he served *soupe de poisson* using only the fish he had caught himself from the cove. He could not, it seems, keep himself from doing this each year. Each year, the *soupe de poisson* did not seem as nice as it had the year before. About a year before Annie left him, she suggested that they should probably stop having that particular dinner party. Sam felt flimflammed.

When Sam returned to the table in the Hot Shoppe on the New Jersey Turnpike after learning about his divorce, Elizabeth didn't look at him.

"I have been practicing different expressions, none of which seem appropriate," Elizabeth said.

"Well," Sam said.

"I might as well be honest," Elizabeth said.

Sam bit into his egg. He did not feel lean and young and unencumbered.

"In the following sentence, the same word is used in each of the missing spaces, but pronounced differently." Elizabeth's head was bowed. She was reading off the place mat. "Don't look at yours now, Sam," she said, "the answer's on it." She slid his place mat off the table, spilling coffee on his cuff in the process. "*A prominent and——— man came into a restaurant at the height of the rush hour. The waitress was———to serve him immediately as she had———.*"

Sam looked at her. She smiled. He looked at the child. The child's eyes were closed and she was moving her thumb around in her mouth as though she were making butter there. Sam paid the bill. The child went to the bathroom. An hour later, just before the Tappan Zee Bridge, Sam said, *"Notable."*

"What?" Elizabeth said.

"Notable. That's the word that belongs in all three spaces."

"You looked," Elizabeth said.

"Goddamn it," Sam yelled. "I did not look!"

"I knew this would happen," Elizabeth said. "I knew it was going to be like this."

It is a very hot night. Elizabeth has poison ivy on her wrists. Her wrists are covered with calamine lotion. She has put Saran Wrap over the lotion and secured it with a rubber band. Sam is in love. He smells the wonderfully clean, sun-and-linen smell of Elizabeth and her calamine lotion.

Elizabeth is going to tell a fairy story to the child. Sam tries to convince her that fables are sanctimonious and dully realistic.

"Tell her any one except 'The Frog King,' " Sam whispers.

"Why can't I tell her that one?" Elizabeth says. She is worried.

"The toad stands for male sexuality," Sam whispers.

"Oh Sam," she says. "That's so superficial. That's a very superficial analysis of the animal-bridegroom stories."

"I am an animal," Sam growls, biting her softly on the collar-bone.

"Oh Sam," she says.

Sam's first wife was very pretty. She had the flattest stomach he had ever seen and very black, very straight hair. He adored her. He was faithful to her. He wrote both their names on the flyleaves of all his books. They were married for six years. They went to Europe. They went to Mexico. In Mexico they lived in a grand room in a simple hotel opposite a square. The trees in the square were pruned in the shape of perfect boxes. Each night, hundreds of birds would come home to the trees. Beside the hotel was the shop of a man who made coffins. So many of the coffins seemed small, for children. Sam's wife grew depressed. She lay in bed for most of the day. She pretended she was dying. She wanted Sam to make love to her and pretend that she was dying. She wanted a baby. She was all mixed up.

Sam suggested that it was the ions in the Mexican air that made her depressed. He kept loving her but it became more and more difficult for them both. She continued to retreat into a landscape of chaos and warring feelings.

Her depression became general. They had been married for almost six years but they were still only twenty-four years old. Often they would go to amusement parks. They liked the bumper cars best. The last time they had gone to the amusement park, Sam had broken his wife's hand when he crashed head-on into her bumper car. They could probably have gotten over the incident had they not been so bitterly miserable at the time.

* * *

In the middle of the night, the child rushes down the hall and into Elizabeth and Sam's bedroom.

"Sam," the child cries, "the baseball game! I'm missing the baseball game."

"There is no baseball game," Sam says.

"What's the matter? What's happening!" Elizabeth cries.

"Yes, yes," the child wails. "I'm late, I'm missing it."

"Oh what is it!" Elizabeth cries.

"The child is having an anxiety attack," Sam says.

The child puts her thumb in her mouth and then takes it out again. "I'm only five years old," she says.

"That's right," Elizabeth says. "She's too young for anxiety attacks. It's only a dream." She takes the child back to her room. When she comes back, Sam is sitting up against the pillows, drinking a glass of Scotch.

"Why do you have your hand over your heart?" Elizabeth asks.

"I think it's because it hurts," Sam says.

Elizabeth is trying to stuff another fable into the child. She is determined this time. Sam has just returned from setting the mooring for his sailboat. He is sprawled in a hot bath, listening to the radio.

Elizabeth says, "There were two men wrecked on a desert island and one of them pretended he was home while the other admitted—"

"Oh Mummy," the child says.

"I know that one," Sam says from the tub. "They both died."

"This is not a primitive story," Elizabeth says. "Colorless, anticlimactic endings are typical only of primitive stories."

Sam pulls his knees up and slides underneath the water. The water is really blue. Elizabeth had dyed curtains in the tub and stained the porcelain. Blue is Elizabeth's favorite color. Slowly, Sam's house is turning blue. Sam pulls the plug and gets out of the tub. He towels himself off. He puts on a shirt, a tie and a white summer suit. He laces up his sneakers. He slicks back his soaking hair. He goes into the child's room. The lights are out. Elizabeth and the child are looking at each other in the dark. There are fireflies in the room.

"They come in on her clothes," Elizabeth says.

"Will you marry me?" Sam asks.

"I'd love to," she says.

Sam calls his friends up, beginning with Peter, his oldest friend. While they have been out of touch, Peter has become a soft contact lenses king.

"I am getting married," Sam says.

There is a pause, then Peter finally says, "Once more the boat departs."

It is harder to get married than one would think. Sam has forgotten this. For example, what is the tone that should be established for the party? Elizabeth's mother believes that a wedding cake is very necessary. Elizabeth is embarrassed about this.

"I can't think about that, Mother," she says. She puts her mother and the child in charge of the wedding cake. At the child's suggestion, it has a jam center and a sailboat on it.

Elizabeth and Sam decide to get married at the home of a justice of the peace. Her name is Mrs. Custer. Then they will come back to their own house for a party. They invite a lot of people to the party.

"I have taken out 'obey,' " Mrs. Custer says, "but I have left in 'love' and 'cherish.' Some people object to the 'obey.' "

"That's all right," Sam says.

"I could start now," Mrs. Custer says. "But my husband will be coming home soon. If we wait a few moments, he will be here and then he won't interrupt the ceremony."

"That's all right," Sam says.

They stand around. Sam whispers to Elizabeth, "I should pay this woman a little something, but I left my wallet at home."

"That's all right," Elizabeth says.

"Everything's going to be fine," Sam says.

They get married. They drive home. Everyone has arrived, and some of the guests have brought their children. The children run around with Elizabeth's child. One little girl has long red hair and painted green nails.

"I remember you," the child says. "You had a kitty. Why didn't you bring your kitty with you?"

"That kitty bought the chops," the little girl says.

Elizabeth overhears this. "Oh my goodness," she says. She takes her daughter into the bathroom and closes the door.

"There is more than the seeming of things," she says to the child.

"Oh Mummy," the child says, "I just want my nails green like that girl's."

"Elizabeth," Sam calls. "Please come out. The house is full of people. I'm getting drunk. We've been married for one hour and fifteen minutes." He closes his eyes and leans his forehead against the door. Miraculously, he enters. The closed door is not locked. The child escapes by the same entrance, happy to be freed. Sam kisses Elizabeth by the shower stall. He kisses her beside the sink and before the full-length mirror. He kisses her as they stand pressed against the windowsill. Together, in their animistic embrace, they float out the window and circle the house, gazing down at all those who have not found true love, below.

WIFE

Norman Fischer

Of all the women
　　Of all the world
Delicate
　　In their various encasings
Of body
　　Of mind
This one
　　Bent asleep before me
On the bed
　　Is the one through whom all must be loved
As I have promised

PART II

THE HOT BED

FIRST KISS

Joan Logghe

Last week was our first kiss. We've been married eighteen years, really only seventeen, but I throw on a year for that kiss. He told me recently, We should go to a sex therapist. I asked why. Because you don't kiss me enough.

So I kissed him hard last week and I tasted, first, his mother. The time he threw the table over in a fight with her, because she brought to his attention all the wrongs of a dozen years in a mental list she'd kept. There was the time he was late for milking, how he read too much, the way he loved the work of Sigmund Freud, which she pronounced "Frood." We lived on the family dairy farm in Wisconsin in early marriage, and she'd relish telling me the crimes of his childhood; the time he cut the tail off the puppy, the time he and his brother crammed a cat in the mailbox. She wondered if I would have married this man if I'd heard about the boy he was.

I learned she used to tell her kids, The devil has got into you. I got it, in that kiss. Why he had a stutter as a child. He had such a blocked tongue that by high school he could barely speak in public and had no one to turn to but himself. He got a record of T. S. Eliot from the library and read aloud with it, recited until he learned elocution, alone on a Wisconsin dairy farm, practicing in the barn. His voice, ever after, has a moo in the vowels and a British accent when he reads me poems.

When you know somebody that deeply, so many bodies lie in the bed alongside. We need a king-sized bed to contain them. Our bed is full of farmland, two hundred acres including the back pasture. And you know, that is where the best sex always is, despite the scent of cows. The Jungians say that in bed there are always at least four people, invisible man and dark surly woman. But in our bed there is a herd—siblings and offspring, his parents, my parents, and the church, full of incense and Latin. My temple, so old it's got the history of God engraved in the bedsheets. It isn't a bed, it's a text, a Russian novel.

And so when I kissed him in our bed, that artifact of repeated love, I finally heard the words, all the lost words. I got the clinkers and the home runs that I never could catch. I got the ashamed red ones and the unexclaimed love words all in a kiss. I ate shame. His shame I could taste in crooked teeth no orthodontist ever saw. He was not perfect and I'd taught him that, too. I counted his not-perfects as a mother does the digits. Only I'm not his mother. Maybe it was then I separated from her.

When we fight he says, I want you to treat me like anyone else. I say, That's impossible. We're married.

He says, If we weren't, maybe we'd be good friends, maybe even lovers.

When I kissed him hard from on top, I got it, it clicked; boyhood, fall from the barn leaving a scar on his back. I smelled coffee his grandmother left on the stove all day. I felt the work ethic squeeze him tight for being a thinker, and then lambaste him for wasting time in bed. And I saw him riding the Ford tractor, plowing for corn with Freud propped in his lap.

By kissing, I begged, Drop down, love, into the heart and live here with me. Drop lower and lower into the deep river of sex and I'll kiss you more. Down out of your large skull, huge as Cro-Magnon, wide as acreage. I'll kiss you like last week when I didn't say a thing, but got a message in a bottle from across the vast ocean of marriage. That is my vow, our future.

From: BEAVER TALES

Elizabeth Hay

A Blood Indian tale. A man and a woman were camped on the shore of a lake and the man was always away hunting. In his absence a beaver came out of the water and made love to the woman. Day after day the beaver returned to her until she finally went away with him. The man came home. He looked for the woman and saw her trail going down to the shore. After a time she came up out of the water "heavy with child." She gave birth to a beaver, which she kept at the head of her bed in a bowl of water.

※

I heard the splash. By the time I reached them he was sitting at the edge of the pond, cradling a woman between his legs.

They got up as I appeared, and we moved in the same direction to the same spot: a large slab of rock in the sun. I sat down with my daughter. He turned and smiled at us both, but especially the little girl. Is the young lady going swimming? he asked. The young lady is, but the old lady isn't. He laughed. Nor will this one, he said of the woman beside him. The woman wore shorts and a sleeveless shirt. Her hair was pulled back and held in place by a large clip. Her legs were scratched in several places, which made the skin look even whiter, more discolored, the veiny patches of middle age. She looked to be in her early forties.

He was tanned. His legs were very brown up to his shorts line, and paler from there to his briefs—all he was wearing. He was about fifty. European, from his accent, even more from his manner: the relaxed way he turned and smiled, the straight white teeth, the eyes, the charm.

I didn't notice his hands, or how much hair was on his chest—things I usually notice right away.

He swam again. The edge of the pond was muddy and rocky, deep with rotting leaves. Is it cold? I asked. Fresh, he answered. He felt his way gingerly before throwing himself out over the lily pads into deeper water.

While he was swimming I watched the woman. He had placed his faded cut-offs against the rock to soften it for her back. She rearranged them, leaned back for a moment, then sat up again and fished for a cigarette. She didn't look my way or watch him swim, even when he swam back towards her. She looked so unhappy. Her body had the loose, unmuscled quality of someone who watches what she eats but doesn't exercise. I imagined them in bed together—he so relaxed, she with that look of strain acquired over many years.

He came out of the water, climbed the rocky slope, put his wet hands on her thighs and stroked them. She twisted away, but laughed as she did so. I love you, he said. That's not a good enough excuse, she answered. Then he came around behind her and settled himself on the rock, pulling her between his legs. He lifted up the back of her blouse and pressed against her. She didn't resist as I had expected but leaned into the embrace.

I thought of him smelling of the lake, and her skin acquiring that smell. Of her tasting his skin, and tasting the lake. Of her hands, as they explored, exploring water. Where we were, in that woods with light breaking through evergreens, we seemed to be under water: something about the light, speckled on needle-deep ground, something liquid.

He did all this—pressing his wet cock against her back, wrapping his arms around her, kissing her neck—as I sat a few feet away. That seemed the most European thing of all.

After we left I imagined him going back to the car, stripping off his briefs, putting on his shorts, going the rest of the day without underwear. Was it that thought that made me shed my own? I walked naked under my sundress, the air lovely, soft, stroking.

✳

When Samuel Hearne lived on the shores of Hudson Bay in the late 1700s, trading furs and exploring, he had, apparently, a number of Indian women as lovers. Hearne doesn't describe the women. He describes the beavers who were their pets. But by making mention of the women—they stayed in the fort all winter—he gave historians cause to write about his "harem."

Indian women, he wrote, nursed beaver orphans at the breast. They would nurse the kit until it was able to eat bark, about six weeks. He describes the women feeding the beaver dainties: rice and plum pudding. And the inordinate affection the beavers showed the women—playing in their laps, crying out when they left.

I was nursing the baby as I read. Lying on the bed, back against the headrest, I wore Alec's big flannel shirt and long underwear. The long underwear had several holes, an especially large one in the crotch. He sat down beside me and slipped his hand through the hole and began to stroke, warm hand on my vulva, and leaning over, he began to suck the other breast.

His sucking was so much more delicate than the baby's. He licked the tip, slid his tongue down the side, massaged the whole of my nipple with his mouth, took it between his teeth—and all the while his fingers were pushing and kneading, spreading me open, going inside. I reached for him, but with the baby on my breast could do little. He undid his fly himself—came into me through the same wide hole in the underwear—balancing so that he didn't disturb the baby. A homely bit of lovemaking.

✳

In a Cree tale a woman married to a pond speaks to her husband by the way she swims in him. There comes a time when there's no rain and the pond dries up. The woman sets off looking for her husband and, after many miles, finds him in a hole. She takes him home little by little in her hands.

✳

I know a woman who swam around an abandoned beaver lodge, entered it through the underwater passage, and climbed up onto the dry ledge inside. It was like a cathedral inside, she told me. Cathedral? An old barn—modifying her description but not losing the image of light drifting dimly through cracks.

For several mornings I got up early and paddled over to the beaver lodge. I heard them talking inside. Two large beavers patrolled behind me, swimming back and forth, about twenty feet away. The lodge was a mound of pale sticks piled up against a rock, a ghostly configuration between two balsam trees. A dead tree jutted up out of the water, and made the lodge easy to find. In fact there were two lodges fifteen feet away from each other, one much smaller than the other—still used. Sometimes beavers entered one, sometimes the other.

I try to remember the description that came to me when I heard the beavers talk—it was indeed as though their tongues had been removed, a low almost birdlike sound.

I ask him to lie on his belly, and reach between his legs with oily hands. He raises himself slightly on one hip and then I can massage his penis, upside down and backwards, pleased by the new perspective and reminded of Old Coyote Man.

Old Coyote Man saw a group of young women picking wild strawberries. Quickly he lay down under the earth and let only the tip of his penis protrude. One of the women saw this large berry and tried to pick it. She called to the other women, who came and pulled at it. It has deep roots, one of them said. They nibbled at it. It weeps, they said. It weeps milk.

More oil, and the thought of castoreum, the liquid in a beaver's scent glands, basis of perfume. The image of a beaver meadow—pungent with musk—of a fallen tree, leafy clearing, Alec's leg pressing up, and me riding it. This image of something male, something which shifts between animal and man—cock erect, or hanging long and low—the shift of myself into something else—this is the sort of loosening I love.

THE FAVORITE SLEEPER

Summer Brenner

every night
we bear down
into some dormant state
on the flats
of mats and beds

it is strange
the stoniness
the form of dream
that every night
we come again
to this repose
of working posture

like great animals
lying in the desert
we monstrously
fill up our sheets

like some plant
impinging on the white garden
we spring
again and again

we lie down
it is ridiculous
this sweetness
this sphinx

THE CORSET

Evan S. Connell

I think that you are, she had said, enunciating each word, unutterably disgusting. I think, to tell the honest truth, that never in my entire life have I heard such an inexpressibly vulgar suggestion. Just in case you care for my opinion, there it is. To think that any man would even propose such an idea, especially to his wife, which, just on the chance that you've forgotten, I happen to be, is, to put it in the simplest possible terms, unutterably disgusting.

Mosher shrugs. Okay, never mind. It was a thought, Alice.

What you did while you were in the Army, and the type of women who prey upon lonesome soldiers in foreign countries, or for that matter, how foreign women in other countries behave with their husbands, are things I'd just as soon not care to hear about. I don't know if I'm making myself clear. It simply does not concern me, first of all, and then too, I don't see why you keep harping on these things, as though I were merely some sort of concubine. I guess that's the word. To be perfectly frank, because certainly I've always wanted you to be frank with me whenever anything was bothering you about our relationship, and I'm sure you've always wanted me to express my feelings just as frankly, I appreciate the fact that you thought enough of me to mention it, but it's just so revolting, I mean, I honestly do not know quite what to say.

I thought it might be fun, says Mosher. Overseas the women would—

Fun! Did you say *fun?* When we've always had such a marvelous relationship? I can't understand you anymore. You've changed. We used to agree that we had the most beautiful relationship in the world, at least you said so every time I asked, but now I don't know whether to believe you or not. I should think you'd want to keep it the way it was. When two people sincerely respect each other they surely oughtn't to jeopardize their affiliation, do you think? A moment ago I could scarcely believe my ears. I never dreamed that you could be so—so—

Vulgar?

Exactly! Not by any stretch of the imagination.

Then you think it's an unreasonable request? asks Mosher after a pause. Listen, Alice—

What you did in Europe is one thing, and I try not to dwell on it, which is more than most wives would do, but now you're home and we ought to go on the way we did before.

Alice, it's a damned strange thing, says Mosher, that my own wife should know less about me than a whore on the Rue de la Paix.

For a moment she gazes at him. Then all at once she remarks: Tell me what you want. I love you, you must know that. I'll do anything on earth for you. Tell me specifically what would please you and I'll agree to do it, on the condition that it means preserving our relationship.

I don't want it that way! Mosher shouts, and bangs his fists together. Can't you understand? Oh my God, don't look so miserable, he adds. You look like I was getting ready to flog you.

That wouldn't surprise me. Nothing you do anymore could possibly surprise me. I don't know what's come over you. Honestly, I don't. You're a perfect stranger.

Mosher, enraged and baffled, lights a cigarette.

Smoking isn't good for you.

I know it isn't, I know, he says, puffing away.

You never listen to me.

Alice, he replies with a gloomy expression, I don't miss a word, not a word. Oh hell, I love you as you are. Don't change. You're probably right, we'll go on like we used to. I don't want you to change. Forget I said anything.

But you *do!* You do want me to change, and I've got to be everything to you, otherwise our—

Don't! Mosher groans, falling back on the bed. Don't keep calling the two of us a relationship, as though we were a paragraph in some social worker's report.

For better or worse, she says as though she had not heard him,

I've made up my mind to behave exactly like one of those European women. I'm quite serious. I mean that.

Mosher, rising on one elbow, gazes at his wife curiously.

I do mean it. I'm going to be every bit as depraved and evil as they are, you just watch!

What the hell's got into you? he demands. You're out of your mind. You're as American as Susan B. Anthony. Then he continues: But if you want to, fine. Go ahead.

What do I do first?

I don't know. Don't you?

No, this was your idea. Give me a suggestion.

Well, says Mosher uneasily, I'm a spectator, so to speak. I don't really know. He realizes that she has started to unbutton her blouse. What do you think you're doing? he asks. I mean, good God, it's three o'clock in the afternoon and the Haffenbecks are coming over.

I don't care, she says. I simply don't care about a thing anymore.

But wait a minute, Alice. We invited them for drinks and a barbecue, remember?

I don't care! I don't care about the Haffenbecks. And she takes off her blouse, asking: Shall I take off everything?

Oh, yes, yes, everything, everything, says Mosher absently, gazing at her shoulders. With his chin propped in his hands he watches her get undressed.

I really should have paid a visit to the beauty parlor this morning, she says. My hair is a fright.

The beauty parlor! he shouts. What the hell has a beauty parlor got to do with this? Life's too short for beauty parlors!

However, she's doing her best, he thinks, all for me, because she does love me and wants to please me, isn't that odd? She's not a bit excited, she's just ashamed and embarrassed, so I am too. He feels deeply touched that his wife is willing to debase herself for him, but at the same time he is annoyed. Her attitude fills him with a sense of vast and unspeakable dismay. In Europe, now, romping in a bedroom, there would be no stilted questions, no apologies or explanations, no pussyfooting about, no textbook psychology, nothing but a wild and fruitful and altogether satisfying game. Alice, though, after the first embrace, customarily looks to see if her clothing is torn or her hair has been mussed.

Why, he asks with a lump like a chestnut in his throat, do you wear that corset?

It isn't a corset, it's a foundation.

Mosher waves impatiently. Alice, I hate these Puritan bones. Those Boston snoods. You haven't the slightest idea how sick and tired I've become of Aunt Martha's prune-whip morals. Whenever I touch you while you're wearing that thing it's like I've got hold of a bag of cement. Didn't I ever tell you how much I hate that corset? Didn't you ever realize? I mean to say, I think of you as flesh and blood, but that freaking thing makes you look like a python that swallowed a pig. Why do you wear it? You have such a marvelous shape all by yourself. It would look wonderful to see you out in public without that damned corset.

I should think a man wouldn't want his wife to be seen on the street bulging at every seam.

Well, I would, says Mosher with great bitterness. I'd love it. Anyway, right now I want you to take that bloody thing off.

She does, with no change of expression; her eyes remain fixed on him rather like the eyes of a frightened tigress, bright and watchful and unblinking.

Do you love me because of this? she asks.

Because of what?

My figure.

Yes, he says earnestly, I certainly do. A moment later, to his amazement, a tear comes wandering down her cheek.

I hoped it was me you loved, she says, weeping a little more but holding her head high.

I should have been a monk, he thinks. I'd have a nice quiet cell with bread and porridge and books to read—it would all be so simple. On the other hand I wouldn't make a very successful monk. I know what I'd spend every day praying for.

You can leave those beads on, Alice, he says, I like the effect.

He gazes at her body with immense interest; it is as pale as a melon. In the undergloom of her belly, he thinks, a little bird has landed—a fierce little falcon with tawny wings. He lifts his eyes once more to her face and sees a lock of hair almost but not quite touching the lobe of her ear. She is as divine and inimitable and perfect as a snow crystal or an April leaf unfolding.

You mentioned some girl over there who was a dancer, who used to dance for the soldiers.

Oh yes, yes, and she was magnificent, Mosher answers. Her name was Zizi. She used to go leaping around like the nymphs on those Greek vases, and when she wriggled across the floor you'd swear she was made out of rubber. I never saw anything like it.

Well, look at me, says Alice. And to Mosher's astonishment she lifts both hands high above her head and turns a perfectly splendid cartwheel.

What do you think of *that*? she demands, on her feet once again, tossing her hair over her shoulders.

I didn't know you could turn a cartwheel, says Mosher. He sits up briskly, spilling cigarette ashes on the bed.

You haven't seen anything yet, she calls from the other side of the room, and bending backward until her palms are flat on the floor, she gives a nimble kick and is upside down.

I didn't know you could stand on your hands, says Mosher, looking at her in stupefaction. Even with your clothes on you never did that.

Does it please you?

I should say it does! Mosher replies.

Men are so peculiar. Why should you want me to do these things?

I don't know, Alice. Somehow it makes me love you all the more.

I simply cannot understand you, she remarks, and begins walking around the bedroom on her hands. Could your old Zizi do this?

I don't know, he mutters. I can't remember. You've got me confused. I don't think I ever saw anything in my life like this.

Not even in Paris?

Not even in Heidelberg. You look strange upside down, Alice. What else can you do?

Just then the doorbell rings.

Oh my word, she exclaims, that must be the Haffenbecks!

No doubt, says Mosher. Either it's the Haffenbecks or the police.

What on earth are we going to do?

THE UNMADE BED

52

I don't know, he replies, unable to stop staring at her. Who cares? Do you?

I suppose not, she answers, still upside down.

The corset is lying on the edge of the bed. Mosher picks it up, flings it out the window and, reclining comfortably, takes a puff at his cigarette.

Now, he commands, turn a somersault.

From: COUPLETS

Robert Mezey

Mouths searching each other for minutes, years
Warmer and warmer, looking for the hidden word.

Arms and legs intertwined, skin sliding on skin,
The blood rushing joyously into its channels.

The breasts open their eyes in the darkness of palms,
The eyes widen at every little touch.

The fingers brush against the mouth of the womb
In the conversation of the deaf and blind.

Yoked by flesh, shaking, hollering praises,
They rise as one body to the opening.

The shining phallus erupts in a spray of stars
Flying into her night at tremendous speed.

If their eyes became the darkness, they would see,
Flaming in the darkness, their blowtorch auras.

Sperm on her lips, her hair, her eyes closed,
His whole body bathed in the odor of the garden,

Wet, motionless, barely breathing,
They fill slowly with the surrounding darkness.

From: THE CALCULUS OF VARIATION

DIANE DI PRIMA

Let me extol your body, the living flesh. The head is small, and turns in to the pillow. As the light turns, falling on your neck. One hand tucked out of sight. The living flesh. What darkness shimmers on your shoulder? Peace, like a child, the long white feet stretch out. Crusted with city dirt, the ankle bone/ streaked.

Gentle soft flesh, thickish about the middle. I slip an arm around you as you sleep. Soft in the middle, gentle, like a girl. Your son is tougher; your son's skin less smooth. LET ME PRAISE LIGHT THAT FALLS ON YOUR MORNING HAIR. Creeps up the edge of buildings, bare brick walls. And falls in pools on the flat tar roof outside.

What joy in the sounds of music, the kings of old/ made no sound richer than what Cecil makes. Playing with one hand on the blurred piano. There is laughter. I think of this. Your soft dull flesh. The variety between your world and mine. Your cock is limp between us. You breathe deep. The wind stirs dust and tar. The cat is stretching. I stroke your hip, the dip and spout of your pelvis.

Mornings are black and white ((oh yes, take sides)). Cat black and white, sheets, black slacks, and white shirt. Roof black, in the white air, like a mountaintop. Brick wall I look at, bathed in a golden light. Bright eyes of Milarepa. Laughing slits.

Clangor. The gongs. The children waking up. What joy we have here/ howls. The shrieks and cries. The names called out/ the shit rubbed in the hair. Black dog on the next roof barks amid green plants. Our cat comes to him, they both lie down. Your eyes, open like slits, the cloudy blue. You smile a little, your mouth tastes of morning.

* * *

The traffic moves through a cloud of sounds like waves. We wake every morning on another beach. The nervous horses dance in the busy streets. The hoods swing out, the cops/ also swing out. A slime like blood falls over everything. Red runs the river, the East River, red. A flame like hearts, like onehand Cecil music. The words John Wieners mumbled after shock. This hymn of joy we're making. Listen close.

My baby laid her head in my lap, she said "what will become of me?" She laughed, she did a dance. A shuffle, in her socks, in the living room. I sleep when I can, the swish of clothesline. The children jumping rope, the swish of traffic. Loud, joyous sounds from the pentecostal churches. Our bright, red car swung over the Brooklyn Bridge. Whom are they hanging where? The children, jumping

> Lady, lady, turn around
> Lady, lady, touch the ground
> Lady, lady, show your shoe
> Lady, lady, I love you . . .

What bright flesh/ turns in the morning air, an offering.

I come to the door of our room. You are still sleeping. The smell of roses hangs in the heavy air. The smell of tar, the musty smell of sheets.

In the high study, warm, I offer incense. My flesh a form of offering, consuming. The smell of musk, the smell of my own death. A formal grace, I turn in the small room. I smell your dream, joyous as shooting stars. We are on a train, outside of salt lake city. Joyous together in some kind of limbo . . .

✳

To come to terms with this, the solstice past. The Darkening of the Light. My place & yours. That our acts should burn, our passions, our clear sight. Until the sun shall come to himself again.

So be it. We play this game of treachery. Of passions running out. Deceit. Of passion. Weeping children. Dripping skies. As if we weren't a single sheet of flame. One body. Fiery garment of the mother. That blows in any wind, the breath of Shiva. As if your ankle I take in my mouth, your sleeping hand, the black fur of the cat. Made something more than pictures on the wall. Shadows projected on a waving cloth. A drape whose folds run sideways.

LET ME DESTROY YOUR BODY, the living flesh. Come, cover it with mine. Our flesh becomes one flame. George, Cecil, Alan. Not many hands have touched as we have touched. Not many gestures cut in flame and stone. Beckon through aeons as our gestures beckon.

POEM TO MY HUSBAND FROM MY FATHER'S DAUGHTER

SHARON OLDS

I have always admired your courage. As I see you
embracing me, in the mirror, I see I am
my father as a woman, I see you bravely
embrace him in me, putting your life in his
hands as mine. You know who I am—you can
see his hair springing from my head like
oil from the ground, you can see his eyes,
reddish as liquor left in a shot-glass and
dried dark, looking out of my face,
and his firm sucking lips, and the breasts
rising frail as blisters from his chest,
tipped with apple-pink. You are fearless, you
enter him as a woman, my sex like a
wound in his body, you flood your seed in his
life as me, you entrust your children to that
man as a mother, his hands as my hands
cupped around their tiny heads. I have never
known a man with your courage, coming
naked into the cage with the lion, I
lay my enormous paws on your scalp I
take my great tongue and begin to
run the rasp delicately
along your skin, humming: as you enter
ecstasy, the hairs lifting
all over your body, I have never seen a
happier man.

From: CHIN MUSIC

James McManus

Teresa can't help it. The churn in her brain has been flashing her back to a series of groaning and sweaty duets, complete with her and Raymondo's most private and personal code words and phrases and rules, to some things that she'd rather not dwell on right now but nonetheless can't quite phase out. It's perverse. Because the harder she struggles to keep certain episodes under, the quicker and fresher the mnemonic bytes effervesce.

For example. Either might balk at the outset, protesting they're GONNA BE LATE, since as often as not it begins as they're on their way out. Ray will be thoroughly naked, having just stepped from out of the shower, and into her own best silk panties will be all the further along she'll have got getting dressed. Somehow or other she'll wind up in front of him on their blue bedroom carpet in the midst of a strenuous set of her best FLEXIONES, making sure that her NIPPLES TOUCH CARPET each time, counting out loud to herself, pumping and straining and sweating. Raymondo JUST WATCHES. When she's done all she can, Raymondo goes to the second small drawer of her dresser and takes out two dice. One die is white, borrowed for keeps several years ago from Ray's uncle's Risk game. The other one's smaller, with more rounded corners, and red. (It was never real clear to her where this second die came from.) They call them ZEE LOGS. Raymondo caresses and rotates them between his huge palms, shakes them around in his fist, looks at her, blows on them, then rolls them out onto the carpet. The number of FLEXIONES she's managed times the number of pips showing on top of ZEE LOGS becomes the MAGIC NUMBER Raymondo will have to perform in order to COME OUT ON TOP. Her average is seven or eight, although when she's desperate to win she has managed as many as twelve. But even if she only does seven, Raymondo, who averages forty-five to fifty, will still have to roll craps or less to keep within striking distance. (One time he'd

THE HOT BED

rolled an eleven after she had done seven and made it all the way up to seventy-three and a half before collapsing. He'd had to pitch that night too.) Once he has started his set, she SUPERVISES every last one very closely, making darn sure those hard concave cheeks DON'T START RISING—if they do they get SNAPPED with his towel—that his chest TOUCHES DOWN every time. He usually is still going strong till around thirty-five, but it's right around then that he starts getting shaky, his rear end STARTS RISING, and so on. SNAP SNAP! By forty his biceps are trembling, his face is all red, and he's gasping. If he fails, as he so often does, to SATISFACTORILY PERFORM THE MAGIC NUMBER, she's got him. WITHOUT HAVING TO BE TOLD, his big chest still heaving, Raymondo rolls over and lies on his back for his TREATMENT, throughout which he stays wholly SERVILE TO HER COY DISDAIN. The first thing she does is she SMOTHERS him by straddling his still-gasping face, propelling herself back and forth over his nose and his mouth and his chin, eventually torquing down to the max in order to keep him from talking or moving or breathing. And meantime, of course, his own NEW DIRECTION is completely IGNORED AND NEGLECTED. The most she'll consent to is lightly and dispassionately running the side of her thumb up and down it, maybe stroking it with her wrist or her palm, BUT THAT'S ALL. And meantime she's riding his face like she's busting a bronco, but harder, till her teeth start to chatter in fact, at which point d'orgue she will jerk off her panties, slide right back up onto his HARDON, continue. If either could take it, this could go on forever, but of course neither can, so it doesn't. When at last she is through with him, Raymondo, UNREQUITED CAMSHAFT and all, is sent back to the shower to cool himself off and get dressed—or whatever. Her reason? THE RULES. And besides. They're ALREADY LATE AS IT IS.

If, on the other hand, Raymondo sur*passes* the MAGIC NUMBER (ties, of course, go to the woman), then it's *she* who's in trouble. BUT NO ROUGH STUFF, she'll say, half kidding, half pleading. No use. WITHOUT FURTHER ADO she'll be DOWN ON HER KNEECAPS and SHLURP-ING. Raymondo's behavior might include anything from straightfor-wardly PROVIDING DIRECTION, caressing her ears with his palms, to grabbing her hair, barking out orders and curses, to wielding the infamous NIPPLEWHIP. It goes without saying that throughout this ordeal her own POOR UNMENTIONABLE gets no stimulation whatever, oral or otherwise. None. She's compelled by THE RULES to continue till she gets him to come, no matter how long he may take. They also provide that she KNOCK IT BACK GRATEFULLY, ALL OF IT, then lick off the series of AFTERSHOCKS. *Yum!*

For the most part these rules get adhered to. The one that gets broken most often, of course, is the one that provides that the loser be COOLLY NEGLECTED throughout the whole session. Her own biggest weakness is for sliding off Raymondo's cleft chin, shimmying down his sleek torso, then swinging around versy-arsy and giddying back up onto his ostensibly off-limits MOONBEAM, meanwhile, to make matters worse, greedily lapping his now comeslick features. DOMESTIC CRUDE city. It's so fun fun fun that 9.9 times out of ten she can't help it. Raymondo's most common transgression gets made in DIRECT RETALIATION, or so he will claim, for being INCISORED too hard, on the basis of which flimsy excuse he will gingerly remove MISTER MIKE from between her sharp choppers, shove her back down off her kneecaps, and pin her young ass to the carpet. Now she is *really* in trouble. For at this point he's got this quick, clever tackle-and-pulley maneuver whereby he forces her legs wide apart by scooping them up and then driving his body between them, shoving her thighs so far back in the process that her knees are on line with her shoulders, while at the same time he pinions her biceps beside her and hoists himself forward by pushing back down off her arms, yanking her torso in one direction while leaning down hard with his chest and his shoulders to double her back in the other. Wrenched open, raised up, defenseless, she hopes that he won't be TOO CRUEL. For Raymondo could sure go to town on her now, give her one real hard time, simply by using the same push-and-pull locomotion to jack up and stretch out her gash as to drive his hard cock down and in, tactically enhancing his thrust-to-weight ratio and at the same time providing for strategically deep penetration. If she's lucky, that is. Because most of the time he just holds her like this for a while, makes her wait, lets that wet helpless feeling soak in. It's her SENTENCE. She can protest all she wants about BREAKING THE RULES, but they both know she's way overmatched now: that the count's 0–2 and THE RULES have gone right out the window: that once she is caught in these hot ineluctable clutches he can tease her and zap her at will. One of his wickedest tricks at this stage is to jam her real slow for a bit, build up some rhythm, pretend that he's finding his stroke, and then suddenly stop and pull out. *O my God!* The soft pulsing void where his hardon just was drives her nuts, but all she can do now is tremble and writhe in short-circuit while he waggles its tip on her stomach, bastes up her thighs with her juices, and asks her HOW BAD DO YOU WANT IT. (She knows that she best keep her throes to a minimum now, but more often than not she just can't.) When she gives him no answer he bites on her nipples, calls her all sorts of lewd names, and jives her with more false alarms: and she *still* won't admit that she wants it. (She likes to make love with her husband, of course, in mature, more conventional manners, but she likes it much better when they fuck with each other, let things get strange and depraved, so it's sinful and painful and raunchy: like they're not really married or something.) When he's darn good and ready he'll stick it back in, lean on her thighs even harder, and then drill her and warp her and rock her, make her quiver and gasp with some extra firm jolts high and tight. Make her ache. Make her shake. Make her come and cry out once or twice, quaking all out of control. Then maybe he'll let up a little, allow her to shiver and shudder, perhaps even put up a (doomed, futile, wonderful) struggle, while he pulls it back out one more time and starts slipping and sliding the whole throbbing length of it upside her clit, back and forth, flaunting his stalwart control, changing speeds, seering her, zinging her, first very slowly, so lightly, so deftly, now faster, now harder, now sideways—by now she is begging him, pleading—or dangles it just out of reach, making her arch up her back even more just to touch it. In the end he will fuck her, of course, long and hard—till she thinks she can't take any more, till she feels like she'll stay fucked forever—but in the frantic and desperate condition in which he's already got her she really can't wait that much longer. She has to, however. She can't, but she has to. She has to.

In any event, whoever has done the most pushups, whoever has broken THE RULES, or even if the dice weren't used in the first place, when they're through with each other Raymondo invariably LIES AND BREATHETH ON HER FACE, and God does she love that. She does.

They do not have a name for this game, but sometimes just the thought of it can burn in Teresa's warm blood like cold powdered glass, and she'll either have to get the game started or, if Ray's not around, just stand there and brace herself, like she's doing right now, rubbing her knuckles and blushing, doing her darnedest to blot out his moonbeam, his breathing, his stubbly slippery frictiony chin, and his face, staring out hard into space, till it passes.

QUEEN

ANNE WALDMAN

My sandpaper husband who
wears sackcloth when I don't behave
says Come sit on rattan, woman
Your will is as brittle as glass
Your mad mouth is untamable
& your heart is always in another country

Your ears are radar stalks
Your eyes magnetize yardmen
& when you sing you shake the house
AHHHHH   AHHHHH   AHHHHH
My wife is a burning house

My silky husband who tends the garden
whose arms shake like branches in a storm
complains I'm a slugabed on his time
He says Wake up woman of sleep & cream
Wake up & sweep back your flickering night-lids

Your hands are leopardesses
Your shins are Cadillacs
Your thighs are palaces of tears
When you weep the house rises
My wife is the Indian Ocean rising

My husband of sacred vows
has October weather in his voice

He says Come to bed, amorous woman
Your ancient desk is covered with leaves
Your tardy poem can't be coaxed
But will come to you like a Queen.

WHEN I SEE YOUR BREASTS I REMEMBER MY HEART'S DESIRE

Norman Fischer

When I see your breasts I remember my heart's desire the place I
want to go to in my dreams
Where all my hopes are completely realized and whatever it is I
want close to me is close to me and what I want pushed away from
me is far away
And I am not confused about anything never disappointed never
dull
never at a loss functioning totally at full tilt all of the time
Your breasts so full and glorious in shape are the breasts I have
seen forever in my dreams and even deeper than my dreams
They are my two great hopes and they are my salvation my respite
from a cruel and fallen world
And they are also my two great fears I am afraid that you will at
some point leave me for another man or that there is something in
your life that is more important than me to you it is another man
isn't it?
So that when I see the outline of your body in the white nightgown
tonight before you go to bed with the lamp on on the table near
the bed so I can see through the nightgown and can make out
perfectly the calming satisfying shape of your breasts except they
are made more mysterious and even more beautiful by the softness
of the fabric
I am lost in this mountainous desire that can never be fulfilled
that aches wounded for you and will probably end up driving you
away
To him it will probably send you right into his arms
But I can't stop feeling it although it terrifies me
And also my hope is that someday my own life will come to a state
of completion I can imagine in a vague way what that would be like

although mainly what it feels like is a state somehow different
from the one I presently inhabit
And my second hope is that this state of completion involves you
we are complete together as intimate as water with water clouds
with clouds flowing in and out of each other
And when you turn your head as you are pinning up your hair and
lifting your arms up over your head in a gesture that is burned
into my mind as an eternal dreamtime image
And I see the outline of your neck and your breasts move higher
and change shape with the movement upward of your arms
Or when the light is a certain way and you are wearing the olive
grey turtleneck shirt I gave you for your birthday several years
ago
Or not that but you are wearing the salmon-colored low-neckline
dress the summer one and also a simple necklace of natural pearls
That accentuates your thick black hair which when worn down full
frames your face and neck so beautifully
Then I think I am going to fly apart with the centrifugal force
created by the pressure of grief within me
Caused by the impossibility of our actually being together in the
way I need you to be with me that kind of constancy and total
fusion
And I am like a woman in a red dress holding a calla lilly at a
funeral
Or a completely set holiday dinner table five minutes before it is
discovered that the guest of honor has suddenly died in a traffic
accident
Or the locker room of a high school football team during halftime
of the city championship game in which it will suffer a stunning
upset defeat
You look different on different days it's so confusing!
Sometimes your hair is short and blonde sometimes it is long and
red all its different colors of blue gold and yellow confused in a
dazzle in the sunlight
You are tall or often quite short and compact ethnic and dark
Scandinavian Russian black
I saw you this morning in my dream you were lovelier than ever and
I could see your breasts through the tee shirt you were wearing it

was you
But at the same time it was my mother when I was a little boy a
deep dream it was my own dream or was it the dream of the race of
all men imagining all women as mothers their breasts huge and
dripping with milk in a world in which there was no other food
and no way to get food other than love and no way to be worthy of
love and no way to keep love from eventually dissolving assuming
you could be worthy of it for a short time
I am wondering whether this passion I feel for you seems
undignified
And whether you can bear it for a single day more

IN THE BLOOD

Jonis Agee

When he had first gotten back, they felt new and strange to each other. It wasn't just that each was five years older, more worn and more certain about life now than in their earlier years. No, it was also the fact of where he had been and how far she had gone on, living in their house and raising their children alone, although for him she was still there as five years before. Somehow he was confident that the threads of feeling remained unbroken and attached as ever between them.

He imagined her body clean lined, though it had never been, and smooth, though she had always had scars and rough, bumpy patches of skin. She was uncomfortable and flattered.

When they made love, she imagined him entering the soft fine bodies of the women he must have known. She imagined him coming at them slowly, his dirty hands and face smudging their cleanness and mingling with their perfume. When he took off his clothes, she tried not to look at the fresh purple scars etched like insect trails along his legs. There had been a wound. A deep and hollow scar, white and strange, stood on one shoulder blade, and if she was not careful, her hand would slip into its cup as she smoothed the muscles on his back. Now she closed her eyes always when they made love. She could not stand the love eating into her like a dog not fed for too many days—this dog living in his eyes, becoming his eyes, the pitiable and the alien, some thirsty and hungry creature intent on feeding itself more than anything else, like the dog she had once accidentally locked in the garage for a weekend when she had gone away, the forgiveness and the starvation together she saw in its face on Monday morning. It had probably stopped howling after a day, when its throat had burned out. She could see the claw marks on the doors and the chewed edges of wood. His teeth had caught and torn the loose skin surrounding his gums. The blood, dried by then, matted the white hairs on his chin. In his frenzy he must have torn out several nails, because his paws were bloody too. And in his anguish of abandonment he had progressed to the diarrhea standing in pools on the concrete floor of the garage, when he must have been certain of his own death. But she had come back, had found him, and had taken him into the house for his food and water, and as he ate, she saw that look—too hungry for what she had offered it.

She felt him feeding on her breasts, biting softly and sucking, trying to drain her into his mouth, and she knew it was not enough. Even when he grew violent, while she lay on her stomach and he hammered himself into her buttocks, she knew that he was growing more afraid of the love he wanted. The only act he really allowed her was to let her use her mouth on him, and after he had emptied himself into her in that way, helpless to her comfort and succored by her tongue, releasing himself into the fear of her teeth, then he could be full. Sometimes he told her afterward that it was like walking down a forest trail, knowing that assassins were waiting for him, yet he could not keep from walking down the trail, smelling the urgent growth of vegetation, seeing the flowers and butterflies, and hearing the birds whose hasty cries could be the end.

She performed this act for him nightly after a while, and somehow it soothed him into his sleep. He could endure the days that way. His life became possible. Like the dog she had recovered from the garage, he became obedient and gentle. But always a little hunger lingered about his mouth, rested in his eyes.

It was two years later that they found out about the thing in his blood. They had gone on with their life, more than less comfortable, accepting the things that had happened, more or less. She sometimes felt tired at night and went to sleep immediately instead of making love with him. These nights he lay awake for hours, but he was beginning to forget the past. What he had lived through had become almost a familiar and comfortable fantasy on those nights of thinking. Often he found that just recalling it would give him an erection, which he would have to somehow dissolve before sleep. A couple of times he watched her sleeping, sometimes frowning, with her mouth slightly open and vulnerable to him at any moment he might choose. The slight pressing of a nipple against her nylon gown as she breathed in and out he would watch for a long time, the rhythm of its coming and going, until he ejaculated. And sometimes, when it was warm and she was in a deep sleep, her eyes fluttering behind the lids in dreaming, he would carefully draw back the covers and hold his penis over her breast or mouth.

Although the cancer in his blood required care from his physician, it didn't stop him from working, only made him tired and sometimes sick. But it also made him more sexual than ever. Now he wanted her all the time. As he lost weight, as he ate less, he grew more frantic about her love and her body. On the other hand, after the disease was discovered, she began to be afraid, even revulsed by the one act which could appease him. As if she now had to feed the dog from her own mouth, eat his fear, she could not bear on her tongue the liquid sex, filled, she imagined, with his blood and webbed with his sickness. She thought of how she had grown afraid of the dog, which, no matter how much she fed it, did not regain its weight. She eventually left the dog in the small wire cage at the Humane Society, panting from its starvation. Now her husband was like a dog let out of a cage, tracking her down, but as if her stomach were always full and bursting, she could not bear to open her mouth to him, and her body ached as if it had been filled with stones.

OLD TIMES NOW

Stephen Rodefer

My wife and I quite often make love in the car on long trips. While driving I mean. I mean usually the children are asleep, but if they're not it hasn't been too hard to avoid their apparent notice. I say apparent because you usually suspect they might well realize but for some reason or other just aren't letting on. I've often wondered if this wasn't some odd ability children have, a general busyness, half aware, that takes its energy from what is not in focus yet; or whether children aren't just more discreet than we give them credit for being. Either way it seems admirable behavior, and is certainly useful for everyone involved.

Of course if they are awake and playing it sets some practical limits on the way you can do it, but everything in the interest of variety seems a fair enough proposition. There are obviously as well the problems of visibility in the daytime. Really it's easier on the thruway. You don't have to pay so much attention to the driving and if you go generally between 50 and 60, passing cars don't have much chance to see anything I don't think. Though it is surprising how many people look back at you even though you're sure they can't know. They seem to sense something. An American habit perhaps, to think people still know when you're doing something amiss, even when they can't; as well as to have that feeling that something is going on even without evidence that it is. At any rate I automatically slow down as they pass, looking at them through my eyeballs.

Trucks and buses, anything that rides high, is what you would worry about obviously. But as I said, there's curiously very little problem, though I've never been stopped by a cop. But then passing through a toll booth has never been a serious interruption either. And every once in a while a brief conversation with Benjamin or Jesse, coming to lean over the front seat to ask what a soft shoulder is, is readily enough dispatched. Where the edge of the road, etc., so cars, go play, etc.

You can see how it's being done of course. Awkward fumbling to begin with. You only have your right hand you understand, but with a moving wife you can soon reach pretty far, she slouching over with her left arm around you and your right palm snailing down the back of her lap, under the elastic of her skirt and into the pants, your middle finger creasing through that straight crack to the wetness further on. I don't want to make it sound quick and determined, even planned. The slower the better, it's a luscious business and to each his own path.

Eventually she has you out, the kids are into their jabbering back of the back seat (it's a station wagon) and while she's opening your shirt and unbuckling your trousers, you're tipping the tips of your fingers with all the saliva that's flowing, and the old right hand can dive right back by now to the perfect place it just left, without bumping into anything. When the juices flow the motor abilities become more accurate and there is no sense of fumbling left.

You can see how snorked into the memory of this I'm getting, and if I go any further I won't be able to keep on typing, or if I could you wouldn't be able to keep reading, if you knew what was good for you. Maybe I better wrap it up.

Once she came four times, starting around Bakersfield, with some variation on the gearshift (floor), and we checked into the first motel in Arizona, to fall totally beyond at the fifth (hers not mine).

THE HOT BED

73

From: ROUGH STRIFE

LYNNE SHARON SCHWARTZ

Caroline and Ivan finally had a child. Conception stunned them; they didn't think, by now, that it could happen. For years they had tried and failed, till it seemed that a special barren destiny was pre-ordained. Meanwhile, in the wide spaces of childlessness, they had created activity: their work flourished. Ivan, happy and moderately powerful in a large foundation, helped decide how to distribute money for artistic and social projects. Caroline taught mathematics at a small suburban university. Being a mathematician, she found, conferred a painful private wisdom on her efforts to conceive. In her brain, as Ivan exploded within her, she would involuntarily calculate probabilities; millions of blind sperm and one reluctant egg clustered before her eyes in swiftly transmuting geometric patterns. She lost her grasp of pleasure, forgot what it could feel like without a goal. She had no idea what Ivan might be thinking about, scattered seed money, maybe. Their passion became courteous and automatic until, by attrition, for months they didn't make love—it was too awkward.

One September Sunday morning she was in the shower, watch-ing, through a crack in the curtain, Ivan naked at the washstand. He was shaving, his jaw tilted at an innocently self-satisfied angle. He wasn't aware of being watched, so that a secret quality, an es-sence of Ivan, exuded in great waves. Caroline could almost see it, a cloudy aura. He stroked his jaw vainly with intense concentration, a self-absorption so contagious that she needed, suddenly, to possess it with him. She stepped out of the shower.

"Ivan."

He turned abruptly, surprised, perhaps even annoyed at the in-terruption.

"Let's not have a baby anymore. Let's just . . . come on." When she placed her wet hand on his back he lifted her easily off her feet with his right arm, the razor still poised in his other, outstretched hand.

"Come on," she insisted. She opened the door and a draft blew into the small steamy room. She pulled him by the hand toward the bedroom.

Ivan grinned. "You're soaking wet." ·

"Wet, dry, what's the difference?" It was hard to speak. She began to run, to tease him; he caught her and tossed her onto their disheveled bed and dug his teeth so deep into her shoulder that she thought she would bleed.

Then with disinterest, taken up only in this fresh rushing need for him, weeks later Caroline conceived. Afterwards she liked to say that she had known the moment it happened. It felt different, she told him, like a pin pricking a balloon, but without the shattering noise, without the quick collapse. "Oh, come on," said Ivan. "That's impossible."

But she was a mathematician, after all, and dealt with infinitesimal precise abstractions, and she did know how it had happened. The baby was conceived in strife, one early October night, Indian summer. All day the sun glowed hot and low in the sky, settling an amber torpor on people and things, and the night was the same, only now a dark hot heaviness sunk slowly down. The scent of the still-blooming honeysuckle rose to their bedroom window. Just as she was bending over to kiss him, heavy and quivering with heat like the night, he teased her about something, about a mole on her leg, and in reply she punched him lightly on the shoulder. He grabbed her wrists, and when she began kicking, pinned her feet down with his own. In an instant Ivan lay stretched out on her back like a blanket, smothering her, while she struggled beneath, writhing to escape. It was a silent, sweaty struggle, interrupted with outbursts of wild laughter, shrieks and gasping breaths. She tried biting but, laughing loudly, he evaded her, and she tried scratching the fists that held her down, but she couldn't reach. All her desire was transformed into physical effort, but he was too strong for her. He wanted her to say she gave up, but she refused, and since he wouldn't loosen his grip they lay locked and panting in their static embrace for some time.

"You win," she said at last, but as he rolled off she sneakily jabbed him in the ribs with her elbow.

"Aha!" Ivan shouted, and was ready to begin again, but she quickly distracted him. Once the wrestling was at an end, though, Caroline found her passion dissipated, and her pleasure tinged with resentment. After they made love forcefully, when they were covered with sweat, dripping on each other, she said, "Still, you don't play fair."

"I don't play fair! Look who's talking. Do you want me to give you a handicap?"

"No."

"So?"

"It's not fair, that's all."

Ivan laughed gloatingly and curled up in her arms. She smiled in the dark.

That was the night the baby was conceived, not in high passion but rough strife.

She lay on the table in the doctor's office weeks later. The doctor, whom she had known for a long time, habitually kept up a running conversation while he probed. Today, fretting over his weight problem, he outlined his plans for a new diet. Tensely she watched him, framed and centered by her raised knees, which were still bronzed from summer sun. His other hand was pressing on her stomach. Caroline was nauseated with fear and trembling, afraid of the verdict. It was taking so long, perhaps it was a tumor.

"I'm cutting out all starches," he said. "I've really let myself go lately."

"Good idea." Then she gasped in pain. A final, sickening thrust, and he was out. Relief, and a sore gap where he had been. In a moment, she knew, she would be retching violently.

"Well?"

"Well, Caroline, you hit the jackpot this time."

She felt a smile, a stupid, puppet smile, spread over her face. In the tiny bathroom where she threw up, she saw in the mirror the silly smile looming over her ashen face like a dancer's glowing grimace of labored joy. She smiled through the rest of the visit, through his advice about milk, weight, travel and rest, smiled at herself in the window of the bus, and at her moving image in the fenders of parked cars as she walked home.

Ivan, incredulous over the telephone, came home beaming stupidly just like Caroline, and brought a bottle of champagne. After dinner they drank it and made love.

"Do you think it's all right to do this?" he asked.

"Oh, Ivan, honestly. It's microscopic."

He was in one of his whimsical moods and made terrible jokes that she laughed at with easy indulgence. He said he was going to pay the baby a visit and asked if she had any messages she wanted delivered. He unlocked from her embrace, moved down her body and said he was going to have a look for himself. Clowning, he put his ear between her legs to listen. Whatever amusement she felt soon ebbed away into irritation. She had never thought Ivan would be a doting parent—he was so preoccupied with himself. Finally he stopped his antics as she clasped her arms around him and whispered, "Ivan, you are really too much." He became unusually gentle. Tamed, and she didn't like it, hoped he wouldn't continue that way for months. Pleasure lapped over her with a mild, lackadaisical bitterness, and then when she could be articulate once more she explained patiently, "Ivan, you know, it really is all right. I mean, it's a natural process."

PART III

THE MARRIAGE BED

LOVE POEM

Ron Padgett

We have plenty of matches in our house.
We keep them on hand always.
Currently our favorite brand is Ohio Blue Tip,
though we used to prefer Diamond brand.
That was before we discovered Ohio Blue Tip matches.
They are excellently packaged, sturdy
little boxes with dark and light blue and white labels
with words lettered in the shape of a megaphone,
as if to say even louder to the world,
"Here is the most beautiful match in the world,
its one and a half inch soft pine stem capped
by a grainy dark purple head, so sober and furious
and stubbornly ready to burst into flame,
lighting, perhaps, the cigarette of the woman you love,
for the first time, and it was never really the same
after that. All this will we give you."
That is what you gave me, I
become the cigarette and you the match, or I
the match and you the cigarette, blazing
with kisses that smoulder toward heaven.

THE ONE

Anselm Hollo

the one
long hair in my beard
this morning
makes me smile:
it's yours

FOR THE WOMAN WITH EVERYTHING

Geoffrey Young

With growing apprehension I thought about Margery's suggestion that I buy Laura a gun for Christmas. Would that be chic? Gun-related accidents in otherwise normal homes produced statistics of national disgrace, as did crimes of passion. And to read in the papers the occasional account of pistol-whipped children was truly upsetting. Still, looking at our life together, and in spite of the distressing paucity of tenderness on all sides lately, I deemed it orderly, respectful, a vessel worthy of the launch.

Was Margery just projecting onto Laura her own desire for a gun? Her knowledge of radical theater tactics was inspiring. Or was this gun suggestion in response to an off-color joke about tacos I had earlier told the Print Center staff at their Christmas party? Margery didn't think it funny, in fact she looked confused, real consternation on her face. Shortly after the laughs faded I noticed she faded from the room. When she returned I remember thinking, she has regrouped her considerable forces in order to study the enemy from behind the blind of a newly adjusted composure. From this observation I gleaned the deduction that Laura needed a gun to protect herself and her sex from a man like me. Ah, Margery *was* being clever!

I drove to the sporting goods store and browsed the hardware. I chose a .22 Browning automatic pistol. It was lovely, especially if you appreciate carved walnut handles, and oily reflections from a gunmetal blue barrel. Along the underside of the barrel were printed the legend and the patent number of this classy little piece. The butt fit perfectly in my hand, and an unmistakable warmth rose to my finger's tip as I squeezed the trigger, ever so lightly, click. Perhaps yes.

And Laura would be excited by the originality of my gift, as well as vaguely threatened by its bravado. She would be eager to tell her family and friends. Her eyes would narrow slightly, and the set of her jaw would soften as she volunteered this new information over the phone to Gloria, to Catherine, to her parents, to Nicole, to Bob. And I could hear Michael's crazed laugh change from hilarity at the image of Laura brandishing a real "peashooter," to nervous distress at the more problematic image of me brandishing it. His son Nathan would not be safe in our house, etc. I imagined Laura's straining to hear whatever minute spasm of shock surfaced in her friends' initial reactions. This would make her happy, but happy with a quizzical expression on her face. And I could eavesdrop the chat that would follow, hearing theoretical conjecture, their armchair attempts to get at my intention (which I would refuse to discuss), and perhaps more importantly the subtextual symbolic meaning lying parallel to the shining pistol, but in some other plane. All this for $162.50, without holster.

I found myself so disoriented, however, at the threshold of this purchase, that I committed the unforgivable sin of saying to the clerk, "Throw in a box of those silver bullets, too." He winced slightly, then worked up a half smile that did no more than reveal an utter exhaustion with seasonal good cheer.

Quickly I tightened up, and reached for my checkbook. Yes, a kind of intimacy would be restored to our life at home, some drastic spiritual charge felt lingering over this revolver like love. The presence of the gun in either of our hands would be a firm reminder to follow the golden rule, no matter how dark the night, or horrible the imagined crime. The gun would unite us, just as the atomic bomb threads all nations together on the same global charm bracelet.

But where was the checkbook? Had I left it in the car? I pulled a measly eleven dollars cash from my wallet, said "fuck" under my breath, then trying to figure what to do, explained to the clerk, "Uh, I can't pay for it right now, my wife must have the checkbook." He stood in the uniform light near the cash register, staring over at me as if I were a cardboard cutout of a man, someone who looked just like me, but who lacked essential human definition.

"Listen, I'll be back, I have to get that gun," I promised him. He saw the arms and legs of the figure begin to back slowly out of the store, when in disgust he turned away, to a burning cigarette.

Outside. Providence? I asked myself. I hadn't gotten the key in the ignition when I flung the car door open and ran back in the store. But I went directly away from the gun counter, moving left· past racks of athletic footwear, to a row of multi-colored jogging suits in small, medium, and large. Under them, into an unfolded pile, I reached, and grabbed a pair of medium-size navy blue "sweat pants" marked 5.95, paid for them with the ten dollar bill, and walked out, knowing how much comfortable wear she would get from them, soft, relaxed in the crotch, and easy to get off.

Selections From: IN BED

Kenneth Koch

MORNINGS IN BED

Are energetic mornings.

*

SNOW IN BED

When we got out of bed
It was snowing.

*

MARRIED IN BED

We'll be married in bed.
The preachers, the witnesses, and all our families
Will also be in bed.

*

ORCHIDS IN BED

She placed orchids in the bed
On that dark blue winter morning.

*

ANGELIC CEREMONY IN BED

Putting on the sheets.

*

THEATRICAL BED

Exceeded expectations
And received applause.

*

COURTSHIP IN BED

"Please. Tell me you like me."
"How did you get in this bed?"

*

LET'S GO TO BED

When the tree
Is blossoming. It will be
A long time
Before it is blossoming again.

*

ADVANCE BED

Advance arm. Advance stairs. Advance power.
Advance bed.

*

CHILD BED

You had two babies
Before we met.

*

ORCHIDS IN BED

She placed orchids on the bed
On a dark red winter afternoon.

*

ENEMIES IN BED

Enemies sleep in separate beds
But in the same part of the city.

*

SUMMER

The bed lies in the room
The way she lies in the bed.

*

ZEN BED

I can't get to bed.
Show me the bed and I will show you how to get to it.

*

SNOW IN BED

When we get out of bed
There is no more bed.

*

MARRIED IN BED

We did not get married
In bed.

*

SHOWER BED

For her engagement they gave her a shower
And for her marriage they went to bed.

*

STREAM BED

In the stream bed
The snails go to sleep.

*

PHILOSOPHY OF BED

A man should be like a woman and a woman should be like an
   animal
In bed is one theory. Another is that they both should be like beds.

*

MALLARMÉ'S BED

An angel came, while Mallarmé lay in bed,
When he was a child, and opened its hands
To let white bouquets of perfumed stars snow down.

*

DAY BED

When I loved you
Then that whole time
Was like a bed
And that whole year
Was like a day bed.

*

DENIED BED

We were not in bed
When summer came.

*

SNOW IN BED

Vanishing snowflakes, rooftops appearing
And sidewalks and people and cars as we get out of bed.

From: FULL OF LIFE

JOHN FANTE

There was also this passionate need for her. I had it from the first time I saw her. She went away that first time, she walked out of her aunt's house where we had met at tea, and I was no good without her, absolutely a cripple until I saw her again. But for her I might have lived out my life in other streams—a reporter, a bricklayer— whatever was at hand. My prose, such as it was, derived from her. For I was always quitting the craft, hating it, despairing, crumpling paper and throwing it across the room. But she could forage through the discarded stuff and come up with things, and I never really knew when I was good, I thought every line I ever wrote was no better than ordinary, for I had no way of being sure. But she could take the pages and find the good stuff and save it, and plead for more, so that it became habitual with me, and I wrote as best I could and handed her the pages, and she did a scissors-and-paste job, and when it was done, with a beginning and middle and end, I was more star-tled than seeing it in print, because at first I couldn't have done it alone.

Three years of this, four, five, and I began to have some no-tions about the craft, but they were her notions, and I never gave much thought to the others who might read my stuff, I only wrote it for her, and if she had not been there I might not have written it at all.

She didn't care to read me while she was pregnant. I brought her sequences from the script and she was not interested. That winter in her fifth month I wrote a short story and she spilled coffee on it—an unheard-of thing, and she read it with yawning attention. Before the baby she would have taken the manuscript to bed with her and spent hours pruning and fixing and making mar-ginal notes.

Like a stone, the child got between us. I worried and wondered if it would ever be the same again. I longed for the old days when I could walk into her room and snatch up some intimacy of hers, a scarf or a dress or a bit of white ribbon, and the very touch had me reeling around, croaking like a bullfrog for the joys of my beloved. The chair she sat upon before the dressing table, the glass that mirrored her lovely face, the pillow upon which she laid her head, a pair of stockings flung to launder, the disarming cunning of her silk pants, her nightgowns, her soap, her wet towels still warm after her bath: I had need for these things; they were a part of my life with her, and the smear of lipstick made no difference, for the red had come from the warm lips of my woman.

Things were changed around there now. Her gowns were specially contrived, with a big hole in front through which leered the bump, her slips were impossible sacks, her flat shoes were strictly for the rice fields, and her blouses were like pup tents. What man could take such a gown and crush it to his face and shudder with the old familiar passion? Everything smelled different too. She used to use some magic called Fernery at Twilight. It was like breathing Chopin and Edna Millay, and when its fragrance rose from her hair and shoulders I knew the flag was up and that she had chosen to be pursued. She didn't use Fernery at Twilight anymore: something else was substituted, a kind of Gayelord Hauser cologne, reeking of just plain good health, clean alcohol and simple soap. There was also the odor of vitamin tablets, of brewer's yeast and blackstrap molasses, and a pale salve to soothe her bursting nipples.

Lying in bed, I used to hear her slushing around, and wonder what was happening to us. I smoked in the darkness and moaned in the belief that she was driving me into another woman's arms. No, she didn't want me anymore, she was forcing me to another woman, a mistress. But what mistress? For years I had been retired from the jungle where bachelors prowled. Where was I to find another woman, even if I wanted one? I saw myself skulking about on Santa Monica Boulevard, drooling at free women in dark, offbeat saloons, sweating out clever dialogue, drinking heavily to hide the stark ugliness of such romances. No, I could not be unfaithful to Joyce. I didn't even want to be unfaithful, and this worried me too. For was it not something of a custom for men to be unfaithful to their wives during confinement? It happened all the time out at the golf club: I heard it from all the guys. Then what was wrong with me? Why wasn't I on the town, chafing for forbidden joys? And so I lay there, trying to coax up a flicker of that flame for strange fruit. But there was none.

LYING UNDER A QUILT

Rachel Hadas

Twilight; a drowsy dim
haven of thick repose
and half the journey done,
we sleepily suppose.
Hidden in either self,
memories lodge in lips,
creased into secret cells;
we're quiet, touching hips,

lying under a quilt,
catted on either flank,
our little boy asleep
on the other side of the wall,
and summer still ungroomed,
bugs in the bushy grass,
rain hanging undecided
whether or not to fall.

I see you—shining islands
haloed with sheer desire!
Unearthly mauve and crimson
sculptings of upper air!
I swoop, I solo float,
I sacrifice it all
for color beyond thought,
gesture, ineffable!

Through empyrean brilliance
our son is cast, a shadow
growing up exiled, empty

of what no one but me
or you can give him. You.
You too were left behind!
My arms are empty. Flailing
I thrash, make up my mind,

clip the wide-flung wings
and fall down the bright air
which speaks to me in light:
Come dive me, plunge me, here.
My purifying fire
gilds all you hope to be,
to travel, to discover,
and everything you've done.

        Again my breast
hardens. Milk comes down.
As constant dripping wears away a stone
so I am hard and softened, bottleful
of riches, magical
and always out of reach
till need uncorks me.

NORTH

Lyn Lifshin

children were wanted

were always close
to their parents'

skin even during
fucking. nobody

put the baby down

except to dip male
babies in the

wind and snow
to make them strong

then close to
the nipple again

BOSS DRAIN

Geoffrey Young

Out of the domestic bed where he lies
mute finger to lips
she steps to put her blue bathrobe on

turning to say through red teary eyes
Don't I look pretty
don't I look real good

He hadn't been looking so he did
She didn't look pretty
she didn't look real good

She was always wrong

PARALLEL BARS

It gets bad and then it gets worse
and then the bottom falls out
but then it gets better, even great, you think
you're there, but then it goes sour, totally alone, hurting,
but it comes back, new breath, friends again,
it's the best it's been in months,
really clicking, it's heaven and then
just about the time you think it's going to stay heaven,
it gets bad, and then it gets worse, and then
the bottom falls out, will it ever get better? and then
it does, it's even great, you blink an eye

and it goes sour, vicious, destructive,
but it comes back, new breath, friends again,
it's the best it's been in months, really clicking,
it's heaven, and then just about the time
you think it's going to stay heaven

From: A COUPLE CALLED MOEBIUS

CAROL BERGÉ

The father, guilty and innocent, moves about the house near the kitchen, carpentering, smoothing, polishing, moving about with his rabbit-beaver stained teeth in the big apartment or in the big advertising agency. His place, his shell, his pride. While the mother moves about the big apartment, cleaning, cleaning, cleaning, endlessly washing, sponging, rubbing, mopping, folding, soaping, polishing, sorting, opening, closing, wrapping, dishing, portioning, fastening, freezing, bottling, pouring, shifting, unwrapping, rewrapping, corking, slicing, grating, blending, mixing, ladling, dicing, slicing, grating, testing, moving, moving, moving. . . . Talking on the phone to her friends, reading recipes, talking to her house-helper, to her children, to her husband.

At the end of the day, the wife and the husband are still awake. They sit at the kitchen table with cups of coffee. Have been married for ten years. Have slept in the same bed for ten years. Have had sex together for ten years, had marital relations, have made love, have had intercourse, have never fucked, have been in rooms near their kitchen table but never on it, never on the kitchen floor in a flurry of excitement, always on their bed, never at the edge of their bed, never with some clothing on, never in the middle of the day, always in either of two usual positions, never the variations, never feeling each other till they came, never taking it in the ass, never with the loving mouths, always hidden from their own sight and from the sight of the lover. Not to be discussed. I do not want to know. It is not nice. We do not. Now they sit in their kitchen at the end of the day, it is quiet, the kitchen fan hums softly at the window drawing the air out, she has swept the floor, wet-mopped it, started the dishwasher, it hums at her right, a harder sound than the fan. He has eaten dinner out with his art director, they have accomplished a gratifying amount of work on a certain account, so he has eaten dinner at Pen and Pencil, he reports to her what they ate, but not before she tries to guess, knowing his favorite luxury meal: two very dry martinis, pâté de maison, filet mignon, baked potato, poire hélène, no, he says, went to the P&P, kept it simple, bourbon and branch, tried their chicken, wasn't any damn good, too dry. O too bad, she says. What'd *you* do today, he asks. Not much, she says, it was kind of . . . What do you mean, kind of, he says. O not much, she says, just my way of putting it, that feeling, you know, one of those kind of nothing days, Elsie came in, took the kids out, I had lunch with Sherry, you know, nothing much. Sometimes I just feel like, you know, just taking off and disappearing, she tells her husband, without looking at him. O you don't have to take off to do that, baby, he says, smiling. O boy you're in a lousy mood, she says, I didn't say that to aggravate *you*, you know . . . I just mean. I was just. Feeling like. I don't know what. Getting the hell. Out or something. Something. Sure, he says. Sure you do, baby. It's a tough life for you isn't it. All depends on who's living it, she says. Maybe it's a lot tougher than it looks to you from there. Maybe even tougher than Sherry's, and from what she told me today, she's having it pretty rough lately. Yeah, I'll bet, he says, there's a broad who really has it rough all right. Her old man makes even more dough than I do. Must be hitting fifty grand easy. What the fuck she have to complain about this time?

THE PROMISE

Toi Derricotte

I will never again
expect too much of you. I have
found out the secret of marriage:
I must keep seeing your beauty
like a stranger's, like the face
of a young girl passing on a train
whose moment of knowing illumines
it—a golden letter in a book.
I will look at you in such
exaggerated moments, lengthening
one second and shrinking eternity
until they fit together like man and wife.
My pain is expectation:
I watch you for hours sleeping, wanting
you to roll over
and look me in the eye;
my days are seconds of waiting
like the seconds between the makings
of boiling earth and sweating rivers.
What am I waiting for if not
your face—like a fish rising
to the surface, a known
but forgotten expression that
suddenly appears—or like myself,
in a strip of mirror, when, having
passed, I come back to that image
hoping to find the woman
missing. Why do you think I sleep
in the other room, planets away,
in a darkness where I could die solitary,

an old nun wrapped in clean white sheets?
Because of lies I sucked
in my mother's milk, because
of pictures in my first grade reader—
families in solid towns as if
the world were rooted and grew down
holding the rocks, eternally;
because of rings in jewelers' windows
engraved with sentiments—*I love you
forever*—as if we could survive
any beauty for longer than just after . . .
So I hobble down a hall
of disappointments past where
your darkness and my darkness have
had intercourse with each other.
Why have I wasted my life
in anger, thinking I could have more
than what is glimpsed in recognition?
I will let go, as we must
let go of an angel called
back to heaven; I will not hold
her glittering robe, but let it
drift above me until I see
the last shred of evidence.

GOOD TIMES

Lydia Davis

What was happening to them was that every bad time produced a bad feeling that in turn produced several more bad times and several more bad feelings, so that their life together had become crowded with bad times and bad feelings, so crowded that almost nothing else could grow in that dark field. But then she had a feeling of peace one morning that lingered from the evening before spent sewing while he sat reading in the next room. And a day or two later, she had a feeling of contentment that lingered in the morning from the evening before when he kept her company in the kitchen while she washed the dinner dishes and then later talked to her in bed about this and that. If the good times increased, she thought, each good time might produce a good feeling that would in turn produce several more good times that would produce several more good feelings. What she meant was that the good times might multiply perhaps as rapidly as the square of the square, or perhaps more rapidly, like mice, or like mushrooms springing up overnight from the scattered spore of a parent mushroom which in turn had sprung up overnight with a crowd of others from the scattered spore of a parent, until her life with him would be so crowded with good times that the good times might crowd out the bad as the bad times had by now almost crowded out the good . . .

NEXT DOOR

Tobias Wolff

I wake up afraid. My wife is sitting on the edge of my bed, shaking me. "They're at it again," she says.

I go to the window. All their lights are on, upstairs and down, as if they have money to burn. He yells, she screams something back, the dog barks. There is a short silence, then the baby cries, poor thing.

"Better not stand there," says my wife. "They might see you."

I say, "I'm going to call the police," knowing she won't let me.

"Don't," she says.

She's afraid that they will poison our cat if we complain.

Next door the man is still yelling, but I can't make out what he's saying over the dog and the baby. The woman laughs, not really meaning it, "*Ha! Ha! Ha!*," and suddenly gives a sharp little cry. Everything goes quiet.

"He struck her," my wife says. "I felt it just the same as if he struck me."

Next door the baby gives a long wail and the dog starts up again. The man walks out into his driveway and slams the door.

"Be careful," my wife says. She gets back into her bed and pulls the covers up to her neck.

The man mumbles to himself and jerks at his fly. Finally he gets it open and walks over to the fence. It's a white picket fence, ornamental more than anything else. It couldn't keep anyone out. I put it in myself, and planted honeysuckle and bougainvillea all along it.

My wife says, "What's he doing?"

"Shh," I say.

He leans against the fence with one hand and with the other he goes to the bathroom on the flowers. He walks the length of the fence like that, not missing any of them. When he's through he gives Florida a shake, then zips up and heads back across the driveway. He almost slips on the gravel but he catches himself and curses and goes into the house, slamming the door again.

When I turn around, my wife is leaning forward, watching me. She raises her eyebrows. "Not again," she says.

I nod.

"Number one or number two?"

"Number one."

"Thank God for small favors," she says, settling back. "Between him and the dog it's a wonder you can get anything to grow out there."

I read somewhere that human pee has a higher acid content than animal pee, but I don't mention that. I would rather talk about something else. It depresses me, thinking about the flowers. They are past their prime, but still. Next door the woman is shouting. "Listen to that," I say.

"I used to feel sorry for her," my wife says. "Not anymore. Not after last month."

"Ditto," I say, trying to remember what happened last month to make my wife not feel sorry for the woman next door. I don't feel sorry for her either, but then I never have. She yells at the baby, and excuse me, but I'm not about to get all excited over someone who treats a child like that. She screams things like *"I thought I told you to stay in your bedroom!"* and here the baby can't even speak English yet.

As far as her looks, I guess you would have to say she's pretty. But it won't last. She doesn't have good bone structure. She has a soft look to her, like she has never eaten anything but donuts and milk shakes. Her skin is white. The baby takes after her, not that you would expect it to take after *him*, dark and hairy. Even with his shirt on you can tell that he has hair all over his back and on his shoulders, thick and springy like an Airedale's.

Now they're all going at once over there, plus they've got the hi-fi turned on full blast. One of those bands. "It's the baby I feel sorry for," I say.

My wife puts her hands over her ears. "I can't stand another minute of it," she says. She takes her hands away. "Maybe there's something on TV." She sits up. "See who's on Johnny."

I turn on the television. It used to be down in the den but I brought it up here a few years ago when my wife came down with an illness. I took care of her myself—made the meals and everything. I got to where I could change the sheets with her still in the bed. I always meant to take the television back down when my wife recovered from her illness, but I never got around to it. It sits between our beds on a little table I made. Johnny is saying something to Sammy Davis, Jr. Ed McMahon is bent over laughing. He is always so cheerful. If you were going to take a really long voyage you could do worse than bring Ed McMahon along.

"Sammy," says my wife. "Who else is on besides Sammy?"

I look at the TV guide. "A bunch of people I never heard of." I read off their names. My wife hasn't heard of them either. She wants to know what else is on. " 'El Dorado,' " I read. " 'Brisk adventure yarn about a group of citizens in search of the legendary city of gold.' It's got two and a half stars beside it."

"Citizens of what?" my wife asks.

"It doesn't say."

Finally we watch the movie. A blind man comes into a small town. He says that he has been to El Dorado, and that he will lead an expedition there for a share of the proceeds. He can't see, but he will call out the landmarks one by one as they ride. At first people make fun of him, but eventually all the leading citizens get together and decide to give it a try. Right away they get attacked by Apaches and some of them want to turn back, but every time they get ready the blind man gives them another landmark, so they keep riding.

Next door the woman is going crazy. She is saying things to him that no person should ever say to another person. It makes my wife restless. She looks at me. "Can I come over?" she says. "Just for a visit?"

I pull down the blankets and she gets in. The bed is just fine for one, but with two of us it's a tight fit. We are lying on our sides with me in back. I don't mean for it to happen but before long old Florida begins to stiffen up on me. I put my arms around my wife. I move my hands up onto the Rockies, then on down across the Plains, heading south.

"Hey," she says. "No Geography. Not tonight."

"I'm sorry," I say.

"Can't I just visit?"

"Forget it. I said I was sorry."

The citizens are crossing a desert. They have just about run out of water, and their lips are cracked. Though the blind man has delivered a warning, someone drinks from a poisoned well and dies horribly. That night, around the campfire, the others begin to quarrel. Most of them want to go home. "This is no country for a white man," one says, "and if you ask me nobody has ever been here before." But the blind man describes a piece of gold so big and pure that it will burn your eyes out if you look directly at it. "I ought to know," he says. When he is finished the citizens are silent: one by one they move away and lie down on their bedrolls. They put their hands behind their heads and look up at the stars. A coyote howls.

Hearing the coyote, I remember why my wife doesn't feel sorry for the woman next door. It was a Monday evening, about a month ago, right after I got home from work. The man next door started to beat the dog, and I don't mean just smacking him once or twice. He was beating him, and he kept beating him until the dog couldn't even cry anymore; you could hear the poor creature's voice breaking. It made us very upset, especially my wife, who is an animal lover from way back. Finally it stopped. Then a few minutes later, I heard my wife say, "Oh!" and I went into the kitchen to find out what was wrong. She was standing by the window, which looks into the kitchen next door. The man had his wife backed up against the fridge. He had his knee between her legs and she had her knee between his legs and they were kissing, really hard, not just with their lips but rolling their faces back and forth one against the other. My wife could hardly speak for a couple of hours afterwards. Later she said that she would never waste her sympathy on that woman again.

It's quiet over there. My wife has gone to sleep and so has my arm, which is under her head. I slide it out and open and close my fingers, considering whether to wake her up. I like sleeping in my own bed, and there isn't enough room for the both of us. Finally I decide that it won't hurt anything to change places for one night.

I get up and fuss with the plants for a while, watering them and moving some to the window and some back. I trim the coleus, which is starting to get leggy, and put the cuttings in a glass of water on the sill. All the lights are off next door except the one in their bedroom window. I think about the life they have, and how it goes on and on, until it seems like the life they were meant to live. Everybody is always saying how great it is that human beings are so adaptable, but I don't know. A friend of mine was in the Navy and he told me that in Amsterdam, Holland, they have a whole section of town where you can walk through and from the street you can see women sitting in rooms, waiting. If you want one of them you just go in and pay, and they close the drapes. This is nothing special to the people who live in Holland. In Istanbul, Turkey, my friend saw a man walking down the street with a grand piano on his back. Everyone just moved round him and kept going. It's awful, what we get used to.

I turn off the television and get into my wife's bed. A sweet, heavy smell rises off the sheets. At first it makes me dizzy but after that I like it. It reminds me of gardenias.

The reason I don't watch the rest of the movie is that I can already see how it will end. The citizens will kill each other off, probably about ten feet from the legendary city of gold, and the blind man will stumble in by himself, not knowing that he has made it back to El Dorado.

I could write a better movie than that. My movie would be about a group of explorers, men and women, who leave behind their homes and their jobs and their families—everything they have known. They cross the sea and are shipwrecked on the coast of a country which is not on their maps. One of them drowns. Another gets attacked by a wild animal, and eaten. But the others want to push on. They ford rivers and cross an enormous glacier by dog sled. It takes months. On the glacier they run out of food, and for a while there it looks like they might turn on each other, but they don't. Finally they solve their problem by eating the dogs. That's the sad part of the movie.

At the end we see the explorers sleeping in a meadow filled with white flowers. The blossoms are wet with dew and stick to their bodies, petals of columbine, clematis, blazing star, baby's breath, larkspur, iris, rue—covering them completely, turning them white so that you cannot tell one from another, man from woman, woman from man. The sun comes up. They stand and raise their arms, like white trees in a land where no one has ever been.

SONNET

Lewis Warsh

If I turn into you
By force of habit, dint
Of luck, or just
Normally, as the occasion warrants
Not romantically, but because
Sifting through myself, I find
I'm thinking your thoughts, and you mine,
So it's possible both to inhabit
The body that sleeps beside you
And the concise fragments of the person
You thought you were, part in-
decision, part desire, part heavenly
Love, or all these things
Scattered over the earth, like sparks.

WANTING ALL

Alicia Ostriker

> More! More! is the cry of a mistaken soul,
> less than All cannot satisfy Man.
> —William Blake

Husband, it's fine the way your mind performs
Like a circus, sharp
As a sword somebody has
To swallow, rough as a bear,
Complicated as a family of jugglers,
Brave as a sequined trapeze
Artist, the only boy I ever met
Who could beat me in argument
Was why I married you, isn't it,
And you have beaten me, I've beaten you,
We are old polished hands.

Or was it your body, I forget, maybe
I foresaw the thousands on thousands
Of times we have made love
Together, mostly meat
And potatoes love, but sometimes
Higher than wine,
Better than medicine.
How lately you bite, you baby,
How angels record and number
Each gesture, and sketch
Our spinal columns like professionals.

Husband, it's fine how we cook
Dinners together while drinking,

How we get drunk, how
We gossip, work at our desks, dig in the garden,
Go to the movies, tell
The children to clear the bloody table,
How we fit like puzzle pieces.

The mind and body satisfy
Like windows and furniture in a house.
The windows are large, the furniture solid.
What more do I want then, why
Do I prowl the basement, why
Do I reach for your inside
Self as you shut it
Like a trunkful of treasures? *Wait,*
I cry, as the lid slams on my fingers.

PART IV

THE BOVARY BED

From: THE BLOOD ORANGES

John Hawkes

Love weaves its own tapestry, spins its own golden thread, with its own sweet breath breathes into being its mysteries—bucolic, lusty, gentle as the eyes of daisies or thick with pain. And out of its own music creates the flesh of our lives. If the birds sing, the nudes are not far off. Even the dialogue of the frogs is rapturous.

As for me, since late boyhood and early manhood, and throughout the more than eighteen years of my nearly perfect marriage, I always allowed myself to assume whatever shape was destined to be my own in the silken weave of Love's pink panorama. I always went where the thread wound. No awkward hesitation, no prideful ravaging. At an early age I came to know that the gods fashion us to spread the legs of woman, or throw us together for no reason except that we complete the picture, so to speak, and join loin to loin often and easily, humbly, deliberately. Throughout my life I have never denied a woman young or old. Throughout my life I have simply appeared at Love's will. See me as small white porcelain bull lost in the lower left-hand corner of that vast tapestry, see me as great white creature horned and mounted on a trim little golden sheep in the very center of Love's most explosive field. See me as bull, or ram, as man, husband, lover, a tall and heavy stranger in white shorts on a violet tennis court. I was there always. I completed the picture. I took my wife, took her friends, took the wives of my friends and a fair roster of other girls and women, from young to old and old to young, whenever the light was right or the music sounded.

✳

The sun was setting, sinking to its predestined death, and to the four of us, or at least to me, that enormous smoldering sun lay on the horizon like a dissolving orange suffused with blood. The tide was low, the smooth black oval stones beneath us were warm to the flesh, we could hear the distant sounds of the three girls playing with the dog behind the funeral cypresses. Fiona, wearing a pale lemon-colored bra and pale lemon-colored briefs for the beach, and I in my magenta trunks as sparse and thick and elastic as an athletic supporter, and Hugh in his long-sleeved cotton shirt and loose gray trunks like undershorts, and Catherine dressed in her faded madras halter and swimming skirt and shorts—together we sat with legs outstretched, soles of our feet touching or nearly touching, a four-pointed human starfish resting together in the last vivid light of the day.

No one moved. Without calculation, almost without consciousness, Fiona lay propped on her elbows and with her head back, her eyes closed, her tense lips gently smiling. Even Catherine appeared to be sunk in a kind of worried slumber, aware somehow of the thick orange light on her knees. Prone bodies, silence hanging on the children's voices and scattered barking of their old black dog, the empty wine bottles turning to gold. All of us felt the inertia, suspension, tranquillity, though I found myself tapping out a silent expectant rhythm with one of my big toes while Hugh's narrow black eyes were alert, unresting, I noticed, and to me revealed only too clearly his private thoughts. But the small black oval stones we lay on were for us much better than sand. Our beach, as we called it, was a glassy volcanic bed that made us draw closer together to touch toes, to dream. With one hand I was carelessly crushing a few thin navy-blue seashells, making a small pile of crushed shell on my naked navel. And yet it was the sun, the sun alone that filled all our thoughts and was turning the exposed skin of all four bodies the same deepening color. The lower the sun fell the more it glowed.

I felt someone's foot recoil from mine and then return. Even the tiny black ringlets in Hugh's beard were turning orange. I could hear the powdery shells collecting in the well of my belly and I realized that all four of us were together on a black volcanic beach in the hour when fiercely illumined goats stand still and huddle and the moon prepares to pour its milk on the fire.

"Cyril. We don't have to go back yet, do we?"

I glanced at Fiona, heard the matter-of-fact whisper and saw that her expression had not changed, that her lips had not moved. But rolling onto one hip, propping myself on one elbow, brushing away crushed shells with a hasty stroke of one hand, I saw also that there was movement in the curve of her throat and that the sun had saturated one of her broad white shoulders. And before I could answer, Fiona giggled. My sensible, stately, impatient, clear-bodied wife giggled, as if in a dream a small bird had alighted on her belly. Giggled for no reason apparently, she whose every impulsive gesture was informed with its own hidden sense, and at the sound Hugh became suddenly rigid, Catherine opened her eyes. I knew what to do.

In silence, while the sun flushed us most deeply and unrecognizably with orange light, I got to my knees beside Fiona, who did not move, and with a flick of my hand untied the silken strings of her pale lemon-colored halter, those thin silken cords knotted in a bow behind her bent neck and curving back, and then with a few more skillful movements removed altogether Fiona's little lemon-colored bra. Then I folded this the briefest of all Fiona's half-dozen bathing bras, stuck it for safekeeping inside one of my empty shoes, and flowed back slowly into my former position on the hot rocks.

Understandably perhaps, for the first few moments Catherine and even Hugh could not bear to look. I myself hardly dared to look. But then I heard a sound like a finger scratching inside Hugh's throat and our three heads turned furtively, shyly, violently or calmly in my wife's direction. And Fiona's eyes, I saw, were open. We said nothing, Fiona was looking straight at the sun and smiling. But had she wanted me to expose her breasts, I wondered, for Hugh's sake or mine? Or was the exposure purely my own idea and something that entered her consciousness and gave her pleasure only after I had touched her, untied the strings? I could not know. But I knew immediately that it was a good idea.

Fiona's breasts were not large. Yet in the sun's lurid effulgence they glistened, grew tight while the two nipples turned to liquid rings, bands, so that to me Fiona's two firm breasts suddenly became the bursting irises of a young white owl's wide-open eyes, and when in the next moment she giggled again, again apparently without reason, those bright naked eyes, breasts, recorded the little spasms of pleasure that, otherwise unseen, were traveling down Fiona's chest and neck and arms.

"Baby, can't we just stay like this forever?"

We heard the words, we watched the very motion of Fiona's speech in her lips and breasts. In mouth and breasts my wife was singing, and despite the possibility of another unexpected giggle, which no doubt would be accompanied by another small eruption of rolling or bouncing in the lovely breasts as well as a slight twisting in the slope of the shoulders, despite all this or perhaps because of it the preciousness of what Fiona said maintained the silence, prevented the rest of us from talking. I could see the thin white edge of Fiona's teeth between the slightly parted lips, the voice was soft and clear, the naked orange breasts were unimaginably free, her eyes were partially open. Even in the silence she was singing, and the rest of us were listening, watching.

Then suddenly Hugh began to scratch viciously at himself beneath the loose gray shorts, and Catherine moved. With a brief flashing sensation of regret, it occurred to me that she was about to climb heavily, angrily to her feet and leave. She too could hear that in the distance the children were beginning to quarrel, beginning to tease the dog. But I was wrong, and she merely drew herself slowly out of her supine state, raised her back and lifted up her long heavy legs and sat upright with her thighs pressed together on the black rocks and her knees bent and her strong calves crossed at the ankles.

And then Hugh spoke. Stopped scratching himself and spoke, while Catherine's unreadable eyes met mine and I smiled, allowed my large right orange hand to lie comfortably where my upper thighs, which were about twice the girth of even Catherine's thighs, joined in special harmony the inverted apex of my own magenta briefs for the beach.

"That's it. All these years you've been castrating him!"

On this occasion it was hardly what I thought he would say. Was this the extent of the private thoughts I had been watching all this time in his black eyes? But then I laughed, because Hugh had been staring all this time at the bare breasts of my wife and because he was thin and because despite the ringlets of his beard and curls of black hair across his forehead he was nonetheless wearing the long gray shapeless bathing trunks and the white cotton collarless shirt with the right sleeve pinned up with one of Catherine's large steel safety pins. Perhaps he did not enjoy the sight of Fiona as much as I did, or would not admit that he did. Nonetheless, that he could lie in my shadow and stare at my wife as he was in fact staring at her, and then pronounce what he had just pronounced, aroused in me new admiration for so much craft, for so much comic design.

"Cyril is virile, baby. He really is."

The absolute certainty of the soft voice which in timbre matched the curve of Fiona's throat, the pleasing brevity of the assertion, the mild sex-message of the accompanying giggle, which was more than the giggle of a mere girl, the fact that Fiona still had not moved but lay back on her elbows with one slender leg raised at the knee and her breasts falling imperceptibly to either side—at that moment I could not have loved Fiona more or felt more affection for my courageous, self-betraying Saint Peter, as I had come to call Hugh mentally whenever our quaternion reached special intensity or special joy.

Suspension, suffusion, peace for the four of us on that black beach. But it was all beginning to pass, I knew, and still I waited, now hearing the older girl shouting at the smaller girls behind the funeral cypresses. Shifting a little, growing mildly impatient myself, I waited, wondering if this momentary idyll would pass before the rose and golden metallic threads could begin to spin our separate anatomies forever into the sunset scene, would come to a sudden conclusion, incomplete, unbalanced. What was the matter with Hugh? Why was he not holding up his end?

I could understand Hugh's affected lack of gratitude, could enjoy his efforts to conceal his feelings on seeing Fiona without her bra. And of course Hugh could not possibly know that I was well aware of the fact that he had already seen Fiona's naked breasts, had already held her breasts in his good hand, so that in taking off her halter I knew full well that I was violating no confidence and was merely extending naturally the pleasures of a treat already quite familiar to the two of us. And I realized also that Hugh did not know that already I was as familiar with Catherine's naked breasts as he was with Fiona's, so that the baring of Catherine's breasts would be no surprise for me. Was he then thoughtless? Selfish? Without even the crudest idea of simple reciprocity? Certainly he must have known that it was up to him, not me, to unfasten Catherine's overly modest halter and take it off. What was holding him back? Could he not see that Catherine herself was puzzled, uncomfortable? Could he deliberately mean to embarrass his wife and to tamper with the obviously intended symmetry of our little scene on the beach? Hugh was unmusical, but I had hoped I could count on him for at least a few signs of romantic temperament. After all, how could any man love my wife and yet fail to appreciate simple harmonious arrangements of flesh, shadow, voice, hair, which were as much the result of Fiona's artistry as of mine. But perhaps I had been wrong. Perhaps Hugh had no eye for the sex-tableau.

I yawned, glanced at the finely muscled music of Fiona's breathing, began crushing another pile of shells. Back at the villas one of the smaller girls was now shrieking distantly in short monotonous bursts of pain.

And then, nearly too late, Catherine acted on her own behalf, brought herself to do what Hugh should have done, and out of feelings of exclusion or possibly pleasure or more likely irritable retaliation, managed to complete the picture that Hugh had almost destroyed. She frowned, tightened her lips, took a short breath and, crooking her elbows so that her bent arms became the rapidly moving wings of some large bird, reached behind her back and quickly, without help, unfastened her halter and pulled it off. It was an awkward, rapid, determined, self-sufficient gesture of compliance, and I was proud of her. And even though in that first moment of exposure she looked as if she wanted nothing more than to cross her arms and conceal beneath the flesh of her arms the flesh of her breasts, still she sat up straight and kept herself uncovered. I was proud of her.

And though I had already known what we would see when she finally bared herself, could visualize to the last detail the surfaces of Catherine's nakedness, still it pleased me to see the round rising breasts and the nipples that resembled small dark rosebuds tightly furled, and to see all this, not at night in their villa, but here at sunset on the polished black stones born of the volcano's chaotic fire.

How long would we manage to preserve this balance of nudity? For how long would we be allowed to appreciate the fact that the nude breathing torsos of these two very different women simply enhanced each other? I could not know. But here, at least, was the possibility of well-being, and though Catherine sat with eyes averted and arms straight and the large halter half-wadded, clutched, in one large hand in her lap, still at that moment I found myself tingling with the realization that Hugh's wife had acted deliberately and in large part for me. And now, this instant, if Catherine had been able, say, to cup her breasts in her hands with Fiona's thoughtless exhilaration, might not the sight of Catherine be as stimulating as that of Fiona? Then again, wasn't the naturalness of Catherine's slight lingering discomfort exactly as stimulating as the naturalness of my own wife's erotic confidence? I smiled, I found that the ball of my right foot was pressed gently to the solid front of one of Catherine's knees, I heard Fiona giggling and saw that Hugh's blue-gray ankle was now trapped, so to speak, between both of Fiona's energetic feet, and again I began to hope that I had not overestimated Hugh after all.

But rolling onto my hands and knees, getting to my feet with a cheerful groan, lumbering to cut off the oldest girl who was running toward us out of the cypresses and shouting for Catherine, and stopping her and displaying friendliness and knowing that when I turned to wave I would see distant gestures of busy hands fastening big and little halters once again into place—still I could only smile and do a few dancing bear steps for the angry child, because no sex-tableau was ever entirely abortive and because ahead of us lay an unlimited supply of dying suns and crescent moons which Fiona, and Catherine too, would know how to use.

A MYTHOLOGICAL SUBJECT

Laurie Colwin

It is often to the wary that the events in life are unexpected. Looser types—people who are not busy weighing and measuring every little thing—are used to accidents, coincidences, chance, things getting out of hand, things sneaking up on them. They are the happy children of life, to whom life happens for better or worse.

Those who believe in will, in meaning, in intentionality, who brood, reflect, and contemplate, who believe there are no accidents, who are born with clear vision or an introspective temperament or a relentless consciousness are quite another matter.

I am of the former category, a cheerful woman. The first man who asked me to marry him turned out to be the perfect mate. It may be that I happily settled for what came my way, but in fact my early marriage endured and prospered. As a couple we are even-tempered, easy to please, curious, fond of food and gossip. My husband Edward runs his family's import business. We have three children, all away at school. We are great socializers, and it is our chief entertainment to bring our interesting friends together.

Of our set, the dearest was my cousin Nellie Felix. I had known her as a child and was delighted when she came to New York to live and study. After all, few things are more pleasing than an attractive family member. She was full of high spirits and emotional idealism. What would become of her was one of our favorite topics of conversation.

In her twenties she had two dramatic love affairs. These love affairs surprised her: she did not think of herself as a romantic, but as someone seeking honor and communion in love. Her idealism in these matters was sweet and rather innocent. That a love affair could lead to nothing stumped her. When she was not seriously attached she was something of a loner, although she had a nice set of friends.

At the age of thirty Nellie fell in love with a lawyer named

Joseph Porter. He was lovable, intelligent, and temperamental enough to make life interesting. With him Nellie found what she had been looking for, and they were married. Nellie believed in order, in tranquillity, in her household as a safe haven, and she worked harder than even she knew to make sure she had these things. She taught three days a week at a women's college an hour outside New York. Her students adored her. She and Joseph expanded their circle, and eventually they had a child, an enchanting daughter named Jane. They lived in a town house and their life was attractive, well organized, comfortable, and looked rather effortless.

But Nellie did not feel that it was effortless. She had so ardently wanted the life she had, but she felt that she had come close to not having it; that her twenties had not been a quest for love but a romantic shambles; that there was some part of her that was not for order and organization but for chaos. She believed that the neat and tidy surfaces of things warded off misery and despair, that she had to constantly be vigilant with everything, especially herself. She once described to me a fountain she had seen on her honeymoon in the close of the Barcelona Cathedral. It was an ornamental fountain that shot up a constant jet of water. On top of this jet bobbled an egg. This seemed to Nellie a perfect metaphor to express the way she felt about her life. Without constant vigilance, self-scrutiny, accurate self-assessment, and a strong will, whatever kept the egg of her life aloft would disappear and the egg would shatter. She knew the unexamined life was not worth living. She never wanted to do things for the wrong reason, or for no reason or for reasons she did not understand. She wanted to be clear and unsentimental, to believe things that were true and not things that it consoled her to believe. When her colleague Dan Hamilton said to her: "You're very rough on me," she said: "I'm rougher on myself, I promise you."

My husband and I introduced Nellie to Dan Hamilton. We had been planning to get the Porters and the Hamiltons together for some time, but the Hamiltons were hard to pin down. Miranda Hamilton was a designer whose work frequently took her abroad. Dan was a historian. Once every three or four years he would produce a popular and successful book on some figure in colonial history. Over the years these books had made him rich, and he had become a sort of traveling scholar. Now that their three sons were grown up and married they had more or less settled down in New York. Dan had taken a sabbatical from writing and was the star appointment at Nellie's college—all the more reason to bring the two couples together.

They got along famously. My husband and I looked down from our opposite ends of the table flushed with the vision of a successful dinner party. How attractive they all looked in the candlelight! Joseph, who was large, ruddy, and beautifully dressed, sat next to Miranda. They were talking about Paris. Miranda wore her reddish hair in a stylish knot. She was wiry and chic and smoked cigarettes in a little black holder. Nellie sat next to Dan. Her clothes, as always, were sober and she looked wonderful. She had straight ashy hair that she pulled back off her face, and hazel eyes full of motion and expression. Dan, who sat next to her, was her opposite. As Nellie was immaculate and precise, Dan looked antic and boyish. He had a mop of curly brown, copper, and grey hair, and he always looked a little awry. His tie was never quite properly tied, and the pockets of his jackets sagged from carrying pipes and books and change in them. He and Nellie and my husband were being silly about some subject or other at their end of the table, and Nellie was laughing.

Over coffee it was discovered that Nellie and Dan shared the same schedule. Dan said: "In that case I ought to drive you up to school. I hate to drive alone and the trains are probably horrible." At this Miranda gave Dan a look which Nellie registered against her will. She imagined that Dan was famous for loving to drive alone and that he was teasing Miranda by flirting.

But the idea of being driven to school was quite heavenly. The trains were awful. The first week of Dan and Nellie's mobile colleagueship was a great success. They talked shop, compared notes on faculty and classes and family. Dan knew some of the people who had taught Nellie at college. The time, on these trips, flew by.

After two weeks Nellie became uneasy about the cost of gas and tolls and insisted on either paying for them or splitting them. Dan would not hear of this so Nellie suggested that she give him breakfast on school days to even up the score. Dan thought this was a fine idea. Nellie was a good plain cook. She gave Dan scones, toasted cheese, sour cream muffins, and coffee with hot milk. On Thursdays when they did not have to be at school until the afternoon they got into the habit of having lunch at Nellie's. They sat in the kitchen dining off the remains of last night's dinner party.

A million things slipped by them. Neither admitted how much they looked forward to their rides to school, or their breakfasts or their unnecessary Thursday lunches. Nellie told herself that this arrangement was primarily a convenience, albeit a friendly one.

One stormy autumn night, full of purple clouds and shaking branches, Nellie and Dan sat for longer than usual in front of Nellie's house. They were both restless, and Nellie's reluctance to get out of the car and go home disturbed her. Every time she got set to leave, Dan would say something to pull her back. Finally she knew she had to go, and on an unchecked impulse she reached for Dan's hand. On a similarly unchecked impulse, Dan took her hand and kissed it.

What happened was quite simple. Nellie came down with the flu—no wonder she had felt so restless. She canceled her classes and called Dan to tell him. He sounded rather cross, and it was clear he did not like to have his routines interrupted.

On Thursday she was all recovered, but Dan turned up in a terrible mood. He bolted his breakfast and was anxious to get on the road. Once they hit the highway he calmed down. They discovered that both Miranda and Joseph were away on business and that Jane was on an overnight school trip. They decided to stop for dinner at the inn they always passed, to see if it was any good.

That day Nellie felt light and clear and full of frantic energy. She taught two of the best classes she had ever taught, but she was addled. She who never lost anything left her handbag in her office and her class notes in the dining commons. Although she and Dan usually met in the parking lot, they had arranged to meet in front of the science building, but both kept forgetting what the plan was, necessitating several rounds of telephone calls.

Finally they drove through the twilight to the inn. The windows were made of bull's-eye glass, and there were flowers on the sideboard. Nellie and Dan sat by the fireplace. Neither had much in the way of appetite. They talked a blue streak and split a bottle of wine.

Outside it was brilliantly clear. The sky was full of stars, and the frosty, crisp air smelled of apples and woodsmoke. Dan started the car. Then he turned it off. With his hands on the steering wheel he said: "I think I've fallen in love with you and if I'm not mistaken, you've fallen in love with me."

It is true that there is something—there is everything—undeniable about the truth. Even the worst true thing fills the consciousness with the light of its correctness. What Dan said was just plain true, and it filled Nellie with a wild surge of joy.

It explained everything: their giddiness, their unwillingness to part, those unnecessary lunches and elaborate breakfasts.

"My God," she said. "I didn't mean for this to happen." She knew in an instant how much care she had been taking all along— to fill her conversation with references to Joseph and Jane, to say "us" and not "me," not to say any flirtatious or provocative thing. How could she have not seen this coming? Falling in love is very often not flirtatious. It is often rather grave, and if the people falling in love are married the mention of a family is not so much a banner as it is a bulletproof vest.

They sat in the cold darkness. Someone looking in the window might have thought they were discussing a terminal illness. Nellie stared at the floor. Dan was fixated on the dashboard. Neither said a word. They were terrified to look at one another—frightened of what might be visible on the other's face. But these things are irresistible, and they were drawn into each other's arms.

They drove home the long way through little towns and villages. Nellie sat close to Dan, who kept his arm around her and drove with one hand, like a teenage boy. At every stop sign and red light they kissed each other. Both of them were giddy and high. They talked and talked—like all lovers worth their salt they compared notes. They had dreamed and daydreamed about each other. They recited the history of their affections: how Dan had once come close to driving the car off the road because he was staring at Nellie one afternoon; how the sight of Dan with his shirttail out had brought Nellie near to tears she did not understand, and so on.

With their families away they had the freedom to do anything they liked but all they did was to stand in Nellie's kitchen and talk. They never sat down. When they were not talking they were in each other's arms, kissing in that way that is like drinking out of terrible thirst. Twice Nellie burst into tears—of confusion, desire, and the terrible excess of happiness that love and the knowledge that one is loved in return often brings. Nellie knew what she was feeling. That she was feeling it as a married woman upset her terribly, but the feeling was undeniable and she did not have the will to suppress it. They stood on opposite sides of the kitchen—this was Nellie's stage direction—and discussed whether or not they should go to bed. They were both quite sick with desire but what they were feeling was so powerful and seemed so dangerous that the idea of physical expression scared them to death.

Very late at night Nellie sent Dan home. In two separate beds in two separate places, in Nellie's house and Dan's apartment, separated by a number of streets and avenues, these two lovers tossed and ached and attempted to sleep away what little of the night remained to them.

The next morning Nellie woke up exhausted and keen in her empty house. When she splashed water on her face to wake herself up she found that she was laughing and crying at the same time. She felt flooded by emotions, one of which was gratitude. She felt that her life was being handed back to her, but by whom? And from where?

Alone in her kitchen she boiled water for tea and thought about Dan. For a moment he would evaporate and she could not remember what had passed between them. She drank her tea and watched a late autumn fly buzz around the kitchen. When it landed on the table, she observed it. The miraculous nature of this tiny beast, the fact that it could actually fly, the complexities and originality of things, the richness of the world, the amazing beauty of being alive struck Nellie full force. She was filled up, high as a kite. Love, even if it was doomed, gave you a renewed sense of things: it did hand life back to you.

But after a certain age, no joy is unmitigated. She knew that if she did not succeed in denying her feelings for Dan her happiness in his presence would always mix with sadness. She had never been in love with anyone unavailable, and she had never been unavailable herself.

Her heart, she felt, was not beating properly. She did not think that she would take a normal breath until she heard from Dan. When the telephone rang, she knew it was him.

"May I come and have breakfast with you?" he said. "Or do you think it's all wrong?"

Nellie said: "It's certainly all wrong but come anyway."

This was their first furtive meeting. Friday was not a school day: they were meeting out of pure volition. If Joseph asked her what she had been up to she could not say casually: "Dan Hamilton stopped by." It might sound as innocent as milk, but they were no longer innocent.

The sunlight through the kitchen windows suddenly looked threatening. The safe, tidy surfaces suddenly looked precarious and unstable. Her life, the life of a secure and faithful wife, had been done away in an instant, and even if she never saw Dan Hamilton again it was clear that something unalterable had happened to her. She could never again say that she had not been tempted. She felt alone in the middle of the universe, without husband or child, with only herself. Surely at the sight of Dan everything would fall into place and everything would be as it had been a day ago. She would see that Dan was her colleague and her friend, and that a declaration of love would not necessarily have to change everything.

But as soon as she saw him from the window she realized that a declaration does in fact change everything and that Dan was no longer just her colleague and friend. They could not keep out of each other's arms.

"I haven't felt this way since I was a teenager," said Dan. Nellie didn't say anything. She *had* felt this way since she was a teenager.

"It feels sort of heavenly," Dan said.

"It will get a little hellish," Nellie said.

"Really?" said Dan. "It's hard to believe."

"I've felt this way a couple of times," said Nellie. "Back in the world of childhood when everyone was single and nothing got in the way of a love affair. You could spend your every minute with the one you loved. You could have the luxury of getting *tired* of the one you loved. You had endless time. This is the grown-up world of the furtive, adulterous love match. No time, no luxury. I've never met anyone on the sly."

"We don't have to meet on the sly," said Dan. "We're commuters."

"I don't think you realize how quickly these things get out of hand," Nellie said.

"I'd certainly like to find out," said Dan, smiling. "Can't we just enjoy our feelings for a few minutes before all this furtive misery comes crashing down on us?"

"I give it an hour," said Nellie.

"Well, all right then. Let's go read the paper. Let's go into the living room and cozy up on the couch like single people. I can't believe you actually went out this morning and got the paper. You must have it delivered."

"We do," said Nellie.

"We do, too," said Dan.

Miranda was due back the next day, and Joseph in the early evening. Dan and Nellie stretched out on the couch in the sunlight and attempted to browse through the paper. Physical nearness caused their hearts to race. Adulterous lovers, without the errands and goals and plans that make marriage so easy, are left horribly to themselves. They have nothing to do but be—poor things.

"Here we are," said Nellie. "Representatives of two households, both of which get the *Times* delivered, curled up on a couch like a pair of teenagers."

They did not kiss each other. They did not even hold hands. The couch was big enough for both of them, with a tiny space between. They kept that space between them. Everything seemed very clear and serious. This was their last chance to deny that they were anything more than friends. Two gestures could be made: they would become lovers or they would not. It seemed to Nellie a very grave moment in her life. She was no longer a girl with strong opinions and ideals, but a mortal woman caught in the complexities of life. Both Nellie and Dan were silent. Once they were in each other's arms it was all over, they knew, but since falling in love outside of marriage is the ultimate and every other gesture is its shadow, when they could bear it no longer they went upstairs to Nellie's guest room and there became lovers in the real sense of the word.

Of all the terrible things in life, living with a divided heart is the most terrible for an honorable person. There were times when Nellie could scarcely believe that she was the person she knew. Her love for Dan seemed pure to her, but its context certainly did not. There was not one moment when she felt right or justified: she simply had her feelings and she learned that some true feelings make one wretched; that they interfere with life; that they cause great emotional and moral pain; and that there was nothing much she could do about them. Her love for Dan opened the world up in a terrible and serious way and caused her, with perfect and appropriate justification, to question everything: her marriage, her ethics, her sense of the world, herself.

Dan said: "Can't you leave yourself alone for five seconds? Can't you just go with life a little?"

Nellie said: "Don't you want this to have anything to do with your life? Do you think we fell in love for no reason whatsoever? Don't you want to know what this means?"

"I can't think that way about these things," Dan said. "I want to enjoy them."

Nellie said: "I have to know everything. I think it's immoral not to."

That was when Dan had said: "You're very rough on me."

Any city is full of adulterers. They hide out in corners of restaurants. They know the location of all necessary pay telephones. They go to places their friends never go to. From time to time they become emboldened and are spotted by a sympathetic acquaintance who has troubles of his or her own and never says a word to anyone.

There are plain philanderers, adventurers, and people seeking revenge on a spouse. There are those who have absolutely no idea what they are doing or why, who believe that events have simply carried them away. And there are those to whom love comes, unexpected and not very welcome, a sort of terrible fact of life like fire or flood. Neither Nellie nor Dan had expected to fall in love. They were innocents at it.

There were things they were not prepared for. The first time Nellie called Dan from a pay phone made her feel quite awful—Joseph was home with a cold and Nellie wanted to call Dan before he called her. That call made her think of all the second-rate and nasty elements that love outside marriage entails.

The sight of Nellie on the street with Jane upset Dan. He saw them from afar and was glad he was too far off to be seen. That little replica of Nellie stunned him. He realized that he had never seen Jane before: that was how distant he and Nellie were from the true centers of each other's lives. He was jealous of Jane, he realized. Jealous of a small daughter because of such exclusive intimacy.

When Nellie ran into Dan with his middle son Ewan at the liquor store one Saturday afternoon, it had the same effect on her. Both she and Dan were buying wine for dinner parties. Both knew exactly what the other was serving and to whom. This made Nellie think of the thousands of things they did not know and would never know: that family glaze of common references, jokes, events, calamities—that sense of a family being like a kitchen midden: layer upon layer of the things daily life is made of. The edifice that lovers build is by comparison delicate and one-dimensional. The sight of the beloved's child is only a living demonstration that the one you love has a long and complicated history that has nothing to do with you.

They suffered everything. When they were together they suffered from guilt and when apart from longing. The joys that lovers experience are extreme joys, paid for by the sacrifice of everything comfortable. Moments of unfettered happiness are few, and they mostly come when one or the other is too exhausted to think. One morning Nellie fell asleep in the car. She woke up with a weak winter light warming her. For an instant she was simply happy—happy to be herself, to be with Dan, to be alive. It was a very brief moment, pure and sweet as cream. As soon as she woke up it vanished. Nothing was simple at all. Her heart felt heavy as a weight. Nothing was clear or reasonable or unencumbered. There was no straight explanation of anything.

Since I saw remarkably little of Nellie, I suspected something was up with her: she was one of those people who hide out when they are in trouble. I knew that if she needed to talk she would come to see me and eventually she did just that.

It is part of the nature of the secret that it needs to be shared. Without confession it is incomplete. When what she was feeling was too much for her, Nellie chose me as her confidante. I was the logical choice: I was family, I had known Nellie all her life, and I had known Dan for a long time, too.

She appeared early one Friday in the middle of a winter storm. She was expected anyway—she and I were going to pick up Jane later in the afternoon, and then my husband and I, Nellie, Joseph, and Jane were going out for dinner.

She came in looking flushed and *fine*, with diamonds of sleet in her hair. She was wearing a grey skirt, and a sweater which in some lights was lilac and in some the color of a pigeon's wing. She shook out her hair, and when we were finally settled in the living room with our cups of tea I could see that she was very upset.

"You look very stirred up," I said.

"I am stirred up," said Nellie. "I need to talk to you." She stared down into her tea and it was clear that she was composing herself to keep from crying.

Finally she said: "I'm in love with Dan Hamilton."

I said: "Is he in love with you?"

"Yes," said Nellie.

I was not surprised at all, and that I was not surprised upset her. She began to cry, which made her look all the more charming. She was one of those lucky people who are not ruined by tears.

"I'm so distressed," she said. "I almost feel embarrassed to be as upset as I am."

"You're not exempt from distress," I said. "You're also not exempt from falling in love."

"I wanted to be," she said fiercely. "I thought that if I put my will behind it, if I was straight with myself I wouldn't make these mistakes."

"Falling in love is not a mistake."

She then poured forth. There were no accidents, she knew. That she had fallen in love meant something. What did it say about herself and Joseph? All the familiar emotional props of girlhood—will, resolve, a belief in a straight path—were gone from her. She did not see why love had come to her unless she had secretly—a secret from herself, she meant—been looking for it. And on and on. That she was someone who drew love—some people do, and they need not be especially lovable or physically beautiful, as Nellie believed—was not enough of an explanation for her. That something had simply happened was not an idea she could entertain. She did not believe that things simply happened.

She talked until her voice grew strained. She had not spared herself a thing. She said, finally: "I wanted to be like you—steady and faithful. I thought my romantic days were over. I thought I was grown up. I wanted for me and Joseph to have what you and Edward have—a good and uncomplicated marriage."

It is never easy to give up the pleasant and flattering image other people have of one's own life. Had Nellie's distress not been so intense, I would not have felt compelled to make a confession of my own. But I felt rather more brave in the face of my fierce cousin: I was glad she was suffering, in fact. I knew she divided the world into the cheerful slobs like me and the emotional moralists like herself. A serious love affair, I thought, might take some of those sharp edges off.

I began by telling her how the rigorousness with which she went after what she called the moral universe did not allow anyone very much latitude, but nonetheless, I was about to tell her something that might put her suffering into some context.

"I have been in love several times during my marriage," I said. "And I have had several love affairs."

The look on her face, I was happy to see, was one of pure relief.

"But I thought you and Edward were so happy," she said.

"We are," I said. "But I'm only human and I am not looking for perfection. Romance makes me cheerful. There have been times in my life when I simply needed to be loved by someone else and I was lucky enough to find someone who loved me. And look at me! I'm not beautiful and I'm not so lovable, but I'm interested in love and so it comes to find me. There are times when Edward simply hasn't been there for me—it happens in every marriage. They say it takes two and sometimes three to make a marriage work and they're right. But this had nothing to do with you because I picked my partners in crime for their discretion and their very clear sense that nothing would get out of hand. I can see that an affair that doesn't threaten your marriage is not your idea of an affair, but there you are."

This made Nellie silent for a long time. She looked exhausted and tearstained.

"One of the good things about this love affair," she said, "is that it's shot my high horse right out from under me. It's a real kindness for you to tell me what you've just told me."

"We're all serious in our own ways," I said. "Now I think you need a nap. You look absolutely wiped out. I'll go call Eddie and tell him to meet Joseph and then when you wake up we can plot where we're going to take Jane for dinner."

I gave her two needlepoint pillows for her head, covered her with a quilt, then went to call my husband. When I got back I sat and watched my cousin sleeping. The sleety, yellowish light played over her brow and cheekbones.

She was lying on her side with her hand slightly arched and bent. Her hair had been gathered at her neck but a few strands had escaped. She looked like the slain nymph Procris in the Piero di Cosimo painting *A Mythological Subject,* which depicts poor Procris who has been accidentally killed by her husband Cephalus. Cephalus is a hunter who has a spear that never misses its mark. One day he hears a noise in the forest, and thinking that it is a wild beast, he takes aim. But it is not a beast. It is Procris. In the painting a tiny jet of blood sprays from her throat. At her feet is her mournful dog, Lelaps, and at her head is a satyr, wearing the look of a heartbroken boy. That picture is full of the misery and loneliness romantic people suffer in love.

The lovely thing about marriage is that life ambles on—as if life were some meandering path lined with sturdy plane trees. A love affair is like a shot arrow. It gives life an intense direction, if only for an instant. The laws of love affairs would operate for Nellie and Dan: they would either run off together, or they would part, or they would find some way to salvage a friendship out of their love affair. If you live long enough and if you are placid and easygoing, people tell you everything. Almost everyone I know has confessed a love affair of some sort or another to me.

But I had never discussed my amours with anyone. Would Nellie think that my affairs had been inconsequential? Certainly I had never let myself get into such a swivet over a man, but I had made very sure to pick only those with very secure marriages and a sense of fun. Each union had been the result of one of the inevitable low moments that marriages contain, and each parting, when the right time came to part, had been relatively painless. The fact was, I was not interested in love in the way Nellie was. She was interested in ultimates. I remembered her fifteen years ago, at twenty-three, rejecting all the nice, suitable young men who wanted to take her out for dinner and in whom she had no interest. She felt this sort of socializing was all wrong. When my husband and I chided her, she said with great passion: "I don't want a social life. I want love, or nothing."

Well, she had gotten what she wanted. There she lay, wiped out, fast asleep, looking wild, peaceful, and troubled all at the same time. She had no dog to guard her, no satyr to mourn her, and no bed of wildflowers beneath her like the nymph in the painting.

What a pleasant circumstance to sit in a warm, comfortable room on an icy winter's day and contemplate someone you love whose life has always been of the greatest interest to you. Procris in the painting is half naked, but Nellie looked just as vulnerable.

It would be exceedingly interesting to see what happened to her, but then she had always been a pleasure to watch.

FEELING NORMAL

Gary Soto

I'm unrepentant on a park bench. For every attractive woman who passes, two bad thoughts knock on my forehead and enter, lie down and frolic with a bold nakedness that scares me. It's lunchtime, the sun half-hidden behind clouds but bright enough to do tricks to my senses, and the women, some alone, some in pairs, some in packs, are so beautiful that tears, like a leaky faucet, drip inward. They're unobtainable and, because of that, more desirable, mysterious, dangerous—all the qualities a man builds into what he can't have.

I only have to glance at the woman across form me, glance and look away, and the knocking begins. Her knees are pink, her cheeks pink, her nails a shade of pink, and so it must be that behind her career woman's clothes—the little gray pinstripe suit—she must be pink. Gray and pink. I like those colors, and black too, the color of her briefcase, which winks a yellow light on the brass latches each time she opens it to ruffle through papers. I have to wonder to myself, is that the signal? Would she like me to get up and move closer to her, sit, right next to her? The latches wink, go dead, wink again.

On lunch break she's taking in the sun, no doubt tired of closed-in office smells of Xerox machines and typewriters and greasy phones. Maybe she's a lawyer, an accountant perhaps, someone in merchandising. Whatever she does she seems happy to be outside eating her lunch. She has already finished her sandwich and is now enjoying her peach. She takes a small bite, chews, and runs a slow tongue across her teeth, which seem also to wink with the noontime light. What would Freud say about that? What would my mother say, a young woman like that chewing so lasciviously?

But how should I approach her? What would I say? Hello, this is Mr. Irresistible. Yes, I am an Aries. Pink and gray are my favorite colors. My BMW is in the shop. I could tell her, "I'm from Fresno!" which would lead smoothly right into my saying that they grow peaches there and that the one she is eating is probably from my hometown, was in fact picked by someone I know. Who would ever guess that we had something in common?

Love can start harmlessly, over lunch for instance, and grow into hand-holding walks and dinner. Maybe we can go out tomorrow night, try the Emerald Garden, yet another new Vietnamese restaurant on California. And the Lumiere is just down the street from there. We can see a movie, see ourselves in the movie: I'm the lead actor in a wheelchair, some unfortunate fellow who was pushed under a train by a psychotic; she's the nurse on the night shift whose real interest is not the sick but literature, and she is, in fact, 13 units away from a second degree, this time in English. Together we fall for one another, but not after some jealous rage at a restaurant. I stir my bread pudding into mush when she hints that she has been married before, two times in fact, OK, if you really want to know the truth, three times; she smacks my face when I mention an old love has better teeth.

But I'm going to meet this woman. I've been working out at the Y, and I'm sweaty, sour as a dirty sock, and generally bad to look at. I'm also hungry for lunch, and married, and a father to a great child who's learning about Europe this week. Why should I ruin myself, and others? And what right does this other woman have to enter my life and cause havoc? Shouldn't a single woman know better? And the truth of the matter is that I have to hurry home: jog a little, walk; jog a little, walk. I have to answer a letter and start the stew my wife expects when she comes home, tired of the office smells she endures daily. If it weren't for the sun, none of this enticement would happen. It would be too dreary for these women to leave their workplace ten minutes early and return ten minutes late. They would not swagger by in tight skirts, each new skirt more beautiful. Neither would bad thoughts knock on my forehead, enter and frolic on all fours. No brass latches would wink and tell me "Go ahead, make a fool of yourself, and tell me you're an unmarried Aries with money and kindness and humor and health." And that would be too bad.

From: EMPIRE

RICHARD FORD

He followed Sergeant Benton into the lounge car, which was smoky. The snack bar was closed. Padlocks were on each of the steel cabinets. Two older men in cowboy hats and boots were arguing across a table full of beer cans. They were arguing about somebody named Heléna, a name they pronounced with a Spanish accent. "It'd be a mistake to underestimate Heléna," one of them said. "I'll warn you of that."

"Oh, fuck Heléna," the other cowboy said. "That fat, ugly bitch. I'm not afraid of her *or* her family."

Across from them a young Asian woman in a sari sat holding an Asian baby. They stared up at Sergeant Benton and at Sims. The woman's round belly was exposed and a tiny red jewel pierced her nose. She seemed frightened, Sims thought, frightened of whatever was going to happen next. He didn't feel that way at all, and was sorry she did.

Sergeant Benton led him out into the second, rumbling vestibule, tiptoeing across in her stocking feet and into the sleeping car where the lights were turned low. As the vestibule door closed, the sound of the moving train wheels was taken far away. Sergeant Benton turned and smiled and put her finger to her lips. "People are sleeping," she whispered.

Marge was sleeping, Sims thought, right across the hall. It made his fingers tingle and feel cold. He walked right past the little silver door and didn't look at it. She'll go right on sleeping, he thought, and wake up happy tomorrow.

At the far end of the corridor a black man stuck his bald head out between the curtains of a private seat and looked at Sims and Doris. Doris was fitting a key into the lock of her compartment door. The black man was the porter who'd helped Marge and him with their suitcases and offered to bring them coffee in the morning. Sergeant Benton waved at him and went "shhhh." Sims waved at him, too, though only halfheartedly. The porter, whose name was Lewis, said nothing, and drew his head back inside the curtains.

"Give me your tired, right?" Doris said, and laughed softly as she opened the door. A bed light was on inside, and the bed had been opened and made up—probably, Sims thought, by Lewis. Out the window he could see the empty, murky night and the moon chased by clouds, and the ground shooting by below the grass. It was dizzying. He could see his own face reflected, and was surprised to see that he was smiling. "*Entrez vous,*" Doris said behind him, "or we'll have tomorrow on our hands."

Sims climbed in, then slid to the foot of the bed while Doris crawled around on her hands and knees reaching for things and digging in her purse behind the pillow. She pulled out an alarm clock. "It's twelve o'clock. Do you know where your kids are?" She flashed Sims a grin. "Mine are still out there in space waiting to come in. Good luck to them, is what I say." She went back to digging in her bag.

"Mine, too," Sims said. He was cold in Doris's roomette, but he felt like he should take his shoes off. Keeping them on made him uncomfortable, but it made him uncomfortable to be in bed with Doris in the first place.

"I just couldn't stand it," Doris said. "They're just other little adults. Who needs that? One's enough."

"That's right," Sims said. Marge felt the same way he did. Children made life a misery and, once they'd finished, they did it again. That had been the first thing he and Marge had seen eye to eye on. Sims put his shoes down beside the mattress and hoped they wouldn't start to smell.

"Miracles," Doris said and held up a pint bottle of vodka. "Never fear, Doris is here," she said. "Never a dull moment. Plus there's glasses, too." She rumbled around in her bag. "Right now in a jiffy there'll be glasses," she said. "Never fear. Are you just horribly bored already, Vic? Have I completely blown this? Are you antsy? Are you mad? Don't be mad."

"I couldn't be happier," Sims said. Doris, on her hands and knees in the half-light, turned and smiled at him. Sims smiled back at her.

"Good man. Excellent." Doris held up a glass. "One glass," she said, "the fruit of patience. Did you know I look as good as I did when I was in high school. I've been told that—recently, in fact."

Sims looked at Doris's legs and her rear end. They were both good-looking, he thought. Both slim and firm. "That's easy to believe," he said. "How old *are* you?"

Sergeant Benton narrowed one eye at him. "How old do you think? Or, how old do I look? I'll ask that."

She was taking all night to fix two drinks, Sims thought. "Thirty. Or near thirty, anyway," he said.

"Cute," Sergeant Benton said. "That's extremely cute." She smirked at him. "Thirty-eight is my age."

"I'm forty-two," Sims said.

Doris didn't seem to hear him. "Glass," she said, holding up another one for him to see. "Two glasses. Let's just go on and have a drink, what do you say?"

"Great," Sims said. He could smell Doris's perfume, a sweet flowery smell he liked and that came from her suitcase. He was glad to be here.

Doris turned and crossed her legs in a way that stretched her skirt across her knees. She set both glasses on her skirt and poured two drinks. Sims realized he could see up her skirt if the light in the compartment was any better.

She smiled and handed Sims a glass. "Here's to your wife," Doris said. "May sweet dreams descend."

"Here's to that," Sims said and drank a gulp of warm vodka. He hadn't known how much he'd wanted a drink until this one was down his throat.

"How fast do you think we're going now?" Doris said, peering toward the dark window where nothing was visible.

"I don't know," Sims said. "Eighty, maybe. I'd guess eighty."

"Hurtling through the dark night," Doris said and smiled. She took another drink. "What scares you ought to be interesting, right?"

"Where've you been on this trip?" Sims said.

Sergeant Benton pushed her fingers through her blond hair and gave her head another shake, then sniffed. "Visiting a relative," she said. She stared at Sims and her eyes seemed to blaze at him suddenly and for no reason Sims could see. Possibly this was a sensitive subject. He would be happy to avoid those.

"And where're you going? You told me but I forgot. It seems like a long time ago."

"Would you like to hear a little story?" Sergeant Benton said. "A recent and true-to-life story?"

"Sure." Sims raised his vodka glass to toast a story. Doris extended the bottle and poured in some more, then more for herself.

"Well," she said. She smelled the vodka in her glass, then pulled her skirt up slightly to be comfortable. "I go to visit my father, you see, out on San Juan Island. I haven't seen him in maybe eight years, since before I went in the Army—since I was married, in fact. And he's married now himself to a very nice lady. Miss Vera. They run a boarding kennel out on the island. He's sixty something and takes care of all these noisy dogs. She's fifty something. I don't know how they do it." Doris took a drink. "Or why. She's a Mormon, believes in all the angels, so he's more or less become one, too, though he drinks and smokes. He's not at all spiritual. He was in the Air Force. Also a sergeant. Anyway, the first night I get there we all eat dinner together. A big steak. And right away my father says he has to drive down to the store to get something, and he'll be back. So off he goes. And Miss Vera and I are washing dishes and watching television and chattering. And before I know it, two hours have gone by. And I say to Miss Vera, 'Where's Eddie? Hasn't he been gone a long time?' And she just says, 'Oh, he'll be back pretty soon.' So we pottered around a little more. Each of us smoked a cigarette. Then she got ready to go to bed. By herself. It was ten o'clock, and I said, 'Where's Dad?' And she said, 'Sometimes he stops and has a drink down in town.' So when she's in bed I get in the other car and drive down the hill to the bar. And there's his station wagon in front. Only when I go in and ask, he isn't there, and nobody says they know where he is. I go back outside, but then this guy steps to the door behind me and says, 'Try the trailer, hon. That's it. Try the trailer.' Nothing else. And across the road is a little house trailer with its lights on and a car sitting out front. And I just walked across the road—I still had on my uniform—walked up the steps and knocked on the door. There're some voices inside and a TV. I hear people moving around and a door close. The front door opens then and here's a woman who apparently lives there. She's completely dressed. I'd guess her age to be fifty. She's younger than Vera anyway, with a younger face. She says, 'Yes. What is it?' and I said I was sorry, but I was looking for my father, and I guessed I'd gotten the wrong place. But she says, 'Just a second,' and turns around and says, 'Eddie, your daughter's here.'

"And my father came out of a door to the next room. Maybe it was a closet, I didn't know. I didn't care. He had his pants on and an undershirt. And he said, 'Oh hi, Doris. How're you? Come on in. This is Sherry.' And the only thing I could think of was how thin his shoulders looked. He looked like he was going to die. I didn't even speak to Sherry. I just said no, I couldn't stay. And I drove on back to the house."

"Did you leave then?" Sims said.

"No, I stayed around a couple more days. *Then* left. It didn't matter to me. It made me think, though."

"What did you think?" Sims asked.

Doris put her head back against the metal wall and stared up. "Oh, I just thought about being the other woman, which I've been that enough. Everybody's done everything twice, right? At my age. You cross a line. But you can do a thing and have it mean nothing but what you feel that minute. You don't have to give yourself away. Isn't that true?"

"That's exactly true," Sims said and thought it was right. He'd done it himself plenty of times.

"Where's the real life, right? I don't think I've had mine, yet, have you?" Doris held her glass up to her lips with both hands and smiled at him.

"Not yet, I haven't," Sims said. "Not entirely."

"When I was a little girl in California and my father was teaching me to drive, I used to think, 'I'm driving now. I have to pay strict attention to everything; I have to notice everything; I have to think about my hands being on the wheel; it's possible I'll only think about this very second forever, and it'll drive me crazy.' But I'd already thought of something else." Doris wrinkled her nose at Sims. "That's my movie, right?"

"It sounds familiar," Sims said. He took a long drink of his vodka and emptied the glass. The vodka tasted metallic, as if it had been kept stored in a can. It had a good effect, though. He felt like he could stay up all night. He was seeing things from the outside, and nothing bad could happen to anyone. Everyone was protected. "Most people want to be good, though," Sims said for no reason. Just words under their own command, headed who-knows-where. Everything seemed arbitrary.

"Would you like me to take my clothes off?" Sergeant Benton said and smiled at him.

"I'd like that," Sims said. "Sure." He thought that he would also like a small amount more of the vodka. He reached over, took the bottle off the blanket and poured himself some more.

Sergeant Benton began unbuttoning her uniform blouse. She knelt forward on her knees, pulled her shirttail out, and began with the bottom button first. She watched Sims, still half smiling. "Do you remember the first woman you ever saw naked?" she said, opening her blouse so Sims could see her white brassiere and a line of smooth belly over her skirt.

"Yes," Sims said.

"And where was that?" Sergeant Benton said. "What state was that in?" She took her blouse off, then pulled her strap down off her shoulder and uncovered one breast, then the other one. They were breasts that went to the side and pushed outward. They were nice breasts.

"That was California, too," Sims said. "Near Sacramento, I think."

"What happened?" Sergeant Benton began unzipping her skirt.

"We were on a golf course. My friend and I and this girl. Patsy was her name. We were all twelve. We both asked her to take off her clothes, in an old caddy house by the Air Force base. And she did it. We did too. She said we'd have to." Sims wondered if Patsy's name was still Patsy.

Sergeant Benton slid her skirt down, then sat back and handed it around her ankles. She had on only panty hose now and nothing beyond that. You could see through them even in the dim light. She leaned against the metal wall and looked at Sims. He could touch her now, he thought. That was what she would like to happen. "Did you like it?" Sergeant Benton asked.

"Yes, I liked it," Sims said.

"It wasn't disappointing to you?"

"It was," Sims said. "But I liked it. I knew I was going to." Sims moved close to her, lightly touched her ankle, then her knee, then the soft skin of her belly and came down with the waist of her hosiery. Her hands touched his neck but didn't feel rough. He heard her breathe and smelled the perfume she was wearing. Nothing seemed arbitrary now.

"Sweet, that's sweet," she said, and breathed deeply once. "Sometimes I think about making love. Like now. And everything tightens up inside me, and I just squeeze and say *ahhhh* without even meaning to. It just escapes me. It's just that pleasure. Someday it'll stop, won't it?"

"No," Sims said. "That won't. That goes on forever." He was near her now, his ear to her chest. He heard a noise, a noise of releasing. Outside, in the corridor, someone began talking in a hushed voice. Someone said, "No, no. Don't say that." And then a door clicked.

"Life's on so thin a string anymore," she whispered, and turned off the tiny light. "Not that much makes it good."

"That's right, isn't it?" Sims said, close to her. "I know that."

"This isn't passion," she said. "This is something different now. I can't lose sleep over this."

"That's fine," Sims said.

"You knew this would happen, didn't you?" she said. "It wasn't a secret." He didn't know it. He didn't try to answer it. "Oh you," she whispered. "Oh you."

Sometime in the night Sims felt the train slow and then stop, then sit still in the dark. He had no idea where he was. He still had his clothes on. Outside there was sound like wind, and for a moment he thought possibly he was dead, that this is how it would feel.

Sergeant Benton lay beside him, asleep. Her clothes were around her. She was covered with a blanket. The vodka bottle was empty on the bed. What had he done here? Sims thought. How had things exactly happened? What time was it? Out the window he could see no one and nothing. The moon was gone, though the sky was red and wavering with a reflected light, as though the wind was moving it.

Sims picked up his shoes and opened the door into the corridor.

The porter didn't appear this time, and Sims closed the door softly and carried his shoes down to the washroom by the vestibule. Inside, he locked the door, ran water on his hands, then rubbed soap on his face and his ears and his neck and into his hairline, then rinsed them with water out of the silver bowl until his face was clean and dripping, and he could stand to see it in the dull little mirror: a haggard face, his eyes red, his skin pale, his teeth gray and lifeless. A deceiver's face, he thought. An adulterer's face, a face to turn away from. He smiled at himself and then couldn't look. He was glad to be alone. He wouldn't see this woman again. He and Marge would get off in a few hours, and Doris would sleep around the clock.

Sims let himself back into the corridor. He thought he heard noise outside the train, and through the window to the vestibule he saw the Asian woman, standing and staring out, holding her little boy in her arms. She was talking to the conductor. He hoped there was no trouble. He wanted to get to Minot on time and get off the train.

When he let himself into Marge's roomette, Marge was awake. And out the window he saw the center of everyone's attention. A wide fire was burning on the open prairie. Out in the dark, men were moving at the edges of the fire. Trucks were in the fields and high tractors with their lights on, and dogs chasing and rumbling in the dark. Far away he could see the white stanchions of high-voltage lines traveling off into the distance.

"It's thrilling," Marge said and turned and smiled at him. "The tracks are on fire ahead of us. I heard someone outside say that. People are running all over. I watched a house disappear. It'll drive you to your remotest thoughts."

"What about *us?*" Sims said, looking out the window into the fire.

"I didn't think of that. Isn't that strange?" Marge said. "It didn't even seem to matter. It should, I guess."

The fire had turned the sky red and the wind blew flames upwards, and Sims imagined he felt heat, and his heart beat faster with the sight—a fire that could turn and sweep over them in a moment, and they would all be caught, asleep and awake. He thought of Sergeant Benton alone in her bed, dreaming dreams of safety and confidence. Nothing was wrong with her, he thought. She should be saved. A sense of powerlessness and despair rose in him, as if there was help but he couldn't offer it.

"The world's on fire, Vic," Marge said. "But it doesn't hurt anything. It just burns until it stops." She raised the covers. "Get in bed with me, sweetheart," she said, "you poor thing. You've been up all night, haven't you?" She was naked under the sheet. He could see her breasts and her stomach and the beginnings of her white legs.

He sat on the bed and put his shoes down. His heart beat faster. He could feel heat now from outside. But, he thought, there was no threat to them, to anyone on the train. "I slept a little," he said.

Marge took his hand and kissed it and held it between her hands. "When I was in my remote thoughts, you know, just watching it burn, I thought about how I get in bed sometimes and I think how happy I am, and then it makes me sad. It's crazy, isn't it? I'd like life to stop, and it won't. It just keeps running by me. It makes me jealous of Pauline. She makes life stop when she wants it to. She doesn't care what happens. That's just a way of looking at things. I guess I wouldn't want to be like her."

"You're not like her," Sims said. "You're sympathetic."

"She probably thinks no one takes her seriously."

"It's all right," Sims said.

"What's going to happen to Pauline now?" Marge moved closer to him. "Will she be all right? Do you think she will?"

"I think she will," Sims said.

"We're out on a frontier here, aren't we, sweetheart? It feels like that." Sims didn't answer. "Are you sleepy, hon?" Marge asked. "You can sleep. I'm awake now. I'll watch over you." She reached and pulled down the shade, and everything, all the movement and heat outside, was gone.

He touched Marge with his fingers—the bones in her face and her shoulders, her breasts, her ribs. He touched the scar, smooth and rigid and neat under her arm, like a welt from a mean blow. This can do it, he thought, this can finish you, this small thing. He held her to him, her face against his as his heart beat. And he felt dizzy, and at that moment insufficient, but without a memory of life's having changed in that particular way.

Outside on the cold air, flames moved and divided and swarmed the sky. And Sims felt alone in a wide empire, removed and afloat, calmed, as if life was far away now, as if blackness was all around, as if stars held the only light.

From: THE PERPLEXING HABIT OF FALLING

Rosemarie Waldrop

Your arms were embracing like a climate that does not require being native. They held me responsive, but I still wondered about the other lives I might have lived, the unused cast of characters stored within me, outcasts of actuality no stranger than my previous selves. As if a word should be counted a lie for all it misses. I could imagine my body arching up toward other men in a high-strung vertigo that scored a virtual accompaniment to our real dance, deep phantom chords echoing from nowhere though with the force of long acceleration, of flying home from a lost wedding. Stakes and mistakes. Big with sky, with bracing cold, with the drone of aircraft, the measures of distance hang in the air before falling in thick drops. The child will be pale and thin. Though it had infiltrated my bones, the thought was without marrow. More a feeling that might accompany a thought, a ply of consonants, an outward motion of the eye.

✳

Many questions were left in the clearing we built our shared life in. Later sheer size left no room for imagining myself standing outside it, on the edge of an empty day. I knew I didn't want to part from this whole which could be said to carry its foundation as much as resting on it, just as a family tree grows downward, its branches confounding gravitation and gravidity. I wanted to continue lying alongside you, two parallel, comparable lengths of feeling, and let the stresses of the structure push our sleep to momentum and fullness. Still, a fallow evening stretches into unknown elsewheres, seductive with possibility, doors open onto a chaos of cul-de-sacs, of could-be, of galloping off on the horse in the picture. And whereto? A crowning mirage or a question like What is love? And where?

Does it enter with a squeeze, or without, bringing, like interpretation, its own space from some other dimension? Or is it like a dream corridor forever extending its concept toward extreme emptiness, like that of atoms?

SIGNS OF DEVOTION

Maxine Chernoff

While Dave was away and I was asleep, a sniper fired two shots on our block. The next morning a neighbor child found bullets under Carla and Stanley Penn's magnolia. Harmless as snails, they hadn't come close to a house. The police theorize that it was a prankster. I must confess I wasn't that sniper, though I wish I were as I wipe off the counter, as I slip off my tee shirt, as Jeff entangles me with his sensitive nerves. I mention the sniper because he signals a change in my relationship with Dave. I used to be afraid to go to bed before my husband was home. For seventeen years, I listened to my tight heartbeat drumming like a toy until I worried him through the door. Something terrible might happen that I might have prevented awake.

Jeff is my first lover, Dave's visiting cousin. After Jeff's marriage failed, he decided to make a tour of all the states he'd never visited. His old Datsun contains souvenirs for Billy: deerskin Indian moccasins from Nebraska, a doll face made of dried apples from Iowa, and a plastic bust of Abraham Lincoln, mole and all, from Springfield, Illinois. Leonora, his ex, has taken little Billy back to Hattiesburg, where she'll live with her mother until they can't stand each other. Leonora's a muralist and needs big walls to keep her happy. I don't think she'll find what she needs in Hattiesburg.

Jeff's sitting on the couch reading the *Journal of Psychomotor Disorders*. When he relaxes, he slouches like laundry. When he slouches, he resembles Dave. "Listen to this," he'll say, and read me a paragraph on facial tics. He'll exaggerate the details, and if I consent to watch, act them out with precision. I pretend that I'm enthused. It makes things work more smoothly.

Whenever the phone rings, it's Irene, who uses her radar to call at the worst moments.

"Hi, Irene," I say.

"I'll be late again," Dave replies.

"Call when you'll be on time. It'll save your firm money."

Dave's seeing Donna. She's a cost accountant with turquoise contact lenses and a wet smile. She used to come to family gatherings with Glen, who's British. She'd get a lot of attention showing him off.

"Say *laboratory*," she'd tell him. "Say *aluminum*."

He'd do exactly as she asked. When Glen's mom died of emphysema and he returned to Birmingham last fall, Donna stopped visiting us. I thought it was unfair that she should feel unwelcome without Glen, so I called her.

"This is hard to believe," she said. "Dave claimed you knew."

When I finally understood her meaning, I reeled around the kitchen feeling myself diminished to a dark hot stone. For months when people spoke, I wondered how they could see me.

Dave doesn't know that Donna told me. He's so cordial that I've begun to feel relieved when he's away. Dave attends sales meetings in the Amazon, at resorts with pineapple-shaped swimming pools. He brings me lizard-skin bags he buys duty-free at the airport. In rooms furnished with mahogany antiques rowed down the river by natives, Dave sleeps with Donna. I can picture them buried under the covers, the air conditioner tweeting. I wonder if Donna thinks about me anymore. At home Dave and I sleep in tense shifts, bumper cars passing in the night.

The first time Jeff fell asleep on our couch, his mouth was an O. His hands, folded in front of him like a diver's, were stiller than hands. He looked like Daniel taking a nap ten years ago, or the little boy I saw in the park asleep under a checkered picnic blanket. When Daniel was small, I used to perform this test: I'd raise his hand above his head, then let it drop. It would fit back in place without disturbing his sleep. He has a pure heart, my sister Irene used to say. Jeff is twenty-nine, too old to seem like a child.

Three days ago, I was sitting on the floor watching Jeff sleep. When he sensed that I was there, he reached over and pulled me on top of him. At first I wondered if he'd done it unconsciously, dreaming that I was Leonora. I thought of those country songs where one or the other says the wrong name in bed.

"What time is it?" he asked after he was inside me.

"Dave's away," I said. "Danny's at school till four."

He dug his head into my hair and said, "Jerri, you're terrific."
It was as simple as that.

The phone rings again. It's really Irene, older than me by twelve years. Irene thinks that Jeff's a nice boy. Her own husband, Clark, left Irene when she was still young. I remember sitting in my mother's house. From the hi-fi in the front room, I could hear Bobby Darin singing "Mack the Knife." Chain-smoking in the kitchen, Irene was telling my mother about Clark. I watched the ash on her cigarette drop onto the green Formica tabletop and thought about Clark's hair. Can elaborately styled hair predict bad character? I considered asking Irene, but she looked too miserable to bother with me. She'd been crying and her eyes were nearly swollen shut. Around her eyes little plateaus of hives had formed.

After Irene left, my mother smoked a rare cigarette. She inhaled like she wanted to swallow the world. Then she began a cleaning frenzy that culminated in defrosting the refrigerator and throwing out the wedding cake top she'd been saving for them. Thinking Irene still might want to keep it, I saved it in my room for a few weeks. When I showed it to Irene, she said, "Dog food."

Irene's worked for years as a secretary to the president of the roofers' union. She attends theater, plays bingo, and talks endlessly to me. She's pieced together a life from others' leftovers: She works for a man whose wife ran off to Scotland with the union treasurer. Her theater companions are widows who call themselves by their husbands' names, Mrs. John Merllman, Mrs. Norman DeBianca. She plays bingo at an old people's home, cheating to make herself lose. Irene's never been wise about capital. My dad called Clark a jack-of-no-trades. When air-conditioning spread, Clark considered refrigeration, but he moved slower than industry. Besides, there was a place for him in Dad's firm. Soon Dad died and Cress Industries was found to be insolvent. Some evidence pointed to Clark's having mishandled the books. After he took off, there were a few letters, and on their third anniversary, a monkey-faced bank made of a coconut with Irene's name etched on it.

Irene gave the bank to Daniel when he was little. He keeps it on his dresser. He's home now, studying in his room with the door bolted. When he was younger, he'd tie a rope to the chair to assure his privacy. Once, I opened the door and upset the chair.

"Expecting terrorists?" I asked him.

"I'm expecting my rights," he countered.

How could I argue?

Daniel's thirteen. Tall for his age, blue-eyed, he has Dave's easy charm and icy way of turning it off. Alone in the bedroom, he's singing along to his radio earphones. His voice is high, sweet even in mimicry. He excels in math and science and hangs Black Hole posters all over his room where I once hung Natalie Wood.

Now I say good-bye to Irene, knowing she'll remember something later and call back.

"Did you hear anything more about the sniper?" she asks before hanging up.

"It happened because I was asleep."

"I don't get it. Was it one of your crazy students?"

My job demands that I be perfectly literal, steady as concrete, since I teach disturbed children. No humor, puns, asides. I finish a joke, lose speed, return to normal gear; they race ahead, overtake me, crash at a curve. Most of the time I give simple orders in an emotionless voice: "Put down that ruler, Tanya. Rulers are for measuring, not for striking other children."

Alex sets fires, but he's careful to choose self-limiting objects. He has burnt towels in a washroom, containing them in a sink. Once, he set fire to a window shade, burning it down to the circular drawstring where the flames stopped, nowhere to spread. The other children I teach are sullen and quiet twelve-year-olds, each with a diagnosis. We're most successful with delinquents like Craig. His minor life of crime is absorbed in building a defense against the biters, the kickers, the glass breakers.

In the morning Dave says hello. I no longer wake up when he gets into bed. Just before the alarm rings, he could walk in, undress and slip under the sheets, and I wouldn't know he hadn't slept with me. But this morning I can tell by the way he ignores the newspaper that he's had a bad night and that he wants to talk.

"I got in after one," he explains. "Wouldn't you know that as soon as I open the door the phone rings? It's for Daniel. I shout up the stairs to him. I ask him why he's up so late."

"What's it your business?" Daniel calls down.

"So I count to ten, Jerri, and decide not to kill him. I'll do something useful. I go outside and dig up some holes to plant the new rosebushes, but I feel stupid digging at two in the morning so I come inside and take a shower. Jeff's up too. He pours me a big glass of milk and we talk about when we were kids. He remembers us playing *The Count of Monte Cristo* in his yard in Spokane. I don't remember reading it, but he says I stood on the porch stairs and acted like the director."

"You're best at that," I tell him.

"Say something to Daniel this morning. He listens to you."

But Daniel's asleep when I'm ready to leave, and our garden looks like it's barely survived a meteor shower.

Rays of sun filtering through the leaded glass windows of the Shedd Aquarium intersect at the coral reef in the lobby. I'm in charge of Alex, the pyromaniac. Since my job will be easy in an aquarium, I relax as he presses his cheek to the huge convex glass of the coral reef. He shouts in pretended terror when a saw-nosed shark brushes past his face. Following him from room to room, I put my hand on his windbreaker when he allows me. Sometimes he brushes me away with a fly-flicking motion neither of us is supposed to acknowledge.

In the room of smaller tanks we now enter, the angelfish seem suspended in water. Only their undulating antennae indicate life. "They're shaped like triangles," I tell Alex, remembering how Daniel liked to distinguish the form of objects when he was younger. Alex drums his long fingers, nails bitten to the quick, against the glass. The fish aren't bothered.

"They like you," I tell him.

Inside their display a tiny ceramic diver stretches his hand in front of me. He's pointing outside of the tank. Water bubbles from his head. In the next tank two lamprey eels poke their rubbery heads out of a clay cylinder. Alex's laugh is so strong that I'm embarrassed by my own weak silence. Running from display to display, the carpeted floor absorbing his steps, Alex is the only moving object in the room of slow water-breathers. He lunges toward the angelfish, which never move. He darts to the eels, bobbing to their own un-gainly rhythm. He shoots out into the hallway to press his face against the reef. Angelfish, eels, reef is his path all morning. Back at school Alex hands me a picture he's drawn, two angelfish facing each other, silver with black stripes, perfect triangles.

That evening Daniel stays at a friend's. The daily paper has dropped the sniper story though the local paper still claims he's at large.

"I wouldn't be surprised if the guy isn't a terrorist," Irene says.

"How do you know it's not a woman?"

I pour a bath, climb in and lean my head back on the clammy porcelain. In walks Jeff holding two tall gin and tonics on a tray.

"I don't drink." I smile.

He pours mine into the water. "Bathtub gin," he says. "May I join you?" He's already taken off his shoes. He's unbuttoning his shirt.

"Can I meet you later?" I ask.

This time Jeff's carrying teacups and some generic sandwich cookies I often give Daniel for lunch. I think of a cat I had when we lived in California that used to bring me dead wading birds, egrets and herons, as signs of devotion. I think of telling Jeff about her, but knowledge is only a complication.

"It's hard to believe I'll be leaving soon."

"Right."

"Too bad I can't stay."

"Let's not talk," I say, stirring my tea with a cookie. Then we both laugh without really knowing why.

As soon as Jeff leaves, I'll speak to Dave. I'll tell him it doesn't matter what he does with Donna. There's so much trouble in the world that a little more confusion can't hurt. If Dave tells me I'm generous, I'll leave him. If he knows to be quiet, maybe I'll let him stay.

From: ADULTERY

ANDRE DUBUS

In the winter and into the spring when snow melted first around the trunks of trees, and the ice on the Merrimack broke into chunks that floated seaward, and the river climbed and rushed, there was a girl. She came uninvited in Christmas season to a party that Edith spent a day preparing; her escort was uninvited too, a law student, a boring one, who came with a married couple who were invited. Later Edith would think of him: if he had to crash the party he should at least have been man enough to keep the girl he crashed with. Her name was Jeanne, she was from France, she was visiting friends in Boston. That was all she was doing: visiting. Edith did not know what part of France she was from nor what she did when she was there. Probably Jeanne told her that night while they stood for perhaps a quarter of an hour in the middle of the room and voices, sipping their drinks, nodding at each other, talking the way two very attractive women will talk at a party: Edith speaking and even answering while her real focus was on Jeanne's short black hair, her sensuous, indolent lips, her brown and mischievous eyes. Edith had talked with the law student long enough—less than a quarter of an hour—to know he wasn't Jeanne's lover and couldn't be; his confidence was still young, wistful, and vulnerable; and there was an impatience, a demand, about the amatory currents she felt flowing from Jeanne. She remarked all of this and recalled nothing they talked about. They parted like two friendly but competing hunters after meeting in the woods. For the rest of the night—while talking, while dancing— Edith watched the law student and the husbands lining up at the trough of Jeanne's accent, and she watched Jeanne's eyes, which appeared vacant until you looked closely at them and saw that they were selfish: Jeanne was watching herself.

And Edith watched Hank, and listened to him. Early in their marriage she had learned to do that. His intimacy with her was private; at their table and in their bed they talked; his intimacy with men was public, and when he was with them he spoke mostly to them, looked mostly at them, and she knew there were times when he was unaware that she or any other woman was in the room. She had long ago stopped resenting this; she had watched the other wives sitting together and talking to one another; she had watched them sit listening while couples were at a dinner table and the women couldn't group so they ate and listened to the men. Usually men who talked to women were trying to make love with them, and she could sense the other men's resentment at this distraction, as if during a hand of poker a man had left the table to phone his mistress. Of course she was able to talk at parties; she wasn't shy and no man had ever intentionally made her feel he was not interested in what she had to say; but willy-nilly they patronized her. As they listened to her she could sense their courtesy, their impatience for her to finish so they could speak again to their comrades. If she had simply given in to that patronizing, stopped talking because she was a woman, she might have become bitter. But she went further: she watched the men, and saw that it wasn't a matter of their not being interested in women. They weren't interested in each other either. At least not in what they said, their ideas; the ideas and witticisms were instead the equipment of friendly, even loving, competition, as for men with different interests were the bowling ball, the putter, the tennis racket. But it went deeper than that too: she finally saw that. Hank needed and loved men, and when he loved them it was because of what they thought and how they lived. He did not measure women that way; he measured them by their sexuality and good sense. He and his friends talked with one another because it was the only way they could show their love; they might reach out and take a woman's hand and stroke it while they leaned forward, talking to men; and their conversations were fields of mutual praise. It no longer bothered her. She knew that some women writhed under these conversations; they were usually women whose husbands rarely spoke to them with the intensity and attention they gave to men.

But that night, listening to Hank, she was frightened and angry. He and Jeanne were watching each other. He talked to the men but he was really talking to her; at first Edith thought he was showing off; but it was worse, more fearful: he was being received and he knew it and that is what gave his voice its exuberant lilt. His eyes met Jeanne's over a shoulder, over the rim of a lifted glass. When Jeanne left with the law student and the invited couple, Edith and Hank told them goodbye at the door. It was only the second time that night Edith and Jeanne had looked at each other and spoken; they smiled and voiced amenities; a drunken husband lurched into the group; his arm groped for Jeanne's waist and his head plunged downward to kiss her. She quickly cocked her head away, caught the kiss lightly on her cheek, almost dodged it completely. For an instant her eyes were impatient. Then that was gone. Tilted away from the husband's muttering face, she was looking at Hank. In her eyes Edith saw his passion. She reached out and put an arm about his waist; without looking at him or Jeanne she said goodnight to the law student and the couple. As the four of them went down the walk, shrugging against the cold, she could not look at Jeanne's back and hair; she watched the law student and wished him the disaster of bad grades. Be a bank teller, you bastard.

She did not see Jeanne again. In the flesh, that is. For now she saw her in dreams: not those of sleep which she could forget but her waking dreams. In the morning Hank went to his office at school to write; at noon he and Jack ran and then ate lunch; he taught all afternoon and then went to the health club for a sauna with Jack and afterward they stopped for a drink; at seven he came home. On Tuesdays and Thursdays he didn't have classes but he spent the afternoon at school in conferences with students; on Saturday mornings he wrote in his office and, because he was free of students that day, he often worked into the middle of the afternoon, then called Jack to say he was ready for the run, the sauna, the drinks. For the first time in her marriage Edith thought about how long and how often he was away from home. As she helped Sharon with her boots she saw Jeanne's brown eyes; they were attacking her; they were laughing at her; they sledded down the hill with her and Sharon.

When she became certain that Hank was Jeanne's lover she could not trust her certainty. In the enclosed days of winter she imagined too much. Like a spy, she looked for only one thing, and she could not tell if the wariness in his eyes and voice were truly there; making love with him she felt a distance in his touch, another concern in his heart; passionately she threw herself against that distance and wondered all the time if it existed only in her own quiet and fearful heart. Several times, after drinks at a party, she nearly asked Jack if Hank was always at school when he said he was. At home on Tuesday and Thursday and Saturday afternoons she wanted to call him. One Thursday she did. He didn't answer his office phone; it was a small school and the switchboard operator said if she saw him she'd tell him to call home. Edith was telling Sharon to get her coat, they would go to school to see Daddy, when he phoned. She asked him if he wanted to see a movie that night. He said they had seen everything playing in town and if she wanted to go to Boston he'd rather wait until the weekend. She said that was fine.

In April he and Jack talked about baseball and watched it on television and he started smoking Parliaments. She asked him why. They were milder, he said. He looked directly at her but she sensed he was forcing himself to, testing himself. For months she had imagined his infidelity and fought her imagination with the absence of evidence. Now she had that: she knew it was irrational but it was just rational enough to release the demons: they absorbed her: they gave her certainty. She remembered Jeanne holding a Parliament, waiting for one of the husbands to light it. She lasted three days. On a Thursday afternoon she called the school every hour, feeling the vulnerability of this final prideless crumbling, making her voice as casual as possible to the switchboard operator, even saying once it was nothing important, just something she wanted him to pick up on the way home, and when he got home at seven carrying a damp towel and smelling faintly of gin she knew he had got back in time for the sauna with Jack and had spent the afternoon in Jeanne's bed. She waited until after dinner, when Sharon was in bed. He sat at the kitchen table, talking to her while she cleaned the kitchen. It was a ritual of theirs. She asked him for a drink. Usually she didn't drink after dinner, and he was surprised. Then he said he'd join her. He gave her the bourbon, then sat at the table again.

"Are you having an affair with that phony French bitch?"

He sipped his drink, looked at her, and said: "Yes."

The talk lasted for days. That night it ended at three in the morning after, straddling him, she made love with him and fell into a sleep whose every moment, next morning, she believed she remembered.

She had slept four hours. When she woke to the news on the radio she felt she had not slept at all, that her mind had continued the talk with sleeping Hank. She did not want to get up. In bed she smoked while Hank showered and shaved. At breakfast he did not read the paper. He spoke to Sharon and watched Edith. She did not eat. When he was ready to leave, he leaned down and kissed her and said he loved her and they would talk again that night.

All day she knew what madness was, or she believed she was at least tasting it and at times she yearned for the entire feast. While she did her work and made lunch for Sharon and talked to her and put her to bed with a coloring book and tried to read the newspaper and then a magazine, she could not stop the voices in her mind: some of it repeated from last night, some drawn up from what she believed she had heard and spoken in her sleep, some in anticipation of tonight, living tonight before it was there, so that at two in the afternoon she was already at midnight and time was nothing but how much pain she could feel at once. When Sharon had been in bed for an hour without sleeping, Edith took her for a walk and tried to listen to her and said yes and no and I don't know, what do you think? and even heard most of what Sharon said and all the time the voices would not stop. All last night while awake and sleeping and all day she had believed it was because Jeanne was pretty and Hank was a man. Like any cliché, it was easy to live with until she tried to; now she began to realize how little she knew about Hank and how much she suspected and feared, and that night after dinner which she mostly drank she tucked in Sharon and came down to the kitchen and began asking questions. He told her he would stop seeing Jeanne and there was nothing more to talk about; he spoke of privacy. But she had to know everything he felt; she persisted, she harried, and finally he told her she'd better be as tough as her questions were, because she was going to get the answers.

Which were: he did not believe in monogamy. Fidelity, she said. You see? he said. You distort it. He was a faithful husband. He had been discreet, kept his affair secret, had not risked her losing face. He loved her and had taken nothing from her. She accused him of having a double standard and he said no; no, she was as free as she was before she met him. She asked him how long he had felt this way, had he always been like this or was it just some French bullshit he had picked up this winter. He had always felt this way. By now she could not weep. Nor rage either. All she could feel and say was: Why didn't I ever know any of this? You never asked, he said.

It was, she thought, like something bitter from Mother Goose: the woman made the child, the child made the roof, the roof made the woman, and the child went away. Always she had done her housework quickly and easily; by ten-thirty on most mornings she had done what had to be done. She was not one of those women whose domesticity became an obsession; it was work that she neither liked nor disliked and, when other women complained, she was puzzled and amused and secretly believed their frustration had little to do with scraping plates or pushing a vacuum cleaner over a rug. Now in April and May an act of will got her out of bed in the morning. The air in the house was against her: it seemed wet and gray and heavy, heavier than fog, and she pushed through it to the bathroom where she sat staring at the floor or shower curtain long after she was done; then she moved to the kitchen and as she prepared breakfast the air pushed down on her arms and against her body. *I am beating eggs*, she said to herself, and she looked down at the fork in her hand, yolk dripping from the tines into the eggs as their swirling ceased and they lay still in the bowl. *I am beating eggs*. Then she jabbed the fork in again. At breakfast Hank read the paper. Edith talked to Sharon and ate because she had to, because it was morning, it was time to eat, and she glanced at Hank's face over the newspaper, listened to the crunching of his teeth on toast, and told herself: *I am talking to Sharon*. She kept her voice sweet, motherly, attentive.

Then breakfast was over and she was again struck by the seductive waves of paralysis that had washed over her in bed, and she stayed at the table. Hank kissed her (she turned her lips to him, they met his, she did not kiss him) and went to the college. She read the paper and drank coffee and smoked while Sharon played with toast. She felt she would fall asleep at the table; Hank would return in the afternoon to find her sleeping there among the plates and cups and glasses while Sharon played alone in a ditch somewhere down the road. So once again she rose through an act of will, watched Sharon brushing her teeth (*I am watching . . .*), sent her to the cartoons on television, and then slowly, longing for sleep, she washed the skillet and saucepan (*always scramble eggs in a saucepan*, her mother had told her; *they stand deeper than in a skillet and they'll cook softer*) and scraped the plates and put them and the glasses and cups and silverware in the dishwasher.

Then she carried the vacuum cleaner upstairs and made the bed Hank had left after she had, and as she leaned over to tuck in the sheet she wanted to give in to the lean, to collapse in slow motion face down on the half-made bed and lie there until—there had been times in her life when she had wanted to sleep until something ended. Unmarried in Iowa, when she missed her period she wanted to sleep until she knew whether she was or not. Now *until* meant nothing. No matter how often or how long she slept she would wake to the same house, the same heavy air that worked against her every move. She made Sharon's bed and started the vacuum cleaner. Always she had done that quickly, not well enough for her mother's eye, but her mother was a Windex housekeeper: a house was not done unless the windows were so clean you couldn't tell whether they were open or closed; but her mother had a cleaning woman. The vacuum cleaner interfered with the cartoons and Sharon came up to tell her and Edith said she wouldn't be long and told Sharon to put on her bathing suit—it was a nice day and they would go to the beach. But the cleaning took her longer than it had before, when she had moved quickly from room to room, without lethargy or boredom but a sense of anticipation, the way she felt when she did other work which required neither skill nor concentration, like chopping onions and grating cheese for a meal she truly wanted to cook.

Now, while Sharon went downstairs again and made lemonade and poured it in the thermos and came upstairs and went down again and came up and said yes there was a little mess and went downstairs and wiped it up, Edith pushed the vacuum cleaner and herself through the rooms and down the hall, and went downstairs and started in the living room while Sharon's voice tugged at her as strongly as hands gripping her clothes, and she clamped her teeth on the sudden shrieks that rose in her throat and told herself: *Don't: she's not the problem*; and she thought of the women in supermarkets and on the street, dragging and herding and all but cursing their children along (one day she had seen a woman kick her small son's rump as she pulled him into a drugstore), and she thought of the women at parties, at dinners, or on blankets at the beach while they watched their children in the waves, saying: *I'm so damned bored with talking to children all day—no,* she told herself, *she's not the problem.* Finally she finished her work, yet she felt none of the relief she had felt before; the air in the house was like water now as she moved through it up the stairs to the bedroom, where she undressed and put on her bathing suit. Taking Sharon's hand and the windbreakers and thermos and blanket, she left the house and blinked in the late morning sun and wondered near-prayerfully when this would end, this dread disconnection between herself and what she was doing. At night making love with Hank she thought of him with Jeanne, and her heart, which she thought was beyond breaking, broke again, quickly, easily, as if there weren't much to break anymore, and fell into mute and dreary anger, the dead end of love's grief.

In the long sunlit evenings and the nights of May the talk was sometimes philosophical, sometimes dark and painful, drawing from him details about him and Jeanne; she believed if she possessed the details she would dispossess Jeanne of Hank's love. But she knew that wasn't her only reason. Obsessed by her pain, she had to plunge more deeply into it, feel all of it again and again. But most of the talk was abstract, and most of it was by Hank. When she spoke of divorce he calmly told her they had a loving, intimate marriage. They were, he said, simply experiencing an honest and healthful breakthrough. She listened to him talk about the unnatural boundaries of lifelong monogamy. He remained always calm. Cold, she thought. She could no longer find his heart.

At times she hated him. Watching him talk she saw his life: with his work he created his own harmony, and then he used the people he loved to relax with. Probably it was not exploitative; probably it was the best he could do. And it was harmony she had lost. Until now her marriage had been a circle, like its gold symbol on her finger. Wherever she went she was still inside it. It had a safe, gentle circumference, and mortality and the other perils lay outside of it. Often now while Hank slept she lay awake and tried to pray. She wanted to fall in love with God. She wanted His fingers to touch her days, to restore meaning to those simple tasks which now drained her spirit. On those nights when she tried to pray she longed to leave the world: her actions would appear secular but they would be her communion with God. Cleaning the house would be an act of forgiveness and patience under His warm eyes. But she knew it was no use: she had belief, but not faith: she could not bring God under her roof and into her life. He waited her death.

Nightly and fearfully now, as though Hank's adulterous heart had opened a breach and let it in to stalk her, she thought of death. One night they went with Jack and Terry Linhart to Boston to hear Judy Collins. The concert hall was filled and darkened and she sat in the sensate, audible silence of listening people and watched Judy under the spotlight in a long lavender gown, her hair falling over one shoulder as she lowered her face over the guitar. Soon Edith could not hear the words of the songs. Sadly she gazed at Judy's face, and listened to the voice, and thought of the voice going out to the ears of all those people, all those strangers, and she thought how ephemeral was a human voice, and how death not only absorbed the words in the air, but absorbed as well the act of making the words, and the time it took to say them. She saw Judy as a small bird singing on a wire, and above her the hawk circled. She remembered reading once of an old man who had been working for twenty-five years sculpting, out of a granite mountain in South Dakota, a 563-foot-high statue of Chief Crazy Horse. She thought of Hank and the novel he was writing now, and as she sat beside him her soul withered away from him and she hoped he would fail, she hoped he would burn this one too: she saw herself helping him, placing alternate pages in the fire. Staring at the face above the lavender gown, she strained to receive the words and notes into her body.

She had never lied to Hank and now everything was a lie. Beneath the cooking of a roast, the still-affectionate chatting at dinner, the touch of their flesh, was the fact of her afternoons ten miles away in a New Hampshire woods where, on a blanket among shading pines and hemlocks, she lay in sin-quickened heat with Jack Linhart. Her days were delightfully strange, she thought. Hank's betrayal had removed her from the actions that were her life; she had performed them like a weary and disheartened dancer. Now, glancing at Hank reading, she took clothes from the laundry basket at her feet and folded them on the couch, and the folding of a warm towel was a manifestation of her deceit. And, watching him across the room, she felt her separation from him taking shape, filling the space between them like a stone. Within herself she stroked and treasured her lover. She knew she was doing the same to the self she had lost in April.

There was a price to pay. When there had been nothing to lie about in their marriage and she had not lied, she had always felt nestled with Hank; but with everyone else, even her closest friends, she had been aware of that core of her being that no one knew. Now she felt that with Hank. With Jack she recognized yet leaped into their passionate lie: they were rarely together more than twice a week; apart, she longed for him, talked to him in her mind, and vengefully saw him behind her closed eyes as she moved beneath Hank. When she was with Jack their passion burned and distorted their focus. For two hours on the blanket they made love again and again, they made love too much, pushing their bodies to consume the yearning they had borne and to delay the yearning that was waiting. Sometimes under the trees she felt like tired meat. The quiet air which she had broken in the first hour with moans now absorbed only their heavy breath. At those moments she saw with detached clarity that they were both helpless, perhaps even foolish. Jack wanted to escape his marriage; she wanted to live with hers; they drove north to the woods and made love. Then they dressed and drove back to what had brought them there.

This was the first time in her life she had committed herself to sin, and there were times when she felt her secret was venomous. Lying beside Terry at the beach she felt more adulterous than when she lay with Jack, and she believed her sun-lulled conversation was somehow poisoning her friend. When she held Sharon, salty and cold-skinned from the sea, she felt her sin flowing with the warmth of her body into the small wet breast. But more often she was proud. She was able to sin and love at the same time. She was more attentive to Sharon than she had been in April. She did not have to struggle to listen to her, to talk to her. She felt cleansed. And looking at Terry's long red hair as she bent over a child, she felt both close to her yet distant. She did not believe women truly had friends among themselves; school friendships dissolved into marriages; married women thought they had friends until they got divorced and discovered other women were only wives drawn together by their husbands. As much as she and Terry were together, they were not really intimate; they instinctively watched each other. She was certain that Terry would do what she was doing. A few weeks ago she would not have known that. She was proud that she knew it now.

With Hank she loved her lie. She kept it like a fire: some evenings after an afternoon with Jack she elaborately fanned it, looking into Hank's eyes and talking of places she had gone while the sitter stayed with Sharon; at other times she let it burn low, was evasive about how she had spent her day, and when the two couples were together she bantered with Jack, teased him. Once Jack left his pack of Luckies in her car and she brought them home and smoked them. Hank noticed but said nothing. When two cigarettes remained in the pack she put it on the coffee table and left it there. One night she purposely made a mistake: after dinner, while Hank watched a ball game on television, she drank gin while she cleaned the kitchen. She had drunk gin and tonic before dinner and wine with the flounder and now she put tonic in the gin, but not much. From the living room came the announcer's voice, and now and then Hank spoke. She hated his voice; she knew she did not hate him; if she did, she would be able to act, to leave him. She hated his voice tonight because he was talking to ballplayers on the screen and because there was no pain in it while in the kitchen her own voice keened without sound and she worked slowly and finished her drink and mixed another, the gin now doing what she had wanted it to: dissolving all happiness, all peace, all hope for it with Hank and all memory of it with Jack, even the memory of that very afternoon under the trees. Gin-saddened, she felt beyond tears, at the bottom of some abyss where there was no emotion save the quivering knees and fluttering stomach and cold-shrouded heart that told her she was finished. She took the drink into the living room and stood at the door and watched him looking at the screen over his lifted can of beer. He glanced at her, then back at the screen. One hand fingered the pack of Luckies on the table, but he did not take one.

"I wish you hadn't stopped smoking," she said. "Sometimes I think you did it so you'd outlive me."

He looked at her, told her with his eyes that she was drunk, and turned back to the game.

"I've been having an affair with Jack." He looked at her, his eyes unchanged, perhaps a bit more interested; nothing more. His lips showed nothing, except that she thought they seemed ready to smile. "We go up to the woods in New Hampshire in the afternoons. Usually twice a week. I like it. I started it. I went after him, at a party. I told him about Jeanne. I kept after him. I knew he was available because he's unhappy with Terry. For a while he was worried about you but I told him you wouldn't mind anyway. He's still your friend, if that worries you. Probably more yours than mine. You don't even look surprised. I suppose you'll tell me you've known it all the time."

"It wasn't too hard to pick up."

"So it really wasn't French bullshit. I used to want another child. A son. I wouldn't want to now: have a baby in this."

"Come here."

For a few moments, leaning against the doorjamb, she thought of going upstairs and packing her clothes and driving away. The impulse was rooted only in the blur of gin. She knew she would get no farther than the closet where her clothes hung. She walked to the couch and sat beside him. He put his arm around her; for a while she sat rigidly, then she closed her eyes and eased against him and rested her head on his shoulder.

From: MARRY ME

JOHN UPDIKE

When they first began to make love, she had felt through his motions the habitual responses his wife must make; while locked in this strange man's embrace she struggled jealously against the outline of the other woman. On her part she bore the impress of Richard's sexual style, so that in the beginning four contending persons seemed involved on the sofa or in the sand, and a confused, half-Lesbian excitement would enclose her. Now these blurs were burned away. On the brightening edge of the long June day that followed the third night they had ever spent together, Jerry and Sally made love lucidly, like Adam and Eve when the human world was of two halves purely. She watched his face, and involuntarily cried out, pierced by the discovery, "Jerry, your eyes are so sad!"

The crooked teeth of his grin seemed Satanic. "How can they be sad when I'm so happy?"

"They're *so* sad, Jerry."

"You shouldn't watch people's eyes when they make love."

"I always do."

"Then I'll close mine."

Oh Sally, my lost only Sally, let me say now, now before we both forget, while the spark still glitters on the waterfall, that I loved you, that the sight of you shamed my eyes. You were a territory where I went on tiptoe to steal a magic mirror. You were a princess married to an ogre. I would go to meet you as a knight, to rescue you, and would become instead the dragon, and ravish you. You weighed me out in jewels, though ashes were what I could afford. Do you remember how, in our first room, on the second night, I gave you a bath and scrubbed your face and hands and long arms with the same methodical motions I used on my children? I was trying to tell you then. I was a father. Our love of children implies our loss of them. What a lazy lovely naked child you were, my mistress and momentary wife; your lids were lowered, your cheek rested on the steaming sheet of bathwater. Can I forget, forget though I live forever in Heaven among the chariots whose wheels are all eyes giving God the glory, how I saw you step from a tub, your body abruptly a waterfall? Like a man you tucked a towel about your woman's hips, and had me enter the water your flesh had charmed to a silvery opacity. I became your child. With a drenched blinding cloth that searched out even the hollows of my ears, you, my mother, my slave, dissolved me in tender abrasions. I forgot, sank. And we dried each other's beaded backs, and went to the bed as if to sleep instantly, two obedient children dreaming in a low tent drumming with the excluded rain.

✳

Later she wondered how she could have been so blind, and blind so long. The signs were abundant: the sand, his eccentric comings and goings, his giving up smoking, his triumphant exuberance whenever Sally was at the same party, the tender wifely touch (this glimpse had stung at the time, to endure in Ruth's memory) with which Sally on one occasion had picked up Jerry's wrist, inviting him to dance. Jerry's obsession with death the spring before had seemed to her so irrational, so unreachable, that she dismissed as also mysterious his new behavior: his new timbre and strut, his fits of ill temper with the children, his fits of affection with her, the hungry introspective tone he brought to their private conversations, his insomnia, the easing of his physical demands on her, and a new cool authority in bed, so that at moments it seemed she was with Richard again. How could she have been so blind? At first she thought that, having gazed so long at her own guilt, she mistook for an afterimage what was in truth a fresh development. She admitted to herself, then, what she could never admit to Jerry, that she did not think him capable of it. . . .

Jerry asked for a divorce on a Sunday, the Sunday after a week in which he had been two days in Washington, and had returned to her in an atmosphere of hazard, on a late flight. There had been a delay, the airlines were jammed up, and she met plane after plane at LaGuardia. When at last his familiar silhouette with its short hair and thin shoulders cut through the muddled lights of the landing field and hurried toward her, her heart surprised her with a groveling gladness. Had she been a dog, she would have jumped and licked his face; being only a wife, she let herself be kissed, led him to the car, and listened as he described his trip—the State Department, a hurried visit to the Vermeers in the National Gallery, his relative lack of insomnia in the hotel, the inadequate gifts for the children he bought at a drugstore, the maddening wait in the airport. As the city confusion diminished behind them, his talking profile, in the warm vault of the car, shed its halo of wonder for her, and by the time they crackled to a stop in their driveway, both felt tired; they had chicken soup and bourbon and fumbled into a cold bed. Yet afterward this homecoming of his was to seem enchanted, a last glimpse of solid headland before, that rainy Sunday afternoon, she embarked on the nightmare sea that became her habitat.

In the morning, she and the children went to the beach. Jerry wanted to go to church. The summer services began at nine-thirty and ended at ten-thirty. She did not think it fair to the children to make them wait that long, especially since the pattern of the summer days was to dawn clear and cloud over by noon. So they dropped him off in his good suit and drove on.

The clouds materialized earlier than usual; little upright puffs at first, like puffs of smoke from a locomotive starting its run around the horizon, then clouds, increasingly structural and opaque, castles, continents that, overhead, grew as they moved, keeping the sun behind them. Waiting for the gaps of sunshine between the clouds was a game for the beach mothers. The clouds blew eastward, so their eyes scouted the west, where a swathe of advancing gold would first ignite the roofs of the cottages on Jacob's Point; then the great green water tower that supplied the cottages would be liberated into light, and like an arrived Martian spaceship the egg of metal on its stilts would glow; then like an onrushing field of unearthly wheat the brightness would roll, in steady jerks like strides, up the mile of sand, and overhead the sun would burn free of the struggling tendrils at the cloud's edge and skyey loops of iridescence would be spun between the eyelashes of the mothers. On this Sunday morning the gaps between the clouds closed more quickly than usual and by eleven-thirty it was clearly going to rain. Ruth and the children went home. They found Jerry sitting in the living room reading the Sunday paper. He had taken off his suit coat and loosened the knot of his tie, but his hair, still combed flat with water, made him look odd to Ruth. He seemed distracted, brittle, hostile; he acted as if they personally had consumed the few hours of beach weather there would be that day. But often he was irritable after attending church.

She took the roast out of the oven and all except Jerry ate Sunday dinner in bathing suits. This was the one meal of the week for which Jerry asked grace. As he began, "Heavenly Father," Geoffrey, who was being taught bedtime prayers, said aloud, "Dear God . . ." Joanna and Charlie burst into giggling. Jerry hurried his blessing through the interference, and Geoffrey, eyes tight shut, fat hands clasped at his plate, tried to repeat it after him and, unable, whimpered, "I can't say it!"

"Amen," Jerry said and, with stiff fingers, slapped Geoffrey on the top of his head. "Shut up." Earlier that week the boy had broken his collarbone. His shoulders were pulled back by an Ace bandage; he was tender all over.

Swallowing a sob, Geoffrey protested, "You said it too fast!"

Joanna explained to him, "You're stupid. You think you're supposed to say grace after Daddy."

Charlie turned and a gleeful taunting sound, "K-k-k," scraped from the roof of his mouth.

The insults were coming too fast for Geoffrey to absorb; he overflowed. His face blurred and crumpled into tears.

"Jerry, I'm amazed," Ruth said. "That was a sick thing to do."

Jerry picked up his fork and threw it at her—not at her, over her head, through the doorway into the kitchen. Joanna and Charlie peeked at each other and their cheeks puffed out in identical smothered explosions. "Goddamn it all," Jerry said, "I'd rather say grace in a pigpen. You all sitting here stark naked."

"The child was trying to be good," Ruth said. "He doesn't understand the difference between grace and prayers."

"Then why the fuck don't you teach him? If he had any decent even half-ass Christian kind of a mother he'd know enough not to interrupt. Geoffrey," Jerry turned to say, "you must stop crying, to make your collarbone stop hurting."

Stunned by his father's unremittingly angry tone, the child tried to enunciate a sentence: "I—I—I—"

"I—I—I—" Joanna mocked.

Geoffrey screamed as if stabbed.

Jerry stood and tried to reach Joanna to slap her. She shied away, upsetting her chair. Something about her expression of terror made Jerry laugh. As if this callous laugh released all the malign spirits at the table, Charlie turned, said "Crybaby," and punched Geoffrey in the arm, jarring his collarbone. Before the child could react, his mother screamed for him; Charlie shouted, "I forgot, I forgot!" Wild to stop this torrent of injury at its source, Ruth, still holding the serving spoon, left her place and moved around the table, so swiftly she felt she was skating. She swung the hand not holding the spoon at Jerry's face. He saw it coming and hid his face between his shoulders and hands, showing her the blank hairy top of his skull, with its helpless amount of gray. His skull was harder than her hand; she jammed her thumb; pain pressed behind her eyes. Blindly she flailed, again and once again, at the obstinate lump of his cowering head, unable with one hand, while the other still clutched the serving spoon, to claw her way into his eyes, his poisonous mouth. The fourth time she swung, he stood up and caught her wrist in midair and squeezed it so hard the fine bones ground together.

"You pathetic frigid bitch," he said levelly. "Don't touch me again." He gave each word an equal weight, and his face, uncovered at last, showed a deadly level calm, though flushed—the face of a corpse, rouged. The nightmare had begun.

Part V

THE BROKEN BED

THERE'S AN OLD . . .

Bobbie Louise Hawkins

There's an old Texas saying that I think I may be the only one who remembers it.

It goes "I've enjoyed just about as much of this as I can stand."

It's a magic formula that lets you head for the door past all the frenzy of any minute now it's going to get significant. It's a way to say that whatever you had in mind this ain't it. It lets you stop eating slop that needs a palate and a vocabulary.

I've enjoyed just about as much of this as I can stand.

LOVE TOO LONG

Barry Hannah

My head's burning off and I got a heart about to bust out of my ribs. All I can do is move from chair to chair with my cigarette. I wear shades. I can't read a magazine. Some days I take my binoculars and look out in the air. They laid me off. I can't find work. My wife's got a job and she takes flying lessons. When she comes over the house in her airplane, I'm afraid she'll screw up and crash.

I got to get back to work and get dulled out again. I got to be a man again. You can't walk around the house drinking coffee and beer all day, thinking about her taking her brassiere off. We been married and divorced twice. Sometimes I wish I had a sport. I bought a croquet set on credit at Penney's. First day I got so tired of it I knocked the balls off in the weeds and they're out there rotting, mildew all over them, I bet, but I don't want to see.

Some afternoons she'll come right over the roof of the house and turn the plane upside down. Or maybe it's her teacher. I don't know how far she's got along. I'm afraid to ask, on the every third night or so she comes in the house. I want to rip her arm off. I want to sleep in her uterus with my foot hanging out. Some nights she lets me lick her ears and knees. I can't talk about it. It's driving me into a sorry person. Maybe Hobe Lewis would let me pump gas and sell bait at his service station. My mind's around to where I'd do nigger work now.

I'd do Jew work, Swiss, Spanish. Anything.

She never took anything. She just left. She can be a lot of things—she got a college degree. She always had her own bank account. She wanted a better house than this house, but she was patient. She'd eat any food with a sweet smile. She moved through the house with a happy pace, like it meant something.

I think women are closer to God than we are. They walk right out there like they know what they're doing. She moved around the house, reading a book. I never saw her sitting down much, unless she's drinking. She can drink you under the table. Then she'll get up on the spot of eight and fix you an omelet with sardines and peppers. She taught me to like this, a little hot ketchup on the edge of the plate.

When she walks through the house, she has a roll from side to side. I've looked at her face too many times when she falls asleep. The omelet tastes like her. I go crazy.

There're things to be done in this world, she said. This love affair went on too long. It's going to make us both worthless, she said. Our love is not such a love as to swell the heart. So she said. She was never unfaithful to me that I know. And if I knew it, I wouldn't care because I know she's sworn to me.

I am her always and she is my always and that's the whole trouble.

For two years I tried to make her pregnant. It didn't work. The doctor said she was too nervous to hold a baby, first time she ever had an examination. She was a nurse at the hospital and brought home all the papers that she forged whenever I needed a report. For example, when I first got on as a fly in elevated construction. A fly can crawl and balance where nobody else can. I was always working at the thing I feared the most. I tell you true. But it was high pay out there at the beam joints. Here's the laugh. I was light and nimble, but the sun always made me sick up there under its nose. I got a permanent suntan. Some people think I'm Arab. I was good.

When I was in the Navy, I finished two years at Bakersfield Junior College in California. Which is to say, I can read and feel fine things and count. Those women who cash your check don't cause any distress to me, all their steel, accents and computers. I'll tell you what I liked that we studied at Bakersfield. It was old James Joyce and his book *The Canterbury Tales*. You wouldn't have thought anybody would write "A fart that well nigh blinded Absalom" in ancient days. All those people hopping and humping at night, framming around, just like last year at Ollie's party that she and I left when they got into threesomes and Polaroids. Because we loved each other too much. She said it was something you'd be sorry about the next morning.

Her name is Jane.

Once I cheated on her. I was drunk in Pittsburgh. They bragged on me for being a fly in the South. This girl and I were left together in a fancy apartment of the Oakland section. The girl did everything. I was homesick during the whole time for Jane. When you get down to it, there isn't much to do. It's just arms and legs. It's not worth a damn.

The first thing Jane did was go out on that houseboat trip with that movie star who was using this town we were in in South Carolina to make his comeback film. I can't tell his name, but he's short and his face is old and piglike now instead of the way it was in the days he was piling up the money. He used to be a star and now he was trying to return as a main partner in a movie about hatred and backstabbing in Dixie. Everybody on board made crude passes at her. I wasn't invited. She'd been chosen as an extra for the movie. The guy who chose her made animalistic comments to her. This was during our first divorce. She jumped off the boat and swam home. But that's how good-looking she is. There was a cameraman on the houseboat who saw her swimming and filmed her. It was in the movie. I sat there and watched her when they showed it local.

The next thing she did was take up with an architect who had a mustache. He was designing her dream house for free and she was putting money in the bank waiting on it. She claimed he never touched her. He just wore his mustache and a gold medallion around his neck and ate yogurt and drew houses all day. She worked for him as a secretary and landscape consultant. Jane was always good about trees, bushes, flowers and so on. She's led many a Spare That Tree campaign almost on her own. She'll write a letter to the editor in a minute.

Only two buildings I ever worked on pleased her. She said the rest looked like death standing up.

The architect made her wear his ring on her finger. I saw her wearing it on the street in Biloxi, Mississippi, one afternoon, coming out of a store. There she was with a new hairdo and a narrow halter and by God I was glad I saw. I was in a bus on the way to the Palms House hotel we were putting up after the hurricane. I almost puked out my kidneys with the grief.

Maybe I need to go to church, I said to myself. I can't stand this alone. I wished I was Jesus. Somebody who never drank or wanted nooky. Or knew Jane.

She and the architect were having some fancy drinks together at a beach lounge when his ex-wife from New Hampshire showed up naked with a single-shotgun gun that was used in the Franco-Prussian War—it was a quaint piece hanging on the wall in their house when he was at Dartmouth—and screaming. The whole bar cleared out, including Jane. The ex-wife tried to get the architect with the bayonet. She took off the whole wall mural behind him and he was rolling around under tables. Then she tried to cock the gun. The policeman who'd come in got scared and left. The architect got out and threw himself into the arms of Jane, who was out on the patio thinking she was safe. He wanted to die holding his love. Jane didn't want to die in any fashion. Here comes the nude woman, screaming with the cocked gun.

"Hey, hey," says Jane. "Honey, you don't need a gun. You got a hell of a body. I don't see how Lawrence could've left that."

The woman lowered the gun. She was dripping with sweat and pale as an egg out there in the bright sun over the sea. Her hair was nearabout down to her ass and her face was crazy.

"Look at her, Lawrence," said Jane.

The guy turned around and looked at his ex-wife. He whispered: "She was lovely. But her personality was a disease. She was killing me. It was slow murder."

When I got there, the naked woman was on Lawrence's lap. Jane and a lot of people were standing around looking at them. They'd fallen back in love. Lawrence was sucking her breast. She wasn't a bad-looking sight. The long gun lay off in the sand. No law was needed. I was just humiliated. I tried to get away before Jane saw me, but I'd been drinking and smoking a lot the night before and I gave out this ninety-nine-year-old cough. Everybody on the patio except Lawrence and his woman looked around.

But in Mobile we got it going together again. She taught art in a private school where they admitted high-type Negroes only. And I was a fly on the city's first high-rise parking garage. We had so much money we ate out even for breakfast. She thought she was pregnant for a while and I was happy as hell. I wanted a heavenly blessing—as the pastors say—with Jane. I thought it would form the living chain between us that would never be broken. It would be beyond biology and into magic. But it was only eighteen months in Mobile and we left on a rainy day in the winter without her pregnant. She was just lean and her eyes were brown diamonds like always, and she had begun having headaches.

Let me tell you about Jane drinking punch at one of the parties at the University of Florida where she had a job. Some hippie had put LSD in it and there was nothing but teacher types in the house, leaning around, commenting on the azaleas and the evil of the administration. I never took any punch because I brought my own dynamite in the car. Here I was, complimenting myself on holding my own with these profs. One of the profs looked at Jane in her long gown, not knowing she was with me. He said to another: "She's pleasant to look at, as far as *that* goes." I said to him that I'd heard she was smart too, and had taken the all-Missouri swimming meet when she was just a junior in high school. Another guy spoke up. The LSD had hit. I didn't know.

"I'd like to stick her brain. I'll bet her brain would be better than her crack. I'd like to have her hair falling around my honker. I'd love to pull on those ears with silver loops hanging around, at, on, above—what is it?—*them.*"

This guy was the chairman of the whole department.

"If I was an earthquake, I'd take care of her," said a fellow with a goatee and an ivory filter for his cigarette.

"Beauty is fleeting," said his ugly wife. "What stays is your basic endurance of pettiness and ennui. And perhaps, most of all, your ability to hide farts."

"Oh, Sandra!" says her husband. "I thought I'd taught you better. You went to Vassar, you bitch, so you wouldn't say things like that."

"I went to Vassar so I'd meet a dashing man with a fortune and a huge cucumber. Then I came back home, to assholing Florida and you," she said. "Washing socks, underwear, arguing with some idiot at Sears."

I met Jane at the punch bowl. She was socking it down and chatting with the librarian honcho who was her boss. He was a

Scotsman with a mountain of book titles for his mind. Jane said he'd never read a book in thirty years, but he knew the hell out of their names. Jane truly liked to talk to fat and old guys best of all. She didn't ever converse much with young men. Her ideal of a conversation was when sex was nowhere near it at all. She hated all her speech with her admirers because every word was shaded with lust implications. One of her strange little dreams was to be sort of a cloud with eyes, ears, mouth. I walked up on them without their seeing and heard her say: "I love you. I'd like to pet you to death." She put her hand on his poochy stomach.

So then I was hitting the librarian in the throat and chest. He was a huge person, looked something like a statue of some notable gentleman in ancient history. I couldn't do anything to bring him down. He took all my blows without batting an eye.

"You great bastard!" I yelled up there. "I believed in You on and off all my life! There better be something up there like Jane or I'll humiliate You! I'll swine myself all over this town. I'll appear in public places and embarrass the shit out of You, screaming that I'm a Christian!"

We divorced the second time right after that.

Now we're in Richmond, Virginia. They laid me off. Inflation or recession or whatever rubbed me out. Oh, it was nobody's fault, says the boss. I got to sell my third car off myself, says he. At my house, we don't eat near the meat we used to, says he.

So I'm in this house with my binoculars, moving from chair to chair with my cigarettes. She flies over my house upside down every afternoon. Is she saying she wants me so much she'd pay for a plane to my yard? Or is she saying: Look at this, I never gave a damn for anything but fun in the air?

Nothing in the world matters but you and your woman. Friendship and politics go to hell. My friend Dan three doors down, who's also unemployed, comes over when he can make the price of a six-pack.

It's not the same.

I'm going to die from love.

THE BROKEN BED

TO HAVE & TO HOLD

CHRISTINE SCHUTT

I have accidents in the Fifth Avenue kitchen—cuts, falls, scaldings. What could I be thinking of when I scissor through a plugged cord? My sleeve catches fire on the burner, and all I do is watch its crinkling into nothing. Fast as paper, it burns, filling the kitchen with a stink of burnt hair, my hair, and that is what finally makes me run for the salt, the smell of me catching fire.

Worse things happen in the kitchen—my husband tells me he is in love with someone else, and what do I do? I go out and buy he- and she-gerbils to make us feel more like a family.

I hate the gerbils. Nothing about them is cute; they twitch and gnaw. The animals live in a plastic, night-glow cage set next to the stove, because this kitchen is small, even if it is on Fifth Avenue, and here they scrabble and play and shred their tray paper—dirty animals that eat their own tails.

The girl was the first at it. One morning I found her dragging her rump through the shavings, scooting around the cage, past the boy. His tail was whole; hers was stubbed, pink, wet-looking. I saw her dizzying chase of it. I thought, maybe this is a mating ritual, maybe this is natural. What do I know? Except a few days later, some of the boy's tail was missing; now both of these cannibals are nearly tailless.

This eating has nothing to do with making baby gerbils. I don't think they even like one another. When the gerbils escape from their cage, and they escape every night, squiggling through a gnawed- away part, I never find them huddling. I might find the boy under the sink, the girl near the warm and coiled back of the refrigerator. I catch them up with a dishcloth; I can't stand to touch these silly savages—who could?—especially since they started eating themselves.

I want to know why my husband picked this woman to love, this woman who has been in my kitchen, who once helped me dry the silverware. This woman my husband loves is always, always on my mind here in the kitchen, where she once hugged me good-bye in her fur and pearls. I split open the coals of feeling to feel the buckle on her belt heat up in my hand. I touch her skirt and the stitched spine of her high heels. I am in a kind of hurry. I snatch at her nylons, her bag. Her bag is the color of toffee; I could eat it, I could gnaw off the clip to where the lining riffles with the scent of her, perfume and pennies and lipstick. Would she want to trade her clothes for my kitchen? Does she want babies?

The Fifth Avenue kitchen is so bright and clean. My husband says the counters are still gritty with cleanser. He says the food's embarrassed to be seen.

I admit it, I am driven. Last thing I do each night is wash my floor. One of the reasons the gerbils are such a problem is that they are so ridiculously dirty.

I should get out of the kitchen.

I should set the gerbils free.

I should let the scrub pads rust and the inky vouchers stain the counters. I should mess up.

My husband says the fridge door reads like an advertisement. He says the door is not a bulletin board. He says, Why don't you get a datebook, act like other people?

I thought that's what I was doing—acting like other people. So much space glinting off the white dune of Fifth Avenue, I thought, other people must want this, but not, it seems, the woman my husband wants. She, he says, wants to pitch her umbrella elsewhere.

Where?

I am standing here with the gerbils, who are loose again and scrabbling over my bare feet.

There is broken glass on the floor.

I can't help what happens.

The kitchen is sprung like an army knife, and I am in a hurry.

I have thrown open the window and am moving fast to catch these gerbils with only my hands. First the girl, who is trembling and trying to nip me, I swing her by the leg and out the window, she is gone. Then I make for the boy, hiding in a corner.

I think he thinks he is safe; he doesn't move. Lost, pointless, filthy boy.

I toss him underhand—just like rice.

THE BROKEN BED

181

DRIVE, IT SAID

Geoffrey Young

I was in love with a song, kept blurting it out, didn't know the words, maybe something about gazing at stars, I do that too, the constellations like old friends, but I might have been in a hot desert wearing snowshoes, the song would not let me go, I was like someone in love, that was the name of the tune in fact, I played it on the trumpet for the ghost of Kenny Dorham, even missing the highest note out of respect for Kenny's "flat on his ass" style, this song was leading me to something, wasn't it? There was no love in my life, or there *was* love, children are loves, brothers and sisters and old friends are love, even the dog is love, but when the fire in the hearth goes out there's no love, no love served at the table, time to get up, time to leave; my candor is true even if my art is grave. Certainly there was no feeling of new love, no baptismal lifeblood romance excitation stirring up the emotions, the months plodding by, celibate eternities curiously bearable, like an experiment in sensory deprivation these months would go on the soul's résumé, though I didn't feel noble, strong or medieval. Rather sad and exhausted, it's hard to swallow a family, tough to cling to what is no longer there. I could ask for a show of hands here, yes, I could ask for a show of hands.

Hollow at the center of the chest, my lungs, and underneath a shirt, my heart hurt. It was a constant pain, it wasn't painful, it was ponderous, I felt closer to everybody on the street, to the people I didn't know, the disfigured and halt, the guy with the huge goiter on his neck standing with his little dog on the storefront sidewalk, I felt tender toward the scruffy kids in the neighborhood whose fathers were in jail or drunk, people who'd gone through it, or were about to, it hurt to see them, one big unhappy family starring everyone. I was poised on that point where measurement fails, the body clamped in on itself, bruised, the little light pleasures of taste and sound were difficult to endure, hard to put two or three thoughts together, reason through an essay, move from sofa to chair, and back, finally standing up to wolf down a sandwich, single people always eat standing up at the sink, just as love compels me to this dialect, says "take a walk, drive around neighborhood, look at houses," their stiff faces, their colors, their porches, if any, glass in windows divided into panes, smoke from chimneys, formal snowshovels. So much was up in the air, so many moments I'd turn to a last falling leaf, or a dashing cat, and want to speak, say "What's up?" or "Where are the boys?" Elements of an unraveling tale written by squirrels in the circular sockets of a brain, I was eager for duties, for the demands of a job, contact with real people around a real table, I am literal, lived in, to think out loud is not to say much until it's written, give me a life in turmoil so I can feel what size brushstrokes will convey its portrait, the set of jaw, eyes the way the painter saw them, slipping. Homemade tapes accompanied my long commutes, driving was music, music never sounded more fundamental, like a dictionary come alive, it entered bodily, it was purposeful direction, all touch and go. I didn't know any teenage girls flipping out, didn't have to include that sound. Sometimes silence and the humming car would take on the shape of domestic anger's impossible heavy life injustice, no one to blame, not even myself, or the culture, a vicious spear thrust into the shell of an alien other, it hit me, I closed up around it, a sea anemone. Why do we hold on to the pain, perform heroic measures to sustain an embalmed identity? Why not melt into it and notice a sea gull's beak?

Or I would begin to flirt with desire for the very change I feared, to be free of the rasps, to be on my own again, be my own boss, make my own clichés, hang my own pictures, dial my own information, less security, but more adventure, less friction, more desire, click the lights off, knock back the heat and slip upstairs to read late into the night, a light that disturbs no one, a few pillows behind the back, a notebook on the nightstand, you can see me here, I'm covered from head to toe, it's an 18th-century classic, it's a copy of *Tears on My Pillow*, it's the neo-wave of the present, I'm wide awake, there's so much to read, so many sentences to speak out loud, words to prowl.

* * *

THE BROKEN BED

The bedside clock ticks, it's a different tune, it sings, "Take care of yourself and get plenty of rest," then sleep like a sponge drops, sops up awareness, involuntary muscular jerks unkink the self, a distant voice whispers, "Take the night off, Lonesome. You can't just have these emotions, you gotta pay for 'em." I was like someone in love falling asleep alone, but only like, there was no one there but memory, but fear, cold mornings the sun would tip through the east-facing windows and arrive on my skin all but extinguished, the light bouncing off the snow was a screaming vitamin, and curious people would tour the little house, it was amusing, I didn't own it, things began to fill it, tables on loan, sofa too, I'd be self-conscious, apologize for the bow in the shelves containing the poetry books, made 'em myself, the rooms so small my eyes could travel the spines, I could jump out of bed and reach a volume of my choice and be back under the covers before the mattress knew I'd left. Sometimes I think everything I know I've learned from poems, then I wake up, I see whole rooms exactly as they were, filled with paintings, I think I'm still in them, the Malevitch room at the Stedelyk in Amsterdam, it's a space station on the trajectory of abstract painting, I sit back down and watch it orbit, it's supreme.

My dreams these mornings weren't spectacular, some revenge, some lust, but the big gnawing fact relentless and obsessive was there to greet me at dawn, a broken record, a tape loop, in the video version the fact planted its green flag in my face, I was its imagery's victim, even as the credits went rolling by, our distant vows went back into the can for the next night's showing, beginning middle and end, finito, history, join the club. I bought a TV set and played the remote buttons like a thumb piano, it broke the silence, it lit the walls, and at dusk I'd say to myself, as I reached for the lamp, "Light the first light of evening," in stentorian tones, or "His gorgeous self-pity." So much for darkness then, but the darkness was only more apparent in the lamplight, I couldn't see where I was going, the body, my own, the room like a cage, moving from chair to sofa, legs tucked up under for warmth, a blanket, a magazine, I was eighty-five years old, I was fifteen, a manuscript was my afghan, a pile of mail, then the hop-up adrenaline of a phone call, let's have another show of hands here, you've been there too, it's ringing just for you, the minuscule bag of groceries, silent rice, passing moments passing, sponged whiteness of stove, sink, all the books filed away, the rug unwalked on, records in alphabetical order, a new ribbon, a stack of envelopes, the liquid paper crust that fell as white dots swept into the trash, I was puttering, not paralyzed, I was waiting, I remembered hitchhiking through Bulgaria with a Lebanese guy in a two-door sedan, and stopping to share cigarettes in a village off the main road. People suddenly materialized, we were surrounded, they looked at our clothes, we exchanged furtive smiles, kidded with the children, then out of nowhere a woman advances, hands us a just-baked loaf of bread, it's big and round and solid and warm and we are immediately touched, we thank them, I shake the woman's hand, it is callused and rough, her eyes are light brown, they are filled with amber lines that seem to spin, while my hands are soft, I'm bookish, I'll sleep tonight on the floor of the train station in Sofia, use my bookbag for a pillow, be up early fully dressed still and away, is there still a crust of that bread? Later picked up in Yugoslavia by a Persian driving a truckload of rugs to Munich, you want to hear about this guy? I believe my senses, I finally had to escape from him in Vienna, completely unstrung me, he was single-minded devotion, we shared five words in English and that's all. One night at a truck stop outside Belgrade, about midnight of a moonless starry night, we stopped to eat, he propositioned our blond waitress, we finished the meal, and she followed us out to the truck, got in between us, we drove a mile down the road, pitch-black. He pulled to the side and stopped. He grabbed a blanket from the cab, they got out, they disappeared into the featureless landscape. Is this the freebooting life of adventure so ably described in the *Tropic of Cancer*? Was I next? Could one say No, in Serbo-Croatian? Is there a God? I can't see them out there. Then just as suddenly as the truck had stopped, and they'd gotten out, she was back, alone, she was furious, she grabbed her jacket from the cab, she was livid, her light summer dress fit her perfectly, she slammed the cab door and took off walking down the highway, back to her truck stop. What had my Persian rug trucker done to earn her disapproval? It was a precipitate disaster. He got back to the truck, threw the blanket in the cab, shrugged his shoulders, and off we drove into the night, there were borders to cross, spring floodwaters rushing off the Alps to admire. But by the time we got to

Vienna, after some harrowing driving routines in dense traffic, some lane-changing leaps of faith that only a true son of Allah's compassionate protection could have gotten away with, he finally pulled off onto a side street, it was about eight o'clock, we stopped, he said, "Girls" (that was one of the five words we shared), and smiled, reached under the front seat, brought out a razor, a mug with soap, a brush, some cold water from a bottle, and a filthy hand towel, and proceeded to lather up the soap for his evening shave, daubing cold water on his bristly dark beard, and glancing over at me as if to indicate, What an Evening We'll Have! But listening to him pull that dull razor across his cold scraped cheeks I nearly gagged, he was really scraping, nicking chin and cheek, his towel on the seat I wouldn't even touch. I had to cut, jam, no time to get sick, I thanked him for the lift, he looked surprised, I was abandoning him! Where was my sense of fun? I grabbed my bag, opened the cab door, swung down, waved once, and took off walking down the city street, it was meant to be, back on my own two feet, and all aboard for the night train to Munich, I was on it, now it's the next day, it's two in the afternoon and I've just eaten a bratwurst and drunk a beer, I turn a corner and nearly bump into the only person I know in all of Germany, a girlfriend named Brigitte Gapp with a Marilyn Monroe–like birthmark on a pale cheek, dark hair, big bright smile, I go crazy, this is serendipity writ large, Jung's magic synchronicity, we fall into each other's arms, we stare, the only person I know, how account for it? The mind entertains a wisdom that the body can't understand.

People would say it takes a year, maybe two, there was money on the table, there were things, what was spoiled needed division, a few rounds of letterhead legality meetings on creamy stationery, the feints and dodges, the disclosures, the aggressive silence, the screaming meemies, the three-piece options expert, the comma that allows, insists, demands another term, something must follow the end of the world, this one here, the oil burner clicks on, these words cost money, it was happening to other people too, it was commonplace, you could join a group and discuss it, commiserating phone calls from old friends long since lost track of, the word spreads, a postcard from a woman in New York wanting to meet, we've mutual friends, let's have a drink, there's one in Stockbridge, you could drive down together, a movie nut uptown, I'd really like her, the chorus chorused, she's just breaking up with, this is the network speaking, it's an erotic universe of random strangers coupling, the matchmakers were lighting up, they closed the cover before striking, life could resume, don't hesitate, change your sheets, act like someone in love would act, get that bounce back into your step, kid, talk funny again, and all so nice and young. *Quel* sequence. It's typical though, isn't it? There's more variety in a crisis, more sense of drama in the pain of a social hello, to be on the crest of a breaking wave, but would you get smashed to the sand and ground up, or ride it for all it's worth into a new life, stolen like fire from the gods one burning finger at a time? Drive, it said, digitalized, accessed, therapied, the talk in every cafe on Main Street. This is our human universe, the glue on a chipped cup, this end that signals a new beginning is the cheapest gas in town. I drink it myself.

THE RIGHT SKATES

Laura Chester

The hand of the famous artist was warm when I met him, but then it was also freezing cold outside. I had written him a fan letter about his recent exhibition, and sent along a book of my own. I think he must have liked the photo on the dust jacket, because he called me immediately, all fired up, and invited me down to the city.

I didn't dare say—I don't really look like that, but suggested we meet at this gallery—the sculptor was a woman friend of mine, and the show was delightful—long, sculpted sticks that had been painted and bent into an airborne dimension.

I felt lively yet relaxed walking around the space, reading the names of the pieces.

"The titles don't matter," the famous artist said. He was almost twenty years older—lanky, severe. "I like this work," he added.

The sculpture reminded me of the arrows of Artemis, of giant ice-fishing hooks. I was pleased he could appreciate the work of a woman, a sure sign of a confident man.

I could have lingered for a while, but he wanted to get going. The heat inside the gallery was making him tired. He had already invited me for Indian food, a little place right around the corner. I'd brought a bottle of champagne. "To celebrate," I said. My husband was getting married.

I know I should say, ex-husband, but that doesn't sound natural. I don't believe in divorce, even if I was the one who left him.

Earlier in the week, I'd gone out and bought a pair of ice skates. It had been a cold, snowless winter, and if I was going to live in this climate, I figured, I should at least be equipped. I bought a pair of black leather figure skates, men's 9's, but when I reached the pond where my husband was meeting me with our ten-year-old son, I discovered both skates were for the right foot. "Can you believe this?" I said to him, though weirder things have happened.

They wanted me to come to their wedding. In fact his sister had asked specifically if she and her family could stay with me. "She can stay," I told him, "whether I'm around or not. But I might be in Siena for the *Palio*. Are you going to take a honeymoon this time?"

Suddenly I felt overwhelmed, and walked over to this bridge where water was leaking, forming stalactite shapes. My son skated over and looked up at me, "Are you crying, Mom?"

"No," I lied. "My skates don't fit."

"Do you want me to push you?" He was such a feeling child and I said yes, and let him push me, though I didn't really want to be shoved across the ice.

My husband offered to let me use his ice skates, and I accepted. We wore the exact same size, but they were hockey skates and didn't have sharp edges. I felt like they could slip out from beneath me. They didn't have those teeth on the front to help you stop, and I didn't want to fall and break something.

The famous artist had age on his mind. He was trying to figure out how old I was by asking me the ages of my children, the year I was pregnant in Paris. I found him very attractive—similar to the looks of my ex-husband actually, and I didn't mind that he was older. I let him order dinner, but he didn't drink, so I'd left the champagne in my car.

I was feeling high anyway, cheerful, alert. I had purposefully tried to look beautiful. This man had been on my mind, even in my dreams. I was amazed that he had responded to my fan note. Now he seemed to be feeling the situation out. He didn't want to fall on ice either.

I told him that I'd had this dream. He was walking through a gallery, an opening full of people, and he had waved at me. I was asked to read "the marriage of true minds," then discovered that all my clothes were lined with poetry. All I had to do was open up and read. I realized this was quite an invention, for I could even go to the bathroom and read poetry in my underpants. "What do you think it means?" I asked.

"I'm sure I don't know, but it sounds pretty good." He went on to describe the different dishes as he knew them—the dry, clay-baked tandoori chicken, the juicier creamed spinach with lamb. I said that I could eat anything, dying for a beer. I was tired of living alone.

I was still very close to my husband, talked to him on the phone at least once a day, but I also got along very well with the woman he was now marrying. We genuinely liked each other. Perhaps I should have minded that she was not at all jealous. She had given me a lambskin cover for my bike seat at Christmas, and I'd given her real turquoise earrings. It would seem odd if I refused to celebrate their marriage, when I was actually glad that she was the one. I'm sure it would be different if I had a partner. I could hobble across the ice, half gliding, but I'd rather not.

I couldn't tell if this famous man was interested in me. There were moments when his eyes lit up, when my thinking brushed up against his. "I grew up in a home where beauty was essential," I told him. "Every painting, each object—it all becomes part of you. Most people pull away from beauty, don't you think? Because they're afraid they might feel something. Pain for instance. But artists have to enter in a state of dilation."

"Yes," he said, in complete agreement. "Though it's sad, most painters squeeze the juice out of their work. They're afraid of appearing sentimental. It can take courage to make something beautiful," he said. "It's more acceptable these days to get ugly."

Whatever he created at this point in his career would undoubtedly be applauded, but still, I could see he continued wrestling with the medium, trying to make it new. I wasn't sure if I should go to the wedding.

The globed lights had come on all around the pond, and our son was skating the periphery. "All our friends would be wondering how I felt, I don't know. I just think it would give you more freedom if I wasn't there." It might also make me very sad.

"Well, you're invited," my husband said, explaining it away. "That was then, and this is now." But everything past still seemed present to me. Even the future was contained in this moment—we just couldn't see the entire panorama, the ribbon that surrounded our lives.

A year ago I saw a psychic who described a tall, married man, older, with glasses and a prominent nose, as if she could actually *see* him. Now I wondered if it was this artist, who fit the description. He was still married, though his wife had left him for a woman less than six months ago.

"It seems that women usually leave men," I said. "Men only leave a marriage if there's something else lined up."

"That's because men associate marriage with the mother," he answered. "And when it's over, believe me, it's almost like death."

I wasn't sure why I felt so comfortable with this man. Most women would feel intimidated, but it seemed as if I almost knew him. He was familiar in this unfamiliar way.

"Do you miss her?" I asked.

"Not at all."

I wondered if this was true. Even though I didn't want my husband back in bed with me, I certainly missed something we'd had—a feeling of wholeness, of skating together, arms linked, feet gliding in tandem.

He asked me if he could have his skates back if I was just going to stand there, shivering. "Sure," I said, and wobbled across the frozen grass to the car. His girlfriend had not shown up. She was making chicken soup because our older son was sick. She was better at mothering than I was, and I was grateful that she cared for my children in my absence.

When my husband put on the skates he was suddenly taller. The famous man *was* taller, and I liked his bony looks, his eyes, when he took off his glasses and left a generous tip. "I hope you enjoyed that. Ready to go?"

He had invited me to stay at his loft—"I've got plenty of room," and though I knew I shouldn't impose, my other city friends were either sick or on vacation, and it was true, he had the entire top floor of this building. One half of it was studio space. Enormous new works were up on the walls—they were like a cross between painting and sculpture. Each canvas had a different object pressing from behind, creating a subtle bulge. I wondered if anything would happen.

I knew men liked me in that way, but I hadn't slept with anyone in over seven months. I'd been writing so much it didn't seem to matter. There were always men interested, hanging around, but for some reason, recently, I hadn't been tempted, and felt like something big was approaching my life. At least that's what I told myself.

As soon as we walked into his living space, the telephone rang. He didn't have an answering machine. He wasn't going to have a machine stand in for him, I guess. "That was my friend," he said, after he had spoken. He didn't elaborate so I didn't ask. Maybe his conscience was getting the better of him. "Do you mind if we don't make a fire?" Having a fireplace was a luxury in New York, and he was almost out of wood. He was not making a move to be romantic.

But the huge space needed warming. "Oh can't we?" I begged.

Once it was lit, he admitted how much he enjoyed watching it, how he didn't do enough for pleasure.

I said, "Pleasure is something we must serve," as if she were a goddess and the fire an offering.

My ex-husband once called me *"la femme de ma vie,"* introducing me to a well-known French poet while his girlfriend was standing right there. It was a slip that slipped by because of the language, but I was flattered, not just the mother of his children.

I wondered if I should tell my husband about the dream I'd had. We were driving together—he was at the wheel and I was sitting very close to him. I kissed him on the cheek and said, *You can never be replaced.* When I woke up, I found myself sobbing.

The next morning I called home and my youngest son answered, informing me, "Dad's getting married. He bought her a ring." I wondered if he had paid for it himself this time.

I said to my son, "Oh, I'm glad! Aren't you?"

"I don't know," he said, honestly.

And I felt myself falling.

"Do you want a divorce?" I asked the artist.

"I don't like to think of anything ending," he said. His statements seemed to contradict, but I could accept that. He went on about the suicide rate for men after divorce, how they didn't fare well. "Most women are relieved."

"Maybe at first," I answered. "A false euphoria."

"I was always wrapped up in my painting." He seemed disconcerted, as if he didn't have much time, and I wondered if he wanted to work that very evening.

He no longer seemed all fired up, just tired, and even the logs had quickly settled. The loft was chilly and too big. I pulled an Indian blanket up over me as I lay back on the sofa, while he sat in his chair. He looked as if he had rested there throughout a very long marriage. He yawned, though it was only ten o'clock. He said that he got up early. That he liked to start painting by seven.

"You can shower." He stood up and showed me the bathroom, got a pillow for the couch. "When you wake," he added, "I'll make you a nice breakfast." He stooped to check the coals. "You're a good fire maker."

"I should be," I answered, "I'm a fire sign."

"Oh, when?" he wanted to know.

"April thirteenth."

"That's *my* birthday." He seemed astounded, as if he owned the date. But I was not so surprised. We were just like that pair of right skates, too similar to be of any use to each other.

"I'm all fire and air. No water anywhere. No earth," I explained, as if I were a female Icarus, flying a bit too high and close to the sun.

He seemed disenchanted, ready for bed. "So is there anything you'd like?" he asked, meaning cider or a magazine.

"I'd like to be *always* in love," I responded.

"Yes," he smiled. "We need that, don't we." He said good night then without giving me a hug, and as soon as he closed the door on the far side of the room, I felt an immense loneliness descending.

The fire had almost burned itself out. It was hardly giving off light or heat. I turned off the lamp and sat in the darkness, wide awake. Then I heard him in his bedroom, talking to someone on the phone. I got up and walked closer, listening for a moment. "I don't care if it's been a year, I just want to see you."

I had this terrible feeling that my presence, my company, had made him feel even more desperate.

I sat back down on the sofa in the darkness, as if I had fallen on the slick, black ice, way out in the middle of nowhere. I could feel the sure cold slowly entering my body, but I did not try to move or make a sound.

SEPARATING

John Updike

The day was fair. Brilliant. All that June the weather had mocked the Maples' internal misery with solid sunlight—golden shafts and cascades of green in which their conversations had wormed unseeing, their sad murmuring selves the only stain in Nature. Usually by this time of the year they had acquired tans; but when they met their elder daughter's plane on her return from a year in England they were almost as pale as she, though Judith was too dazzled by the sunny opulent jumble of her native land to notice. They did not spoil her homecoming by telling her immediately. Wait a few days, let her recover from jet lag, had been one of their formulations, in that string of gray dialogues—over coffee, over cocktails, over Cointreau—that had shaped the strategy of their dissolution, while the earth performed its annual stunt of renewal unnoticed beyond their closed windows. Richard had thought to leave at Easter; Joan had insisted they wait until the four children were at last assembled, with all exams passed and ceremonies attended, and the bauble of summer to console them. So he had drudged away, in love, in dread, repairing screens, getting the mowers sharpened, rolling and patching their new tennis court.

The court, clay, had come through its first winter pitted and windswept bare of redcoat. Years ago the Maples had observed how often, among their friends, divorce followed a dramatic home improvement, as if the marriage were making one last strong effort to live; their own worst crisis had come amid the plaster dust and exposed plumbing of a kitchen renovation. Yet, a summer ago, as canary-yellow bulldozers gaily churned a grassy, daisy-dotted knoll into a muddy plateau, and a crew of pigtailed young men raked and tamped clay into a plane, this transformation did not strike them as ominous, but festive in its impudence; their marriage could rend the earth for fun. The next spring, waking each day at dawn to a sliding sensation as if the bed were being tipped, Richard found the barren tennis court—its net and tapes still rolled in the barn—an environment congruous with his mood of purposeful desolation, and the crumbling of handfuls of clay into cracks and holes (dogs had frolicked on the court in a thaw; rivulets had evolved trenches) an activity suitably elemental and interminable. In his sealed heart he hoped the day would never come.

Now it was here. A Friday. Judith was reacclimated; all four children were assembled, before jobs and camps and visits again scattered them. Joan thought they should be told one by one. Richard was for making an announcement at the table. She said, "I think just making an announcement is a cop-out. They'll start quarreling and playing to each other instead of focusing. They're each individuals, you know, not just some corporate obstacle to your freedom."

"O.K., O.K. I agree." Joan's plan was exact. That evening, they were giving Judith a belated welcome-home dinner, of lobster and champagne. Then, the party over, they, the two of them, who nineteen years before would push her in a baby carriage along Fifth Avenue to Washington Square, were to walk her out of the house, to the bridge across the salt creek, and tell her, swearing her to secrecy. Then Richard Jr., who was going directly from work to a rock concert in Boston, would be told, either late when he returned on the train or early Saturday morning before he went off to his job; he was seventeen and employed as one of a golf-course maintenance crew. Then the two younger children, John and Margaret, could, as the morning wore on, be informed.

"Mopped up, as it were," Richard said.

"Do you have any better plan? That leaves you the rest of Saturday to answer any questions, pack, and make your wonderful departure."

"No," he said, meaning he had no better plan, and agreed to hers, though to him it showed an edge of false order, a hidden plea for control, like Joan's long chore lists and financial accountings and, in the days when he first knew her, her too copious lecture notes. Her plan turned one hurdle for him into four—four knife-sharp walls, each with a sheer blind drop on the other side.

All spring he had moved through a world of insides and outsides, of barriers and partitions. He and Joan stood as a thin barrier between the children and the truth. Each moment was a partition, with the past on one side and the future on the other, a future containing this unthinkable *now*. Beyond four knifelike walls a new life for him waited vaguely. His skull cupped a secret, a white face, a face both frightened and soothing, both strange and known, that he wanted to shield from tears, which he felt all about him, solid as the sunlight. So haunted, he had become obsessed with battening down the house against his absence, replacing screens and sash cords, hinges and latches—a Houdini making things snug before his escape.

The lock. He had still to replace a lock on one of the doors of the screened porch. The task, like most such, proved more difficult than he had imagined. The old lock, aluminum frozen by corrosion, had been deliberately rendered obsolete by manufacturers. Three hardware stores had nothing that even approximately matched the mortised hole its removal (surprisingly easy) left. Another hole had to be gouged, with bits too small and saws too big, and the old hole fitted with a block of wood—the chisels dull, the saw rusty, his fingers thick with lack of sleep. The sun poured down, beyond the porch, on a world of neglect. The bushes already needed pruning, the windward side of the house was shedding flakes of paint, rain would get in when he was gone, insects, rot, death. His family, all those he would lose, filtered through the edges of his awareness as he struggled with screw holes, splinters, opaque instructions, minutiae of metal.

Judith sat on the porch, a princess returned from exile. She regaled them with stories of fuel shortages, of bomb scares in the Underground, of Pakistani workmen loudly lusting after her as she walked past on her way to dance school. Joan came and went, in and out of the house, calmer than she should have been, praising his struggles with the lock as if this were one more and not the last of their long chain of shared chores. The younger of his sons, John, now at fifteen suddenly, unwittingly handsome, for a few minutes held the rickety screen door while his father clumsily hammered and chiseled, each blow a kind of sob in Richard's ears. His younger daughter, having been at a slumber party, slept on the porch hammock through all the noise—heavy and pink, trusting and forsaken. Time, like the sunlight, continued relentlessly; the sunlight slowly slanted. Today was one of the longest days. The lock clicked, worked.

He was through. He had a drink; he drank it on the porch, listening to his daughter. "It was so sweet," she was saying, "during the worst of it, how all the butchers and bakery shops kept open by candlelight. They're all so plucky and cute. From the papers, things sounded so much worse here—people shooting people in gas lines, and everybody freezing."

Richard asked her, "Do you still want to live in England forever?" *Forever*: the concept, now a reality upon him, pressed and scratched at the back of his throat.

"No," Judith confessed, turning her oval face to him, its eyes still childishly far apart, but the lips set as over something succulent and satisfactory. "I was anxious to come home. I'm an American." She was a woman. They had raised her; he and Joan had endured together to raise her, alone of the four. The others had still some raising left in them. Yet it was the thought of telling Judith—the image of her, their first baby, walking between them arm in arm to the bridge—that broke him. The partition between his face and the tears broke. Richard sat down to the celebratory meal with the back of his throat aching; the champagne, the lobster seemed phases of sunshine; he saw them and tasted them through tears. He blinked, swallowed, croakily joked about hay fever. The tears would not stop leaking through; they came not through a hole that could be plugged but through a permeable spot in a membrane, steadily, purely, endlessly, fruitfully. They became, his tears, a shield for himself against these others—their faces, the fact of their assembly, a last time as innocents, at a table where he sat the last time as head. Tears dropped from his nose as he broke the lobster's back; salt flavored his champagne as he sipped it; the raw clench at the back of his throat was delicious. He could not help himself.

His children tried to ignore his tears. Judith, on his right, lit a cigarette, gazed upward in the direction of her too energetic, too sophisticated exhalation; on her other side, John earnestly bent his face to the extraction of the last morsels—legs, tail segments—from the scarlet corpse. Joan, at the opposite end of the table, glanced at him surprised, her reproach displaced by a quick grimace, of forgiveness, or of salute to his superior gift of strategy. Between them, Margaret, no longer called Bean, thirteen and large for her age, gazed from the other side of his pane of tears as if into a shopwindow at something she coveted—at her father, a crystalline heap of splinters and memories. It was not she, however, but John who, in the kitchen, as they cleared the plates and carapaces away, asked Joan the question: *"Why is Daddy crying?"*

Richard heard the question but not the murmured answer. Then he heard Bean cry, "Oh, no-oh!"—the faintly dramatized exclamation of one who had long expected it.

John returned to the table carrying a bowl of salad. He nodded tersely at his father and his lips shaped the conspiratorial words "She told."

"Told what?" Richard asked aloud, insanely.

The boy sat down as if to rebuke his father's distraction with the example of his own good manners. He said quietly, "The separation."

Joan and Margaret returned; the child, in Richard's twisted vision, seemed diminished in size, and relieved, relieved to have had the bogieman at last proved real. He called out to her—the distances at the table had grown immense—"You knew, you always knew," but the clenching at the back of his throat prevented him from making sense of it. From afar he heard Joan talking, levelly, sensibly, reciting what they had prepared: it was a separation for the summer, an experiment. She and Daddy both agreed it would be good for them; they needed space and time to think; they liked each other but did not make each other happy enough, somehow.

Judith, imitating her mother's factual tone, but in her youth off-key, too cool, said, "I think it's silly. You should either live together or get divorced."

Richard's crying, like a wave that has crested and crashed, had become tumultuous; but it was overtopped by another tumult, for John, who had been so reserved, now grew larger and larger at the table. Perhaps his younger sister's being credited with knowing set him off. "Why didn't you *tell* us?" he asked, in a large round voice quite unlike his own. "You should have *told* us you weren't getting along."

Richard was startled into attempting to force words through his tears. "We *do* get along, that's the trouble, so it doesn't show even to us—" *That we do not love each other* was the rest of the sentence; he couldn't finish it.

Joan finished for him, in her style. "And we've always, *especially*, loved our children."

John was not mollified. "What do you care about *us?*" he boomed. "We're just little things you *had.*" His sisters' laughing forced a laugh from him, which he turned hard and parodistic: "Ha ha *ha.*" Richard and Joan realized simultaneously that the child was drunk, on Judith's homecoming champagne. Feeling bound to keep the center of the stage, John took a cigarette from Judith's pack, poked it into his mouth, let it hang from his lower lip, and squinted like a gangster.

"You're not little things we had," Richard called to him. "You're the whole point. But you're grown. Or almost."

The boy was lighting matches. Instead of holding them to his cigarette (for they had never seen him smoke; being "good" had been his way of setting himself apart), he held them to his mother's face, closer and closer, for her to blow out. Then he lit the whole folder—a hiss and then a torch, held against his mother's face. Prismed by his tears, the flame filled Richard's vision; he didn't know how it was extinguished. He heard Margaret say, "Oh stop showing off," and saw John, in response, break the cigarette in two and put the halves entirely into his mouth and chew, sticking out his tongue to display the shreds to his sister.

Joan talked to him, reasoning—a fountain of reason, unintelligible. "Talked about it for years . . . our children must help us . . . Daddy and I both want . . ." As the boy listened, he carefully wadded a paper napkin into the leaves of his salad, fashioned a ball of paper and lettuce, and popped it into his mouth, looking around the table for the expected laughter. None came. Judith said, "Be mature," and dismissed a plume of smoke.

Richard got up from this stifling table and led the boy outside. Though the house was in twilight, the outdoors still brimmed with light, the lovely waste light of high summer. Both laughing, he supervised John's spitting out the lettuce and paper and tobacco into the pachysandra. He took him by the hand—a square gritty hand, but for its softness a man's. Yet, it held on. They ran together up into the field, past the tennis court. The raw banking left by the bulldozers was dotted with daisies. Past the court and a flat stretch where they used to play family baseball stood a soft green rise glorious in the sun, each weed and species of grass distinct as illumination on parchment. "I'm sorry, so sorry," Richard cried. "You were the only one who ever tried to help me with all the goddam jobs around this place."

Sobbing, safe within his tears and the champagne, John explained, "It's not just the separation, it's the whole crummy year, I *hate* that school, you can't make any friends, the history teacher's a scud."

They sat on the crest of the rise, shaking and warm from their tears but easier in their voices, and Richard tried to focus on the child's sad year—the weekdays long with homework, the weekends spent in his room with model airplanes, while his parents murmured down below, nursing their separation. How selfish, how blind, Richard thought; his eyes felt scoured. He told his son, "We'll think about getting you transferred. Life's too short to be miserable."

They had said what they could, but did not want the moment to heal, and talked on, about the school, about the tennis court, whether it would ever again be as good as it had been that first summer. They walked to inspect it and pressed a few more tapes more firmly down. A little stiltedly, perhaps trying now to make too much of the moment, Richard led the boy to the spot in the field where the view was best, of the metallic blue river, the emerald marsh, the scattered islands velvety with shadow in the low light, the white bits of beach far away. "See," he said. "It goes on being beautiful. It'll be here tomorrow."

"I know," John answered, impatiently. The moment had closed.

Back in the house, the others had opened some white wine, the champagne being drunk, and still sat at the table, the three females, gossiping. Where Joan sat had become the head. She turned, showing him a tearless face, and asked, "All right?"

"We're fine," he said, resenting it, though relieved, that the party went on without him.

In bed she explained, "I couldn't cry I guess because I cried so much all spring. It really wasn't fair. It's your idea, and you made it look as though I was kicking you out."

"I'm sorry," he said. "I couldn't stop. I wanted to but couldn't."

"You *didn't* want to. You loved it. You were having your way, making a general announcement."

THE UNMADE BED

"I love having it over," he admitted. "God, those kids were great. So brave and funny." John, returned to the house, had settled to a model airplane in his room, and kept shouting down to them, "I'm O.K. No sweat." "And the way," Richard went on, cozy in his relief, "they never questioned the reasons we gave. No thought of a third person. Not even Judith."

"That *was* touching," Joan said.

He gave her a hug. "You were great too. Very reassuring to everybody. Thank you." Guiltily, he realized he did not feel separated.

"You still have Dickie to do," she told him. These words set before him a black mountain in the darkness; its cold breath, its near weight affected his chest. Of the four children, his elder son was most like a conscience. Joan did not need to add, "That's one piece of your dirty work I won't do for you."

"I know. I'll do it. You go to sleep."

Within minutes, her breathing slowed, became oblivious and deep. It was quarter to midnight. Dickie's train from the concert would come in at one-fourteen. Richard set the alarm for one. He had slept atrociously for weeks. But whenever he closed his lids some glimpse of the last hours scorched them—Judith exhaling toward the ceiling in a kind of aversion, Bean's mute staring, the sunstruck growth of the field where he and John had rested. The mountain before him moved closer, moved within him; he was huge, momentous. The ache at the back of his throat felt stale. His wife slept as if slain beside him. When, exasperated by his hot lids, his crowded heart, he rose from bed and dressed, she awoke enough to turn over. He told her then, "Joan, if I could undo it all, I would."

"Where would you begin?" she asked. There was no place. Giving him courage, she was always giving him courage. He put on shoes without socks in the dark. The children were breathing in their rooms, the downstairs was hollow. In their confusion they had left lights burning. He turned off all but one, the kitchen overhead. The car started. He had hoped it wouldn't. He met only moonlight on the road; it seemed a diaphanous companion, flickering in the leaves along the roadside, haunting his rearview mirror like a pursuer, melting under his headlights. The center of town, not quite deserted, was eerie at this hour. A young cop in uniform kept company with a gang of T-shirted kids on the steps of the bank. Across from the railroad station, several bars kept open. Customers, mostly young, passed in and out of the warm night, savoring summer's novelty. Voices shouted from cars as they passed; an immense conversation seemed in progress. Richard parked and in his weariness put his head on the passenger seat, out of the commotion and wheeling lights. It was as when, in the movies, an assassin grimly carries his mission through the jostle of a carnival—except the movies cannot show the precipitous, palpable slope you cling to within. You cannot climb back down; you can only fall. The synthetic fabric of the car seat, warmed by his cheek, confided to him an ancient, distant scent of vanilla.

A train whistle caused him to lift his head. It was on time; he had hoped it would be late. The slender drawgates descended. The bell of approach tingled happily. The great metal body, horizontally fluted, rocked to a stop, and sleepy teenagers disembarked, his son among them. Dickie did not show surprise that his father was meeting him at this terrible hour. He sauntered to the car with two friends, both taller than he. He said "Hi" to his father and took the passenger's seat with an exhausted promptness that expressed gratitude. The friends got into the back, and Richard was grateful; a few more minutes' postponement would be won by driving them home.

He asked, "How was the concert?"

"Groovy," one boy said from the back seat.

"It bit," the other said.

"It was O.K.," Dickie said, moderate by nature, so reasonable that in his childhood the unreason of the world had given him headaches, stomachaches, nausea. When the second friend had been dropped off at his dark house, the boy blurted, "Dad, my eyes are killing me with hay fever! I'm out there cutting that mothering grass all day!"

"Do we still have those drops?"

"They didn't do any good last summer."

"They might this." Richard swung a U-turn on the empty street. The drive home took a few minutes. The mountain was here, in his throat. "Richard," he said, and felt the boy, slumped and rubbing his eyes, go tense at his tone, "I didn't come to meet you just to make your life easier. I came because your mother and I have some news for you, and you're a hard man to get a hold of these days. It's sad news."

"That's O.K." The reassurance came out soft, but quick, as if released from the tip of a spring.

Richard had feared that his tears would return and choke him, but the boy's manliness set an example, and his voice issued forth steady and dry. "It's sad news, but it needn't be tragic news, at least for you. It should have no practical effect on your life, though it's bound to have an emotional effect. You'll work at your job, and go back to school in September. Your mother and I are really proud of what you're making of your life; we don't want that to change at all."

"Yeah," the boy said lightly, on the intake of his breath, holding himself up. They turned the corner; the church they went to loomed like a gutted fort. The home of the woman Richard hoped to marry stood across the green. Her bedroom light burned.

"Your mother and I," he said, "have decided to separate. For the summer. Nothing legal, no divorce yet. We want to see how it feels. For some years now, we haven't been doing enough for each other as, making each other as happy as we should be. Have you sensed that?"

"No," the boy said. It was an honest, unemotional answer: true or false in a quiz.

Glad for the factual basis, Richard pursued, even garrulously, the details. His apartment across town, his utter accessibility, the split vacation arrangements, the advantages to the children, the added mobility and variety of the summer. Dickie listened, absorbing. "Do the others know?"

"Yes."

"How did they take it?"

"The girls pretty calmly. John flipped out; he shouted and ate a cigarette and made a salad out of his napkin and told us how much he hated school."

His brother chuckled. "He did?"

"Yeah. The school issue was more upsetting for him than Mom and me. He seemed to feel better for having exploded."

"He did?" The repetition was the first sign that he was stunned.

"Yes. Dickie, I want to tell you something. This last hour, waiting for your train to get in, has been about the worst of my life. I hate this. *Hate* it. My father would have died before doing it to me." He felt immensely lighter, saying this. He had dumped the mountain on the boy. They were home. Moving swiftly as a shadow, Dickie was out of the car, through the bright kitchen. Richard called after him, "Want a glass of milk or anything?"

"No thanks."

"Want us to call the course tomorrow and say you're too sick to work?"

"No, that's all right." The answer was faint, delivered at the door to his room; Richard listened for the slam that went with a tantrum. The door closed normally, gently. The sound was sickening.

Joan had sunk into that first deep trough of sleep and was slow to awake. Richard had to repeat, "I told him."

"What did he say?"

"Nothing much. Could you go say good night to him? Please."

She left their room, without putting on a bathrobe. He sluggishly changed back into his pajamas and walked down the hall. Dickie was already in bed, Joan was sitting beside him, and the boy's bedside clock radio was murmuring music. When she stood, an inexplicable light—the moon?—outlined her body through the nightie. Richard sat on the warm place she had indented on the child's narrow mattress. He asked him, "Do you want the radio on like that?"

"It always is."

"Doesn't it keep you awake? It would me."

"No."

"Are you sleepy?"

"Yeah."

"Good. Sure you want to get up and go to work? You've had a big night."

"I want to."

Away at school this winter he had learned for the first time that you can go short of sleep and live. As an infant he had slept with an immobile, sweating intensity that had alarmed his babysitters. In adolescence he had often been the first of the four children to go to bed. Even now, he would go slack in the middle of a television show, his sprawled legs hairy and brown. "O.K. Good boy. Dickie, listen. I love you so much, I never knew how much until now. No matter how this works out, I'll always be with you. Really."

Richard bent to kiss an averted face but his son, sinewy, turned and with wet cheeks embraced him and gave him a kiss, on the lips, passionate as a woman's. In his father's ear he moaned one word, the crucial, intelligent word: *"Why?"*

Why. It was a whistle of wind in a crack, a knife thrust, a window thrown open on emptiness. The white face was gone, the darkness was featureless. Richard had forgotten why.

SONNET

Bernadette Mayer

A thousand apples you might put in your theories
But you are gone from benefit to my love

You spoke not the Italian of Dante at the table
But the stingy notions of the bedded heterosexual

You cursed and swore cause I was later
To come home to you without your fucking dinner

Dont ever return su numero de telefono it is just this
I must explain I dont ever want to see you again

Empezando el 2 de noviembre 1980-something I dont love you
So stick it up your ass like she would say

I'm so mad at you I'm sure I'll take it all back tomorrow
& say then they flee from me who sometime did me seek

Meanwhile eat my existent dinner somebody and life
C'mon and show me something newer than even Dante

INTIMACY

Raymond Carver

I have some business out west anyway, so I stop off in this little town where my former wife lives. We haven't seen each other in four years. But from time to time, when something of mine appeared, or was written about me in the magazines or papers—a profile or an interview—I sent her these things. I don't know what I had in mind except I thought she might be interested. In any case, she never responded.

It is nine in the morning, I haven't called, and it's true I don't know what I am going to find.

But she lets me in. She doesn't seem surprised. We don't shake hands, much less kiss each other. She takes me into the living room. As soon as I sit down she brings me some coffee. Then she comes out with what's on her mind. She says I've caused her anguish, made her feel exposed and humiliated.

Make no mistake, I feel I'm home.

She says, But then you were into betrayal early. You always felt comfortable with betrayal. No, she says, that's not true. Not in the beginning, at any rate. You were different then. But I guess I was different too. Everything was different, she says. No, it was after you turned thirty-five, or thirty-six, whenever it was, around in there anyway, your mid-thirties somewhere, then you started in. You really started in. You turned on me. You did it up pretty then. You must be proud of yourself.

She says, Sometimes I could scream.

She says she wishes I'd forget about the hard times, the bad times, when I talk about back then. Spend some time on the good times, she says. Weren't there some good times? She wishes I'd get off that other subject. She's bored with it. Sick of hearing about it. Your private hobby horse, she says. What's done is done and water under the bridge, she says. A tragedy, yes. God knows it was a tragedy and then some. But why keep it going? Don't you ever get tired of dredging up that old business?

She says, Let go of the past, for Christ's sake. Those old hurts. You must have some other arrows in your quiver, she says.

She says, You know something? I think you're sick. I think you're crazy as a bedbug. Hey, you don't believe the things they're saying about you, do you? Don't believe them for a minute, she says. Listen, I could tell them a thing or two. Let them talk to me about it, if they want to hear a story.

She says, Are you listening to me?

I'm listening, I say. I'm all ears, I say.

She says, I've really had a bellyful of it, buster! Who asked you here today anyway? I sure as hell didn't. You just show up and walk in. What the hell do you want from me? Blood? You want more blood? I thought you had your fill by now.

She says, Think of me as dead. I want to be left in peace now. That's all I want anymore is to be left in peace and forgotten about. Hey, I'm forty-five years old, she says. Forty-five going on fifty-five, or sixty-five. Lay off, will you.

She says, Why don't you wipe the blackboard clean and see what you have left after that? Why don't you start with a clean slate? See how far that gets you, she says.

She has to laugh at this. I laugh too, but it's nerves.

She says, You know something? I had my chance once, but I let it go. I just let it go. I don't guess I ever told you. But now look at me. Look! Take a good look while you're at it. You threw me away, you son of a bitch.

She says, I was younger then and a better person. Maybe you were too, she says. A better person, I mean. You had to be. You were better then or I wouldn't have had anything to do with you.

She says, I loved you so much once. I loved you to the point of distraction. I did. More than anything in the whole wide world. Imagine that. What a laugh that is now. Can you imagine it? We were so *intimate* once upon a time I can't believe it now. I think that's the strangest thing of all now. The memory of being that intimate with somebody. We were so intimate I could puke. I can't imagine ever being that intimate with somebody else. I haven't been.

She says, Frankly, and I mean this, I want to be kept out of it from here on out. Who do you think you are anyway? You think you're God or somebody? You're not fit to lick God's boots, or anybody else's for that matter. Mister, you've been hanging out with the wrong people. But what do I know? I don't even know what I know any longer. I know I don't like what you've been dishing out. I know that much. You know what I'm talking about, don't you? Am I right?

Right, I say. Right as rain.

She says, You'll agree to anything, won't you? You give in too easy. You always did. You don't have any principles, not one. Anything to avoid a fuss. But that's neither here nor there.

She says, You remember that time I pulled the knife on you?

She says this as if in passing, as if it's not important.

Vaguely, I say. I must have deserved it, but I don't remember much about it. Go ahead, why don't you, and tell me about it.

She says, I'm beginning to understand something now. I think I know why you're here. Yes. I know why you're here, even if you don't. But you're a slyboots. You know why you're here. You're on a fishing expedition. You're hunting for *material*. Am I getting warm? Am I right?

Tell me about the knife, I say.

She says, If you want to know, I'm real sorry I didn't use that knife. I am. I really and truly am. I've thought and thought about it, and I'm sorry I didn't use it. I had the chance. But I hesitated. I hesitated and was lost, as somebody or other said. But I should have used it, the hell with everything and everybody. I should have nicked your arm with it at least. At least that.

Well, you didn't, I say. I thought you were going to cut me with it, but you didn't. I took it away from you.

She says, You were always lucky. You took it away and then you slapped me. Still, I regret I didn't use that knife just a little bit. Even a little would have been something to remember me by.

I remember a lot, I say. I say that, then wish I hadn't.

She says, Amen, brother. That's the bone of contention here, if you hadn't noticed. That's the whole problem. But like I said, in my opinion you remember the wrong things. You remember the low, shameful things. That's why you got interested when I brought up the knife.

THE BROKEN BED

She says, I wonder if you ever have any regret. For whatever that's worth on the market these days. Not much, I guess. But you ought to be a specialist in it by now.

Regret, I say. It doesn't interest me much, to tell the truth. Regret is not a word I use very often. I guess I mainly don't have it. I admit I hold to the dark view of things. Sometimes, anyway. But regret? I don't think so.

She says, You're a real son of a bitch, did you know that? A ruthless, coldhearted son of a bitch. Did anybody ever tell you that?

You did, I say. Plenty of times.

She says, I always speak the truth. Even when it hurts. You'll never catch me in a lie.

She says, My eyes were opened a long time ago, but by then it was too late. I had my chance but I let it slide through my fingers. I even thought for a while you'd come back. Why'd I think that anyway? I must have been out of my mind. I could cry my eyes out now, but I wouldn't give you that satisfaction.

She says, You know what? I think if you were on fire right now, if you suddenly burst into flame this minute, I wouldn't throw a bucket of water on you.

She laughs at this. Then her face closes down again.

She says, Why in hell *are* you here? You want to hear some more? I could go on for days. I think I know why you turned up, but I want to hear it from you.

When I don't answer, when I just keep sitting there, she goes on.

She says, After that time, when you went away, nothing much mattered after that. Not the kids, not God, not anything. It was like I didn't know what hit me. It was like I had *stopped living*. My life had been going along, going along, and then it just stopped. It didn't just come to a stop, it screeched to a stop. I thought, If I'm not worth anything to him, well, I'm not worth anything to myself or anybody else either. That was the worst thing I felt. I thought my heart would break. What am I saying? It did break. Of course it broke. It broke, just like that. It's still broke, if you want to know. And so there you have it in a nutshell. My eggs in one basket, she says. A tisket, a tasket. All my rotten eggs in one basket.

She says, You found somebody else for yourself, didn't you? It didn't take long. And you're happy now. That's what they say about you anyway: "He's happy now." Hey, I read everything you send! You think I don't? Listen, I know your heart, mister. I always did. I knew it back then, and I know it now. I know your heart inside and out, and don't you ever forget it. Your heart is a jungle, a dark forest, it's a garbage pail, if you want to know. Let them talk to me if they want to ask somebody something. I know how you operate. Just let them come around here, and I'll give them an earful. I was there. I served, buddy boy. Then you held me up for display and ridicule in your so-called work. For any Tom or Harry to pity or pass judgment on. Ask me if I cared. Ask me if it embarrassed me. Go ahead, ask.

No, I say, I won't ask that. I don't want to get into that, I say.

Damn straight you don't! she says. And you know *why*, too!

She says, Honey, no offense, but sometimes I think I could shoot you and watch you kick.

She says, You can't look me in the eyes, can you?

She says, and this is exactly what she says, You can't even look me in the eyes when I'm talking to you.

So, okay, I look her in the eyes.

She says, Right. Okay, she says. Now we're getting someplace, maybe. That's better. You can tell a lot about the person you're talking to from his eyes. Everybody knows that. But you know something else? There's nobody in this whole world who would tell you this, but I can tell you. I have the right. I *earned* that right, sonny. You have yourself confused with somebody else. And that's the pure truth of it. But what do I know? they'll say in a hundred years. They'll say, Who was she anyway?

She says, In any case, you sure as hell have *me* confused with somebody else. Hey, I don't even have the same name anymore! Not the name I was born with, not the name I lived with you with, not even the name I had two years ago. What is this? What is this in hell all about anyway? Let me say something. I want to be left alone now. Please. That's not a crime.

She says, Don't you have someplace else you should be? Some plane to catch? Shouldn't you be somewhere far from here at this very minute?

No, I say. I say it again: No. No place, I say. I don't have anyplace I have to be.

And then I do something. I reach over and take the sleeve of her blouse between my thumb and forefinger. That's all. I just touch it that way, and then I just bring my hand back. She doesn't draw away. She doesn't move.

Then here's the thing I do next. I get down on my knees, a big guy like me, and I take the hem of her dress. What am I doing on the floor? I wish I could say. But I know it's where I ought to be, and I'm there on my knees holding on to the hem of her dress.

She is still for a minute. But in a minute she says, Hey, it's all right, stupid. You're so dumb, sometimes. Get up now. I'm telling you to get up. Listen, it's okay. I'm over it now. It took me a while to get over it. What do you think? Did you think it wouldn't? Then you walk in here and suddenly the whole cruddy business is back. I felt a need to ventilate. But you know, and I know, it's over and done with now.

She says, For the longest while, honey, I was inconsolable. *Inconsolable*, she says. Put that word in your little notebook. I can tell you from experience that's the saddest word in the English language. Anyway, I got over it finally. Time is a gentleman, a wise man said. Or else maybe a worn-out old woman, one or the other anyway.

She says, I have a life now. It's a different kind of life than yours, but I guess we don't need to compare. It's my life, and that's the important thing I have to realize as I get older. Don't feel *too* bad, anyway, she says. I mean, it's all right to feel a *little* bad, maybe. That won't hurt you, that's only to be expected after all. Even if you can't move yourself to regret.

She says, Now you have to get up and get out of here. My husband will be along pretty soon for his lunch. How would I explain this kind of thing?

It's crazy, but I'm still on my knees holding the hem of her dress. I won't let it go. I'm like a terrier, and it's like I'm stuck to the floor. It's like I can't move.

She says, Get up now. What is it? You still want something from me. What do you want? Want me to forgive you? Is that why you're doing this? That's it, isn't it? That's the reason you came all this way. The knife thing kind of perked you up, too. I think you'd forgotten about that. But you needed me to remind you. Okay, I'll say something if you'll just go.

THE UNMADE BED

She says, I forgive you.

She says, Are you satisfied now? Is that better? Are you happy? He's happy now, she says.

But I'm still there, knees to the floor.

She says, Did you hear what I said? You have to go now. Hey, stupid. Honey, I said I forgive you. And I even reminded you about the knife thing. I can't think what else I can do now. You got it made in the shade, baby. Come on now, you have to get out of here. Get up. That's right. You're still a big guy, aren't you. Here's your hat, don't forget your hat. You never used to wear a hat. I never in my life saw you in a hat before.

She says, Listen to me now. Look at me. Listen carefully to what I'm going to tell you.

She moves closer. She's about three inches from my face. We haven't been this close in a long time. I take these little breaths that she can't hear, and I wait. I think my heart slows way down, I think.

She says, You just tell it like you have to, I guess, and forget the rest. Like always. You been doing that for so long now anyway it shouldn't be hard for you.

She says, There, I've done it. You're free, aren't you? At least you think you are anyway. Free at last. That's a joke, but don't laugh. Anyway, you feel better, don't you?

She walks with me down the hall.

She says, I can't imagine how I'd explain this if my husband was to walk in this very minute. But who really cares anymore, right? In the final analysis, nobody gives a damn anymore. Besides which, I think everything that can happen that way has already happened. His name is Fred, by the way. He's a decent guy and works hard for his living. He cares for me.

So she walks me to the front door, which has been standing open all this while. The door that was letting in light and fresh air this morning, and sounds off the street, all of which we had ignored. I look outside and, Jesus, there's this white moon hanging in the morning sky. I can't think when I've ever seen anything so remarkable. But I'm afraid to comment on it. I am. I don't know what might happen. I might break into tears even. I might not understand a word I'd say.

She says, Maybe you'll be back sometime, and maybe you won't.

This'll wear off, you know. Pretty soon you'll start feeling bad again. Maybe it'll make a good story, she says. But I don't want to know about it if it does.

I say good-bye. She doesn't say anything more. She looks at her hands, and then she puts them into the pockets of her dress. She shakes her head. She goes back inside, and this time she closes the door.

I move off down the sidewalk. Some kids are tossing a football at the end of the street. But they aren't my kids, and they aren't her kids either. There are these leaves everywhere, even in the gutters. Piles of leaves wherever I look. They're falling off the limbs as I walk. I can't take a step without putting my shoe into leaves. Somebody ought to make an effort here. Somebody ought to get a rake and take care of this.

OUR FIRST SUMMER

Marie Harris

At a deepening
of the Isinglass River
I lie down in stones and tea-colored water.
I think: be careful; do not say
Home.
The bones of that word mend slowly.

LUCY ORTIZ

Miriam Sagan

Lucy Ortiz backs her blue Hyundai out of its spot in front of the state library and keeps going. A line of cars is parallel-parked along Don Gaspar in front of the Bataan Building and the eternal flame burning under a cottonwood in remembrance of those New Mexicans forced on a death march in such a hot and sticky place. The blue Hyundai keeps going until it stops with its back fender neatly rammed into the door of an old station wagon. Too late, Lucy hits the brakes and then puts her head down on the steering wheel in an attitude of prayer.

Lucy Ortiz has not been looking where she is going. She has been thinking instead of Joe Senior, her no-good soon-to-be-ex-husband, her husband she has loved so long and faithfully. Joe Senior has been two-timing her again. He has been two-timing her at the Thunderbird Motel on Cerrillos Road. It is not a nice motel. Lucy likes a nice motel as well as anyone. She likes the Best Western in Carlsbad, where she has gone on a librarians' tour of the radioactive-waste facilities. The radioactive-waste will be stored in salt mines sunk deep in the flat earth. These salt deposits have not moved in half a billion years. Lucy Ortiz thought marriage was forever. Unlike her mother and grandmother, she even expected to be happy. And now Joe Senior has hurt her where no man should hurt a woman. He has hurt her in her dark Spanish pride and in her dark Spanish name: Lucille Baca Serna Ortiz. She wishes she had brothers so they could kill him.

Lucy Ortiz gets out of her car and goes to inspect the damage. The damage is not extensive. The station wagon was already old, chipped, and dented. Lucy's car has only added a bruise the size of her hand. Lucy looks at the dent blankly. Then she looks at the owner of the dent, a tall ordinary enough Anglo guy, all boots and blondish mustache. Lucy touches the Virgin of Guadalupe key chain inside her purse for spiritual aid and bursts into tears. She is still thinking about Joe Senior stretched out on one of the ratty orange bedspreads at the Thunderbird Motel.

"Hey, it's not that bad," he says.

Lucy Ortiz looks down because her eyes are full of tears. She sees her own feet—nice, slightly plump feet in a pair of sheer pantyhose and a librarian's sensible summer sandals with closed toes so as not to upset the patrons. Granted, the shoes are red and have slightly too much heel, but underneath, her toenails are modestly painted mauve. Her feet are planted in the dirt. Visitors might call it earth and remark on its spiritual healing qualities, but to Lucy it is dirt, red dirt, chicken-pecked dirt, cholla cactus dirt, prickly pear dirt, dirt dirt.

"I bet it won't even cost fifty dollars to fix," he says. "Even if you have to pay it against the deductible, it's nothing to cry about."

Lucy Ortiz sobs openly.

"Okay, look," he says, "I won't even bother to get it fixed. That door is pretty dented anyway. I won't even file."

The tears run down her face.

"Come on," he says, "I'll take you to lunch. You eat lunch, don't you? I can't stand to see a pretty woman cry."

Lucy gives him the chilly look of her conquistador forebears and of her paternal grandmother, who was the meanest woman in two counties. "Lunch?"

"Lunch. Like a sandwich. A beer. Chili. Like eating."

"I'm getting divorced," says Lucy Ortiz.

"Oh . . . that," he says. "Well, divorced or married, you still have to eat."

"Where are we going?" asks Lucy.

"I thought maybe to Dave's Not Here. We'll take my car. I'll drive," he adds magnanimously.

Dave's Not Here smells of hamburgers, green chili, lemonade, a week of sunshine. Not adobe chic—the salt, pepper, and ketchup sit right on the table. Like half the restaurants in town it was once part of a coke deal. But the *federales* had caught Dave. When the new owners—formerly, a feminist vegetable Co-op—bought the place, Dave was in jail in El Paso and his creditors were banging on the door. Hence the name—Dave's Not Here.

At Dave's the linoleum is clean and the chocolate cake is as big as the dark side of the moon. Lucy studies the menu even though she knows it by heart. She wants fried onions on her hamburger, but can she eat onions on a date? Does it count as a date if you have sideswiped the guy? Does it count as a date if you haven't had sex with anyone besides your husband in seventeen years?

The guy across the table thinks this is a date. He is even telling her his name, that he works as a surveyor, and that right now he is working for Sandia Pueblo on a boundary line dispute. He listens as Lucy talks about her two children and her job as a state librarian. It turns out they both like hiking and unexcavated archaeological sites—potsherds and bits of volcanic glass. Lucy eats her hamburger as if she were a normal person. She eats her onions because she realizes this is not a date. She hates all men everywhere and could never marry her luncheon companion because he is not Catholic. Then she agrees to go walking with him in the back country at Bandelier next Saturday. That will not be a date either. She is just being nice because she backed into his car.

After lunch the surveyor drops Lucy back at her car. She knows that should she ever overcome her revulsion for handsome men with mustaches and kiss him or even go to bed with him, it would not be a date, because her heart is broken. She decides to take the rest of the day off and call in sick. Divorce has made her sick. She gets into her car, which she loves. It is spotlessly clean. Joe Senior gave her one of those little hand vacuums two Christmases ago, during that good year after he'd stopped sleeping with his secretary and before he'd started sleeping with the family dentist. She loves the vacuum cleaner and uses it weekly.

Just a few miles from her house Lucy is forced to stop by a flooded arroyo. An arroyo is the bed that temporary water makes in a dry place. Three hundred and sixty-four days a year it is dry, but today it is running fast, brown with muddy foam, and carrying the carcass of a cottonwood tree.

Lucy Ortiz stands in the red New Mexico mud. There is no way she can cross the arroyo. She has been married practically her whole life. Lucy Ortiz reaches down and picks up a handful of dirt. Experimentally she squeezes it between her fingers, then she puts a small daub on her cheek. It feels both warm and cool, like kissing a baby.

She rubs a little across her chin and opens her mouth as if she is going to eat some. She unbuttons first the top button of her white rayon blouse and then the next. She takes off her blouse and white bra and begins to cover her breasts with mud. She takes off her tailored purple skirt until she is standing in just her taupe pantyhose and her red shoes. She begins to smear mud over her belly, covering the stretch marks from pregnancy.

Mud trickles under the elastic of her pantyhose. Now Lucy Ortiz slips down the elastic band. The pantyhose begin to run as she tears off one foot, then the other. She covers her ankles, knees, and thighs with mud. She stands stark naked, covered with mud, in the middle of the New Mexico afternoon, between her car and the flooding arroyo. But she is still a sensible woman. She will not throw herself in the arroyo. She will not believe that death is as easy as taking off her pantyhose. She reminds herself that she was not a virgin when she married Joe Senior, despite the long white veil. She will wash in the water of the arroyo and put on her skirt and drive home barefoot the long way round. She will make tortillas by hand and cook beans for her children. She will marry the next man who asks her. She will be a good wife, but not yet. She stands naked, her thirty-seven-year-old body covered in mud that trickles down her breasts and thighs. She isn't crying. She isn't thinking about her no-good ex-husband. Lucy Ortiz is thinking that she isn't the kind of woman who is easy to fool twice.

HURT BOOKS

Edra Ziesk

I know I shouldn't be spending my whole life thinking about Joe and how to get him to come back, but I can't help it. Nothing else really interests me. I've talked to Joe about it and he says it isn't healthy. He says I should go out and get myself a full-time job, then I'd be too busy to think about him and I'd also have a retirement plan and some medical coverage. This is basically Joe's solution to everything, but as I've told him about four thousand times, I'm only twenty-seven. I'm not interested. Besides, I like the job I have. I only have to work three days a week, which gives me time to do other things, even though right now that's mostly thinking about Joe. I'm a secretary to a psychiatrist. I feel secure working in a shrink's office, though it's not the kind of security Joe's talking about. It's like it makes me immune from contracting any kind of mental illness myself. The office is quiet, it's like a club or a library with dark floor-to-ceiling bookcases and green leather chairs. I sit in the waiting room behind a glass-topped mahogany desk that's so large it makes me feel like a child whose feet don't touch the floor. I answer the phone and type Dr. Friedman's notes off a transcribing machine with earphones that look like the paws of small animals. I have a lot of time to think about Joe. I got used to my life being Joe and me—we were married for four and a half years. My life is still Joe and me; being divorced hasn't really changed that. Sometimes I see him doing stuff that's already happened. Like it's the night before he moved out more than a year ago. Joe's standing in our living room looking out the window, even though there's nothing to see in the dark except the lit-up red-pink apartment across the way where, for years, a man wearing only boxer shorts stood at his window and watched us.

"I'm really going to miss this place," Joe says. His voice is low and he speaks without inflection. There's a light on in the kitchen;

it makes the skin of Joe's back look yellow and luminous. I can see the slightly darker alley that travels the length of his spine.

"It's a dump," he says, meaning the apartment. I look up at the large cornflake-shaped strips of paint unrolling from the steam pipe. "But I'm really going to miss it." He pauses. "When I move out," he says. I can hear him forcing himself to use those words and other words—divorce, separate, split, go. When we used to say them about other people, they seemed only tinged with distant menace; now they detonate inside him, leaving his insides stewed and bloodied. I watch myself watching Joe, not knowing what to say. I am the one who decided he should leave; who decided our life, which had felt as safe as a used nest, had suddenly closed up around me. Needing to be by myself felt urgent. I didn't know that as soon as he moved out I would start to want him back.

There's a mantelpiece clock in Dr. F's office, the kind where the slow gold works are visible under a domed crystal. Today—it's a Tuesday—Joe's going out of town. His flight was at 10:40. All day I've been looking at the clock and thinking: now he's leaving for the airport, now he's sitting on the plane. I am ghosting through his life. I can feel the weight of his legs dropping down into the seat; the knobby hardness of his pelvic bones. When he looks out the window, I can see the delicate red threads in the whites of his eyes.

I turn on an all-news radio station every twenty-two minutes, which is how long it takes them to give you the world. They don't say anything about a plane crash. I go home after work and sit on the bed hoping Joe will call. I asked him to, so I'd know he was safe. He got pissed off. "Listen," he said, "we aren't married, you don't have to worry about it anymore." I think he might call anyway. I've always been his check-in point. I sit with my legs crossed and examine the crease behind my knee. The TV is on in the living room. I can make out the commercials because the volume goes up. The rest of the time I just hear an undercurrent of sound like the distant rumble of trucks. I'm jittery and wired. I pick up the phone a few times to make sure it's working, but I'm afraid Joe will be calling me right at that second, so I hang up. I get furious at the phone for not ringing. This is what it would feel like if Joe had died, I tell myself. I start to get breathless and panicky. I get myself some brandy and flip through the TV stations, but I can't stand being this far from the phone, as if the few feet between the living room and the bedroom puts an extra unbearable distance between us. I go back inside and sit on the bed in the same cross-legged position. It makes me a little calmer. I think about calling up every hotel in Los Angeles until I find the one Joe's staying at. That makes me a little calmer too. I wonder how many hotels there are in L.A. I fall asleep with my clothes and all the lights on. The brandy is on the floor next to the bed. When I wake up, a cloud of alcohol blooms up out of the glass.

On Saturday morning the phone rings. "Hi," Joe says. It sounds like two words. On the second, his voice goes up. He's surprised that I'm home. I'm out a lot. I walk around, hang out in bars, so I'll have to spend as little time as possible by myself in the apartment. Joe thinks I'm out with friends, some mysterious collection I've acquired since he moved out. "Like who?" I say. I don't have many friends. I got used to it being just the two of us.

"How ya doing?" Joe says. I hear a chair creak, as if he is settling back.

"Where are you?" I say.

"Home." Home. The word hangs there: home, what place is that? I've never been to the apartment Joe lives in now or seen his furniture, what he has on the walls, the views from his windows. It sounds like a setback, that he has begun to call that place home. "So," I say. "How was the trip?"

"Oh, boring," he says and yawns, as if to prove this. "Same old shit. You know how those conventions are." I do know. We used to work in the same place, this small advertising agency that wouldn't take soap or cigarette or fast-food accounts. I left when we got married—they have this rule about married couples, and everyone knew it was Joe who'd be staying. It was okay, though, since I wanted to do other things. I thought I might try to be a writer. I had a teacher in college who said I had a writerly eye but lacked discipline. Joe said that pretty much summed me up.

"Jackie," he says. "Don't think I'm nuts or anything, but were you *over* here or something lately?"

"Over there?" I say. "You mean your apartment?" I feel odd, as if he found out about this plan I have of going to sit on his front stoop some night, waiting for him to come home.

"Listen to this, this is the weirdest thing," Joe says. "Remember those little books you used to make me?"

"Books?" I say.

"Books. You know. Those drawings?" I used to hide notes when Joe went out of town, in his toiletry case, in the pockets of his shirts. They were small books made out of folded sheets of blue or white Xerox paper. I illustrated them with stick figures of myself—a skinny long-legged person with a mess of wild-looking curly hair. I wrote little stories, stuff the person was up to when Joe went away. In one, she cried so much she filled up two buckets with briny water which she saved to make cucumber pickles. In another, she strapped herself to the underbelly of Joe's plane with leather belts.

"Yeah?" I say.

"Well, I get down to L.A., I'm putting my shit in the bathroom, and I find one."

"Really?" I say. I am pleased this is what Joe has called to tell me. It makes me hopeful. My cheeks feel as pink as cherries. "I wonder how that got there. Osmosis?" I know it's an old note I probably once stuck in his toilet case and he forgot about. I can picture how the red Pentel I used to draw it has bled, turning pink and blurred from the wetness of his toothbrush. "What'd it look like?" I say. "Describe it." I'm sitting on a kitchen stool next to the phone. I look down at my bare thighs spreading across the seat.

"Well, it was you—you know, that stick person—strewing flowers all over the bed or something. You're standing on the bed," he says.

"Yup," I say. "Sounds like me."

"On the outside it says, 'The person who's here wishes to inform the person who's there . . .' and on the inside . . ." I hear him unfolding the paper. It sounds stiff and cracked and old. Sadness shoots through me, quick and delicate, like a feathery crack in an eggshell. It gets my attention. " 'That she hates sleeping alone,' " Joe is saying, " 'and so has decided to turn the bed into a garden.' "

"Not *strewing* flowers," I say. "*Watering* them! And at the bottom it says, 'Consider this fair warning. I miss you, come home,' right?"

"Yeah," Joe says. His voice is low. It is flat and sad and unbearable, as if he has caught himself doing some futile thing.

"Joe," I say, "it's still true. I miss you. More." I draw the sentence out. I can feel him slipping away, like a fast-moving silvery fish.

"Don't start this stuff, okay? What's the point? What's done is done." I try to think of something to say, a way to argue with him, but all I can think of are other little clichés: a stitch in time, a bird in the hand. To Joe, the divorce was huge and catastrophic, like a flood or an earthquake, against which he had no defense. Now it is over. He wants to put it all behind him. He wants—he has told me a hundred times—to get on with it and says I should do the same. If I cry, tell him I wish he would come back, he won't call me for days; if I call him he'll speak in curt sentences and stick to general subjects like sports or the news in the paper. "Look," he says, "let me go, I have stuff to take care of. I haven't even unpacked yet, everything smells like an airport. I'll talk to you next week."

"Next week is your birthday!" I say, trying to keep him on the phone. He'll be thirty-one. "Let's get together and have drinks—notice I put an s on that. On me."

"On you! You don't have two nickels to rub together!"

"I have enough. For drinks."

"Let me see how it goes," Joe says.

"Work, you mean?" I sound too eager. I know he does not mean work. He means if he can take it, being around me, even on neutral territory. "I'd really like to see you," I say. I realize I am sitting here with my fingers crossed.

I buzz Dr. F on the intercom as soon as I know her last patient has left because I see him go out through the side door on Seventy-eighth Street. Dr. F shows her patients out through the side so they won't have to run into each other in the waiting room, their eyes hopping all over like furtive rabbits. I ask her if it's okay if I take a long lunch. I've been trying to buy Joe a birthday present for three days.

I go into Barnes & Noble. They're paving the sidewalk out front and you can only get in or out by walking single file across a raised plank that has too much give and bounces back against you. Everyone crosses it with a loopy, goofy step, looking like cartoon characters.

It's cool inside. There's a crowd of prep-school teenagers hanging out, talking in clear loud voices that sound rude and jarring in a bookstore. The girls are wearing pastel tank tops and dangling earrings made out of beads. I start looking through a table where there's a sign that says "Hurt Books." It's a random collection, in no order. The books cost $1.98. Their covers have small flaps torn in them and are blurred from overhandling. I keep twisting my head from side to side so I can read the titles. I see one called *The Mick* by Mickey Mantle. It jumps right out at me. Mickey Mantle is Joe's all-time favorite hero. One year I gave him a Mickey Mantle key chain. It had a picture of Mantle in a round plastic disc the size of the face of a child's watch. I bought it in a store that sold antique campaign buttons and sports memorabilia. I gave it to Joe in a necklace box. "Oh, wow," he said when he opened it. He sounded awed. "This is the best gift anybody ever gave me." He held the key chain up to the light and looked at it as if it were made out of deep-colored lustrous stones.

Out of nowhere there's this great rolling pain inside me, as intense and as sudden as a fall caused by an invisible slick of ice. It makes me jump back and take two steps away from the table. Everything's mined. There is no thing that has not somehow touched or passed through or surrounded Joe and me during our marriage, and everything—book titles, colors, the heat—everything hurts. I leave the store without buying anything.

It's two days after Joe's birthday. I'm in the coffee shop where I go for lunch every day and eat things with no nutritional value. Today I am having pound cake that came wrapped in a piece of matted plastic and iced tea made from henna-colored powder with sugar and lemon flavoring already mixed in. It leaves a metallic aftertaste.

I didn't send Joe a birthday card. They all seemed tastelessly cheerful. Some didn't have enough space to write anything; some, the blank ones, had too much space. I'd either have to go on and on or leave a large white or blue or salmon-colored gap. My idea was to call Joe and talk him into letting me buy him that drink, but when he heard it was me, all the juice ran out of his voice and I barely got out "Happy birthday" before he hustled me off the phone.

Today, before lunch, I went to a card store. I got a card with a bunch of clocks on the outside, all set at different times like in an airport or a war room. On the inside it said, "I didn't miss your birthday. I got confused." The left side of the card was blank. I decided to draw one of those picture notes. I got out a blue pen. At the top I wrote, "A Dance for Your Birthday," then I started drawing the wild-haired stick figure doing dance steps. She twirled around. She did splits and leaps and cartwheels. When I drew her in a handstand, I turned the card upside down so the twisty curls would fly in the right direction. One of the countermen came over and cocked his head to see what I was doing. "Oooh," he says. "Very bee-you-tee-ful!" I slapped my hand down on the card. The spoon in my iced tea glass jumped.

I was up to the last picture. I was going to draw the little stick figure holding a bouquet of flowers out in front of her with a "Happy Birthday" streamer trailing down. The counterman came back to serve the people sitting next to me. He had a line of large and small dishes up his arm. There was a strong mixed smell of stew and the counterman's sweat. I wanted to get out of there. I wanted to get the card in the mail so I could start thinking about Joe receiving it. I could picture him smiling, starting to melt down, even though I know Joe basically thinks my sending him cards now is like some kind of booby prize. So I rushed the last drawing. I didn't do the hair right, which I drew with three or four squiggly strands like cooked fusilli on either side of this round moon face, and I realized when I finished it that the picture looked like a girl in a dress, holding a bouquet, wearing a veil. It looked like a bride. Forget it, I told myself. Even I knew there was no way I could send Joe a card with a picture of a stick person who was supposed to be me dressed like a bride on it.

So I tore it up. I threw it away in the wire trash can on the corner instead of leaving it on my plate where, I was sure, the counterman would pick it up and paste it back together. I decided I'd go back to Barnes & Noble and buy *The Mick*. I ran the eight blocks to the bookstore. The new sidewalk out front was dry and they'd taken the plank away. I went to the Hurt Books section and started scanning titles but I didn't see it, so I walked around to the other side of the table for a different perspective. I went through the books slowly, one at a time, flipping my fingers along the spines. It wasn't here—I couldn't believe it. For a second I couldn't move. I stood there, my hand hovering above the books as if I was about to bless them. I felt like I'd lost this one chance: if I could just have the right thing to give Joe, everything would be okay. Except, at the same time I'm thinking it, I'm aware of this other thought, right at the edge of my consciousness: that it didn't make any difference. Joe wasn't going to come back.

But I wouldn't let myself think about it. I left the store. By the time I hit the street I had a reserve plan, Plan B. Tonight, after work, I'd go downtown and check out the Barnes & Noble on Eighteenth Street. They'd have it. That store is fucking humongous. They have everything.

Part VI

❦

THE FOREVER BED

I WAS BORN TO SPEAK YOUR NAME

Tom Clark

I knew the tune
It was my song
Even before you came along
Yet only then did I perceive its meaning

This *you* I wished for
This desired Other of whom
I spoke so glowingly in poems
I never knew its name

When I lifted its arms up
I noticed tiny wings
That's all I knew
The rest was Muselike
Anonymous this "you"

So I guess those poems
Were like phonecalls to the future
I think I had your number
Knew what I was looking for
Even before I found it
In the face directory

And luckiest of all
Your human substance
Was life's loveliest
Far as I could see

As if I'd placed
Bones and skin
Together in a dream
You were put together that way
But I wouldn't let it go to my head if I were you

LOVE SONG

Theodore Enslin

Though we have travelled far
we have not reached
the mountains.
                        Mons Veneris,
the mountain of love,
is as far from us now
as when we set out fresh
in the early morning.
Now we are tired, and feel old.
The only things worth looking at
are the mountains:
                        Love's
and a few others,
catching the late flame of the sun,
almost down,
                        behind us.

From: GERALD'S PARTY

Robert Coover

"Somehow," she said now, gazing around wearily (she was standing in front of me, easing her shoes off: I hadn't seen her come up), "parties don't seem as much fun as they used to." She sat down beside me, curling under my arm, the one I could still move, and tucked her feet up. "It's almost as though the parties have started giving us instead of us giving the parties . . ." She loosened my shirt, lay her head sleepily against my chest. "It gives me a . . . funny feeling . . ."

"Yes . . ."

"Still, I guess it's worth it . . ."

The woman in Greece had said something much like that about making love. She'd had an appetite for the unusual, the perverse even, and I too was pretty jaded in those days, frustrated by the commonplaces of sex, bored with all its trite conventions—the state of the art, so to speak—and so in need of ever greater novelty, ever greater risktaking, in order to arouse myself to any kind of performance. What worked for her—and thus for us both—was to be unexpectedly violated in a more or less public place, the key to a successful orgasm being not so much the setting or the use of force as the element of surprise. It was a kind of essential trigger for her—like having to scare someone out of her hiccups. Thus, I might walk her through public parks, churches, department stores, taunting her with exotic possibilities while yet denying her, only to jump on her back in the busy hotel lobby while asking for the key. Or I might arrange a night out at some mysterious destination, coax her into dressing up elaborately, then get her out of the hotel, hail a taxi—and suddenly violate her on the sidewalk just as she was stepping into the cab. I don't know why I thought that pitful of decayed atrocity victims would work. Perhaps because it seemed so unlikely. But nothing happened. In fact it was a disaster. We got filthy, she hurt her back on the bones, got her nose bloodied, I cracked my elbow, we were both choking with dust, and when it was over—or rather, when there was no point in going on—she told me just to leave her alone and go away. I never saw her again, my last vision of her being sprawled out there in the—"*Ouch!*"

"Sorry, Gerald, is something . . . ?" She had been stroking me through the trousers and had caught the place where Jim had nicked me. She opened my trousers carefully, eased my shorts down. "Oh, I see . . ." She licked it gently, then took the crown into her mouth, coating it with warm saliva. "Bat's a bad bwuise, too," she observed, touching my tummy, then let her mouth slide gradually down the shaft. I reached for the hem of her dress and she shifted her hips, turning her knees toward the back of the couch.

There was a sudden crash, the whole house shook—I lurched away, reared up—and then a scraping, another crash, a rumble, something rolling in the street. She closed her mouth around my penis again, curled her hands behind my hips, tugged at the back of my trousers.

"But . . . my god, what *was* that—?!"

"Pwobabwy Chawwey puwwing out ubba dwibe . . ."

"Ah . . ." She eased my trousers down below my hips—outside, there was another crunch, the distant squealing of tires—then pulled them away from between my thighs. She put my hand back on the hem of her dress. There was a tag there, I noticed, stamped by the city police department. "Wewacsh, Gewawd," she whispered. I liked the pushing of her tongue against the consonants and, surrendering to that, slid down toward her knees. "Tell me again . . ."

"Wewacsh, Gewawd . . . ?"

"Yes . . . good . . ." It all comes down to words, as I might have argued with Vic. Or parts of them. "Is this a new dress?"

"Yeumf," she said, working my trousers down to my ankles: I lifted out foot one and raised it to the couch. "Do woo wike it?"

"Right now, it's in my way . . ."

"You say the nicest things, Gerald," she sighed, taking her mouth away. She located the fastener, unhooked it, pushed at the skirt: I pulled it away and, stretching forward, eased it past her feet. "What are you doing with pancake makeup on the back of your neck?" she asked.

"I don't remember."

I tugged at her panty girdle, stretching it down past her soft hips, and she took my penis in her mouth again, warming it all over, closing one hand tenderly around my testicles. She kneaded them softly, pulling them toward her as though gently pumping them, sliding her other hand around to stroke my buttocks, finger my anus. Only one arm worked for getting her clothes off her: I left the dead one between her legs for the time being and she squeezed her thighs around it. "Just . . . a minute . . ." The panties and stockings came off in a tangle. I ran my tongue slowly up her leg from her calf, past her knee, and up the inside of her thigh: she spread her legs and, as I nosed into her vulva, lifted the top one over my head. "Mmmmf!" She had her finger up my anus now and was sucking rhythmically, her mouth full of foamy saliva like a warm bubble bath. I had found the nub of her clitoris with the tip of my tongue and now worked against it as though trying to pry it open. I reached round from behind, dipped my fingers into her moist vagina, pushed one of them up her rectum—"*Ouch!*" she cried, letting my penis go.

"Sorry . . ." I pushed my nose deeper between her thighs to have a closer look: her anus was drawn up in a tight little pucker, inflamed and cracked, slightly discolored as though rubbed with ashes. "How did you—?"

"You know. The police." She paused, holding my penis by the root. Perhaps she was studying it. Or simply reflecting.

I pressed my chin against the hood of her clitoris, gazing thoughtfully at her crinkled anus, remembering now her position on the butcherblock (as though being changed, I'd thought as they lowered her), her thighs stretching back, belly wrinkling, tiny little red lines running down her cheeks. "What . . . what's an exploding sausage . . . ?" I asked uneasily.

"Oh, Gerald!" She laughed and wagged my penis playfully. "Don't you know a joke when you hear one?"

"Ah . . ." I stroked her buttocks gently as my penis returned to its soothing bath, rubbing my chin rhythmically against her pubic knoll. Like veined marble, they'd seemed to me at the time, as I remembered, something like that, though now they sparkled with a kind of fresh dewy innocence (it was the kind of feeling I had between my own legs now) under the bright overhead light. She was beginning to grind vigorously against my chin, thighs cuffing my ears, so I moved my mouth back over her rosy lips, dipping my tongue into their warm mushy depths—I was aswim in warm mushy depths, we were both—

"Say, uh . . . where the hell *is* everybody?" someone asked. I peered up between my wife's convulsing thighs, my own hips bucking against the cushions: it was Knud, standing bleary-eyed over us, rubbing the back of his neck. "Crikey!" he muttered, his voice phlegmy with sleep. "You'll never believe the dream I just had!"

"Everybody's gone home, Knud," I gasped, my chin sliding now in the dense juices beneath it.

"Hunh?" He frowned at his empty wrist. My wife had stopped pumping her head up and down the shaft of my penis, but she was still sucking at it rhythmically and stroking it with her tongue, marking time, as it were, her throbbing clitoris searching for my mouth. "Even Kitty? Jeez, what time is it?"

"*Everybody's* gone, Knud. It's *late.*"

"Holy cow, I must have slept through the whole goldarn party," he rumbled, still staring at his wrist. He yawned, belched. "Boy! What a dream, though!" My wife's hips had stopped pitching. She held my testicles and one buttock firmly, but had let my penis slide past her teeth into one cheek. "I was like in some kind of war zone, see, only everyone was all mixed up and you didn't know who was on your side—"

"Not now, Knud," my wife panted, letting me go and twisting round to look up at him. Her buttocks spread a bit, giving me a clearer view of Knud: he was puffy-eyed and rumpled, tie undone, shirttail out, pants damp and sticky, and he looked like he needed a shave.

"No, listen, it was a lot longer. And really weird. Since you couldn't be sure who anybody was, see, just to be safe you naturally had to kill everyone—right? Ha ha! You wouldn't *believe* the blood and gore! And all in 3-D and full color, too, I kid you not! I kept running into people and asking them: 'Where *am* I?' They'd say: 'What a *loony*,' or something like that—and then I'd chop their heads off, right?"

"Please, Knud—?"

He glanced down at my penis withering in my wife's hand, at

her buttocks flattening out in front of my face. "Oh, right . . . sorry . . ." He gazed around at the living room, running his hand through his snarled hair. "Say, do you remember, was I wearing a watch when I came here tonight?"

"Well . . ." my wife began tentatively, raising herself up on one elbow, and I cut in: "I can't remember, Knud."

He seemed to accept that. He squinted up at the lights on the ceiling for a moment, yawning. "Kitty been gone long?"

"No, you can probably catch her." I was beginning to feel my wife's weight: I gave a little push and she lifted herself off my face. "Don't get up," Knud insisted. "I can find my own way out." He stumbled away, stuffing his shirttail in. My wife, sitting up, let her hand fall idly on my hip. We could hear Knud peeing noisily in the toilet bowl. It was a lonely sound, but not so lonely as the silence all around it. "At least it's working," my wife said. She picked up her stockings and panty girdle, toweled between her legs with them. "Hey, thanks," said Knud from the doorway. "See you at the next one."

"Flush it, please, Knud!" my wife called, but he was already out the door. "Oh well." I curled around her from behind, hugging her close, and she patted my hip with sleepy affection. My penis nuzzled between her cheeks. It felt good there. It was something to think about. "Do you notice a kind of chill in here?" she murmured sleepily.

"Well, all the windowpanes are out," I said. I ran my hand along her thigh where it met the couch. "We could try the TV room now that Knud's vacated it . . ."

She smiled, a bit wearily, then took my good hand and pulled me to my feet. I kicked off the trousers, still tangled around one foot, and, holding hands, we stepped out from under the tented drapes and linens into the glare and wreckage of what was once our living room. She drew close to me suddenly, pressing her naked hip against mine. I was feeling it, too. As though the house had not been emptying out so much as filling up. The windows, stripped bare and paneless, seemed to crowd in on us, letting the dark night at their edges leak in like some kind of deadly miasma. Hugging each other's waists, we picked our way barefoot through the shards of broken pots and glassware, the food squashed into the carpet, the chalk outlines and bent cocktail skewers. The wall next to the dining room doorway was splattered and streaked with a mince pie someone must have thrown, and even that, innocent as it was, seemed to add to our feelings of apprehension and melancholy.

The wall above the dining room sideboard was eloquently vacant, the picture hooks sitting on it like a pair of pinned insects. Bottles lay tipped like fallen soldiers, liquor still, amazingly enough, gurgling from one of the open mouths. "What exactly happened to Vic?" my wife whispered.

"He . . . got shot . . ."

"He makes you think of Tania's painting, doesn't he? The one with the eyes . . ."

"Well . . ."

I tugged her on into the TV room. We seemed safer in here somehow. Maybe because the lights were softer ("Our antique lamps are missing," she remarked quietly as though in explanation) or because the drapes were still on the windows and the furniture more or less where it ought to be. Or just the soothing blueness of the walls. I could feel my wife's hip soften and I too seemed to walk less stiffly, my knees unlocking, my scrotum sliding back into place. Snow played on the TV screen, making a scratchy noise like a needle caught on the outer lip of a record, but I didn't want to turn it off. It was company of sorts. "I'll put a cassette on," I said, letting go her waist, and she sat down on the sofa to wait. "Don't be long, Gerald," she yawned.

I couldn't seem to find any of our old tapes, but there were plenty of new ones scattered about to choose from. "How about 'The Ancient Arse'?" I proposed, reading the labels. "Or 'Cold Show at the Ice Palace'—or here's one: 'The Garden Peers.' "

"I think that's *pee*-ers. I've seen that one. I don't want to see it again." Ah. I understand now. "Below the Stairs," "Butcherblock Blues," "Party Time," "Life's Mysterious Currents," "The Host's Hang-up," they all fell dismally into place. "Candid Coppers." "Some Dish." "Special Favors." I felt defeated even before I'd begun. There were tears in my eyes and a strange airy tingling on my exposed behind, like a ghostly remembrance of cold knuckles. I shuddered. "Put on 'Hidden Treasure,' " my wife suggested, unbuttoning her blouse and jacket.

I searched through the pile of cassettes, intent on doing my best, getting through it somehow, but my appetite had faded. "It . . . it will never be the same again," I muttered, my throat tight.

"Tsk. You said that the last time, Gerald. After Archie and Emma and . . ."

"Yes, well . . ." It was true, I'd all but forgotten. "But Ros, Vic, Tania . . ."

"Roger, Noble . . ."

"Yes, that's right, Roger . . ."

"Fiona . . ."

"Fiona—?" I took off the cassette labeled "The Wayward Finger," and inserted "Hidden Treasure," rewound it to the beginning, punched the "Play" button, wishing it were all so easy as that.

"Yes, that was why Cyril was so upset." She was completely naked now, stretched out on the sofa, hands behind her head, eyes half-closed, scratching the bottom of her foot with one toe. "How do you think Peg found out?"

"Found out what?" I took off my shirt, folded it neatly over the back of the sofa, stalling for time. On the TV, my mother-in-law was getting Mark into his pajama bottoms. "That's better," she was saying. Mark was holding Peedie, which now had one of Sally Ann's patches sewn on its underside. "HOT TWOT," it said.

"Well, she was pregnant."

"Peg was?"

"No, Fiona." I sat down beside her and stroked her thighs, pushing into the warm place between her legs, but my heart wasn't in it. Mark, on the television screen, was asking: "What's a 'twot,' Gramma?" Behind him, his bedroom door was all smashed in. "That's the whole point, Gerald. Didn't you notice? It was very obvious."

"It's a . . . a faraway place," my mother-in-law was explaining. "A kind of secret garden . . ."

"I'm not sure I saw her all night," I said. Maybe it was the scar, cold and bluish in the light from the flickering TV image, that was bothering me. I looked around, spied one of her aprons hanging over the edge of the games table.

"Is it always hot, Gramma?"

"But you heard Peg carrying on when she left—she was telling everybody!"

"No, it's warm. Like a bed. Now you crawl up into yours there, young man."

"I guess I missed that." I brought the apron over: "Listen, do you mind—?"

"But then that's why everyone was feeling so sorry for Cyril after." She raised her hips so I could tie the apron on. "Will I ever go there someday?" Mark was asking. "You know, to lose them both in one night . . ."

"Both—?"

"It seems inevitable, child . . ."

"Yes—my goodness, Gerald, where *were* you?" I slid my hand up under the apron: yes, this was better. There was a faint stirring at last between my legs, which my mother-in-law appeared to be overseeing from the TV screen, her face marked by a kind of compassionate sorrow mixed with amusement. "Tell me a story about it, Gramma," Mark was pleading sleepily, as she led him to the bed. "You missed just about everything!"

"About what?" she asked.

"You know, the Twot," said Mark, as my hand reached my wife's pubis. I let my fingers scratch gently in the hair there, while my thumb slid between her thighs and curled into her vagina. "Well, once upon a time," she began, lifting Mark onto the bed, and I too lifted slightly, then let her down again. "You know . . . sometimes, Gerald . . . ," she sighed, closing her hands gently over mine, . . . "it's almost as if . . ." "There was a young prince . . ."

". . . you were at a different party . . ."

"Was his name Mark?"

I edged closer to my wife's hips, my thumb working rhythmically against the ball of my index finger ("Oh yes . . . good . . ."), and she took my wilted organ in her hand. On the television screen, my mother-in-law was tucking Mark in. "All right then, a young prince named Mark—but get down under the covers, or I won't tell it."

I pushed my thumb as deep as it would go, while at the same time stretching my fingers up her belly, her pubis thrusting at me under the apron, closing around my thumb, her own hand (my mother-in-law had already launched Prince Mark out on his "unique adventure," but Mark wanted to know: "Where's his mommy and daddy? Is he a orphan?") stroking me with a gentle but insistent cadence, slowly helping me forget what I'd been sticking out from under the games table a moment ago when I'd reached for her apron: a foot, wrapped in a plastic bag, one toe poking out. Its nail painted. Cherry red. "No, he was the little boy of Beauty and the—her husband . . ." my mother-in-law was saying, as the prospect of orgasm swelled in my mind like a numbing intuition. I gazed down at my wife, her hair unrolled now and loose about her pale shoulders, her thin lips parted, nostrils flared, and thought I could hear Ros whispering: *Oh yes, let's!*

Oh no . . .

". . . But he was a big boy now and it was time to leave home and seek his own fortune . . ."

I was frightened and wanted to stop ("We are in it, Gerry, we cannot get out of it," I seemed to hear Vic mumble right outside the door—had he moved somehow?!), but my wife was blindly pulling me toward her, spreading her legs, the apron wrinkling up between us, and my genitals, it seemed, were quite willing to carry on without the rest of me. "We can only stand up to it or chicken out . . ."

What? Vic—?

"Was the Beast nice now?"

"Oh yes, yes . . . !" my wife was gasping.

"Most of the time . . ."

I'd let go my thumbhold on her pubic handle and, twisting my hand around, my mouth sucking at a breast now (ah, what was it I *really* wanted? I didn't want to think about it . . .), had slid my handful of fingers down there instead, my bodily parts separating out like a houseful of drunken and unruly guests, everybody on his own. She tugged still at that most prodigious member, the host, as it were ("He paused at the edge of the Enchanted Forest: it was dreary and dangerous and . . ."), pumping it harder and harder, her other hand grasping my testicles like a doorknob: she gave them a turn, opened, and, going up on my knees as though to offer my behind to the invading emptiness ("And . . . dark?" asked Mark fearfully, hugging his Peedie under the blankets), mouth still at her breast, I crossed over between her legs.

"Yes . . . !"

"Hurry, Gerald!"

"I'm afraid, Gramma!"

There was a congestion now of fingers and organs, a kind of rubbery crowding up around the portal ("But he was not alone," my mother-in-law was explaining in an encouraging voice), but then she slipped her hands out to snatch at my buttocks, yanking them fiercely toward her as though to keep them from floating away like hot-air balloons—perhaps I'd been worrying about this, I felt like I was coming apart and falling together at the same time—and as her legs jerked upward ("Little Prince Mark was protected by his faithful companion Peedie the Brave Rabbit . . ."), I dropped in through the ooze as though casting anchor. *This*, I was thinking with some excitement, and with some bewilderment as well—what *is* this "we" when the I's are gone?—is my *wife!*

TRUE LOVE

Sharon Olds

In the middle of the night, when we get up
after making love, we look at each other
in total friendship, we know so fully
what the other has been doing. Bound to each other like
soldiers coming out of a battle,
bound with the tie of the birth-room, we
wander down the hall to the bathroom, I can
hardly walk, we weave through the dark
soft air, I know where you are
with my eyes closed, we are bound to each other with the
huge invisible threads of sex, though our
sexes themselves are muted, dark and
exhausted and delicately crushed, the whole
body is a sex—surely this
is the most blessed time of life,
the children deep asleep in their beds like a
vein of coal and a vein of gold
not discovered yet. I sit on the
toilet in the dark, you are somewhere in the room, I
open the window and the snow has fallen in a
deep drift against the pane, I
look up into it, a
world of cold crystals, silent and
glistening so I call out to you and you
come and hold my hand and I say
I cannot see beyond it! I cannot see beyond it!

THE HEART STUMBLES IN DARKNESS

Nathaniel Tarn

Anxious at every moment of his life, without fail.
Each time, as if he were on the brink of an abyss.
At every moment, lapsing a step into the darkness.
That cavern where consciousness seems to vegetate,
a hollow prison full of dark steps, trip and fall.
"If I could only bury my face in her body — invade
her, hang out for some time as in the sacred river
of salvation bathed in waters as cool as their own
definition, come out on the other side of herself,
like the word having its being in the world, *then*,
I could know that single moment free of it, again,
that moment would spread out everywhere and assume
all time, to home in purified, recovered, reborn."
Little but the week has gone by in his divine city
where men still hear of salvation; the narcissi on
his desk are still pungent and send him, all night
messages of self-pleasure — yet, already he misses
her odors where she sits on the world and makes it
human for him to adopt, be reborn into, as if from
a lifelong death, fear, that companion at his side
walking with deliberate slowness, the black beast,
in pace with him, stalling the outcome of the sun.

BODY

ROBERT CREELEY

Slope of it,
hope of it—
echoes faded,
what waited

up late inside
old desires
saw through
the screwed importunities.

This regret?
Nothing's left.
Skin's old,
story's told—

but still touch,
selfed body,
wants other,
another mother

to him, her
insistent "sin"
he lets in
to hold him.

Selfish bastard,
headless catastrophe.
Sans tits, cunt,
wholly blunt—

fucked it up,
roof top, loving cup,
sweatered room,
old love's tune.

Age dies old,
both men and women cold,
hold at last no one,
die alone.

Body lasts forever,
pointless conduit,
floods in its fever,
so issues others parturient.

Through legs wide,
from common hole site,
aching information's dumb tide
rides to the far side.

WHAT WE TALK ABOUT
WHEN WE TALK ABOUT LOVE

Raymond Carver

My friend Mel McGinnis was talking. Mel McGinnis is a cardiologist, and sometimes that gives him the right.

The four of us were sitting around his kitchen table drinking gin. Sunlight filled the kitchen from the big window behind the sink. There were Mel and me and his second wife, Teresa—Terri, we called her—and my wife, Laura. We lived in Albuquerque then. But we were all from somewhere else.

There was an ice bucket on the table. The gin and the tonic water kept going around, and we somehow got on the subject of love. Mel thought real love was nothing less than spiritual love. He said he'd spent five years in a seminary before quitting to go to medical school. He said he still looked back on those years in the seminary as the most important years in his life.

Terri said the man she lived with before she lived with Mel loved her so much he tried to kill her. Then Terri said, "He beat me up one night. He dragged me around the living room by my ankles. He kept saying, 'I love you, I love you, you bitch.' He went on dragging me around the living room. My head kept knocking on things." Terri looked around the table. "What do you do with love like that?"

She was a bone-thin woman with a pretty face, dark eyes, and brown hair that hung down her back. She liked necklaces made of turquoise, and long pendant earrings.

"My God, don't be silly. That's not love, and you know it," Mel said. "I don't know what you'd call it, but I sure know you wouldn't call it love."

"Say what you want to, but I know it was," Terri said. "It may sound crazy to you, but it's true just the same. People are different, Mel. Sure, sometimes he may have acted crazy. Okay. But he loved me. In his own way maybe, but he loved me. There was love there, Mel. Don't say there wasn't."

Mel let out his breath. He held his glass and turned to Laura and me. "The man threatened to kill me," Mel said. He finished his drink and reached for the gin bottle. "Terri's a romantic. Terri's of the kick-me-so-I'll-know-you-love-me school. Terri, hon, don't look that way." Mel reached across the table and touched Terri's cheek with his fingers. He grinned at her.

"Now he wants to make up," Terri said.

"Make up what?" Mel said. "What is there to make up? I know what I know. That's all."

"How'd we get started on this subject, anyway?" Terri said. She raised her glass and drank from it. "Mel always has love on his mind," she said. "Don't you, honey?" She smiled, and I thought that was the last of it.

"I just wouldn't call Ed's behavior love. That's all I'm saying, honey," Mel said. "What about you guys?" Mel said to Laura and me. "Does that sound like love to you?"

"I'm the wrong person to ask," I said. "I didn't even know the man. I've only heard his name mentioned in passing. I wouldn't know. You'd have to know the particulars. But I think what you're saying is that love is an absolute."

Mel said, "The kind of love I'm talking about is. The kind of love I'm talking about, you don't try to kill people."

Laura said, "I don't know anything about Ed, or anything about the situation. But who can judge anyone else's situation?"

I touched the back of Laura's hand. She gave me a quick smile. I picked up Laura's hand. It was warm, the nails polished, perfectly manicured. I encircled the broad wrist with my fingers, and I held her.

"When I left, he drank rat poison," Terri said. She clasped her arms with her hands. "They took him to the hospital in Santa Fe. That's where we lived then, about ten miles out. They saved his life. But his gums went crazy from it. I mean they pulled away from his teeth. After that, his teeth stood out like fangs. My God," Terri said. She waited a minute, then let go of her arms and picked up her glass.

"What people won't do!" Laura said.

THE FOREVER BED

249

"He's out of the action now," Mel said. "He's dead."

Mel handed me the saucer of limes. I took a section, squeezed it over my drink, and stirred the ice cubes with my finger.

"It gets worse," Terri said. "He shot himself in the mouth. But he bungled that too. Poor Ed," she said. Terri shook her head.

"Poor Ed nothing," Mel said. "He was dangerous."

Mel was forty-five years old. He was tall and rangy with curly soft hair. His face and arms were brown from the tennis he played. When he was sober, his gestures, all his movements, were precise, very careful.

"He did love me though, Mel. Grant me that," Terri said. "That's all I'm asking. He didn't love me the way you love me. I'm not saying that. But he loved me. You can grant me that, can't you?"

"What do you mean, he bungled it?" I said.

Laura leaned forward with her glass. She put her elbows on the table and held her glass in both hands. She glanced from Mel to Terri and waited with a look of bewilderment on her open face, as if amazed that such things happened to people you were friendly with.

"How'd he bungle it when he killed himself?" I said.

"I'll tell you what happened," Mel said. "He took this twenty-two pistol he'd bought to threaten Terri and me with. Oh, I'm serious, the man was always threatening. You should have seen the way we lived in those days. Like fugitives. I even bought a gun myself. Can you believe it? A guy like me? But I did. I bought one for self-defense and carried it in the glove compartment. Sometimes I'd have to leave the apartment in the middle of the night. To go to the hospital, you know? Terri and I weren't married then, and my first wife had the house and kids, the dog, everything, and Terri and I were living in this apartment here. Sometimes, as I say, I'd get a call in the middle of the night and have to go in to the hospital at two or three in the morning. It'd be dark out there in the parking lot, and I'd break into a sweat before I could even get to my car. I never knew if he was going to come up out of the shrubbery or from behind a car and start shooting. I mean, the man was crazy. He was capable of wiring a bomb, anything. He used to call my service at all hours and say he needed to talk to the doctor, and when I'd return the call, he'd say, 'Son of a bitch, your days are numbered.' Little things like that. It was scary, I'm telling you."

"I still feel sorry for him," Terri said.

"It sounds like a nightmare," Laura said. "But what exactly happened after he shot himself?"

Laura is a legal secretary. We'd met in a professional capacity. Before we knew it, it was a courtship. She's thirty-five, three years younger than I am. In addition to being in love, we like each other and enjoy one another's company. She's easy to be with.

"What happened?" Laura said.

Mel said, "He shot himself in the mouth in his room. Someone heard the shot and told the manager. They came in with a passkey, saw what had happened, and called an ambulance. I happened to be there when they brought him in, alive but past recall. The man lived for three days. His head swelled up to twice the size of a normal head. I'd never seen anything like it, and I hope I never do again. Terri wanted to go in and sit with him when she found out about it. We had a fight over it. I didn't think she should see him like that. I didn't think she should see him, and I still don't."

"Who won the fight?" Laura said.

"I was in the room with him when he died," Terri said. "He never came up out of it. But I sat with him. He didn't have anyone else."

"He was dangerous," Mel said. "If you call that love, you can have it."

"It was love," Terri said. "Sure, it's abnormal in most people's eyes. But he was willing to die for it. He did die for it."

"I sure as hell wouldn't call it love," Mel said. "I mean, no one knows what he did it for. I've seen a lot of suicides, and I couldn't say anyone ever knew what they did it for."

Mel put his hands behind his neck and tilted his chair back. "I'm not interested in that kind of love," he said. "If that's love, you can have it."

Terri said, "We were afraid. Mel even made a will out and wrote to his brother in California who used to be a Green Beret. Mel told him who to look for if something happened to him."

Terri drank from her glass. She said, "But Mel's right—we lived like fugitives. We were afraid. Mel was, weren't you, honey? I even called the police at one point, but they were no help. They said they couldn't do anything until Ed actually did something. Isn't that a laugh?" Terri said.

She poured the last of the gin into her glass and waggled the bottle. Mel got up from the table and went to the cupboard. He took down another bottle.

"Well, Nick and I know what love is," Laura said. "For us, I mean," Laura said. She bumped my knee with her knee. "You're supposed to say something now," Laura said, and turned her smile on me.

For an answer, I took Laura's hand and raised it to my lips. I made a big production out of kissing her hand. Everyone was amused.

"We're lucky," I said.

"You guys," Terri said. "Stop that now. You're making me sick. You're still on the honeymoon, for God's sake. You're still gaga, for crying out loud. Just wait. How long have you been together now? How long has it been? A year? Longer than a year?"

"Going on a year and a half," Laura said, flushed and smiling.

"Oh, now," Terri said. "Wait awhile."

She held her drink and gazed at Laura.

"I'm only kidding," Terri said.

Mel opened the gin and went around the table with the bottle.

"Here, you guys," he said. "Let's have a toast. I want to propose a toast. A toast to love. To true love," Mel said.

We touched glasses.

"To love," we said.

Outside in the backyard, one of the dogs began to bark. The leaves of the aspen that leaned past the window ticked against the glass. The afternoon sun was like a presence in this room, the spacious light of ease and generosity. We could have been anywhere, somewhere enchanted. We raised our glasses again and grinned at each other like children who had agreed on something forbidden.

"I'll tell you what real love is," Mel said. "I mean, I'll give you a good example. And then you can draw your own conclusions." He poured more gin into his glass. He added an ice cube and a sliver of lime. We waited and sipped our drinks. Laura and I touched knees again. I put a hand on her warm thigh and left it there.

"What do any of us really know about love?" Mel said. "It seems to me we're just beginners at love. We say we love each other and we do, I don't doubt it. I love Terri and Terri loves me, and you guys love each other too. You know the kind of love I'm talking about now. Physical love, that impulse that drives you to someone special, as well as love of the other person's being, his or her essence, as it were. Carnal love and, well, call it sentimental love, the day-to-day caring about the other person. But sometimes I have a hard time accounting for the fact that I must have loved my first wife too. But I did, I know I did. So I suppose I am like Terri in that regard. Terri and Ed." He thought about it and then he went on. "There was a time when I thought I loved my first wife more than life itself. But now I hate her guts. I do. How do you explain that? What happened to that love? What happened to it, is what I'd like to know. I wish someone could tell me. Then there's Ed. Okay, we're back to Ed. He loves Terri so much he tries to kill her and he winds up killing himself." Mel stopped talking and swallowed from his glass. "You guys have been together eighteen months and you love each other. It shows all over you. You glow with it. But you both loved other people before you met each other. You've both been married before, just like us. And you probably loved other people before that too, even. Terri and I have been together five years, been married for four. And the terrible thing, the terrible thing is, but the good thing too, the saving grace, you might say, is that if something happened to one of us tomorrow, I think the other one, the other person, would grieve for a while, you know, but then the surviving party would go out and love again, have someone else soon enough. All this, all of this love we're talking about, it would just be a memory. Maybe not even a memory. Am I wrong? Am I way off base? Because I want you to set me straight if you think I'm wrong. I want to know. I mean, I don't know anything, and I'm the first one to admit it."

"Mel, for God's sake," Terri said. She reached out and took hold of his wrist. "Are you getting drunk? Honey? Are you drunk?"

THE FOREVER BED

253

"Honey, I'm just talking," Mel said. "All right? I don't have to be drunk to say what I think. I mean, we're all just talking, right?" Mel said. He fixed his eyes on her.

"Sweetie, I'm not criticizing," Terri said.

She picked up her glass.

"I'm not on call today," Mel said. "Let me remind you of that. I am not on call," he said.

"Mel, we love you," Laura said.

Mel looked at Laura. He looked at her as if he could not place her, as if she was not the woman she was.

"Love you too, Laura," Mel said. "And you, Nick, love you too. You know something?" Mel said. "You guys are our pals," Mel said.

He picked up his glass.

Mel said, "I was going to tell you about something. I mean, I was going to prove a point. You see, this happened a few months ago, but it's still going on right now, and it ought to make us feel ashamed when we talk like we know what we're talking about when we talk about love."

"Come on now," Terri said. "Don't talk like you're drunk if you're not drunk."

"Just shut up for once in your life," Mel said very quietly. "Will you do me a favor and do that for a minute? So as I was saying, there's this old couple who had this car wreck out on the interstate. A kid hit them and they were all torn to shit and nobody was giving them much chance to pull through."

Terri looked at us and then back at Mel. She seemed anxious, or maybe that's too strong a word.

Mel was handing the bottle around the table.

"I was on call that night," Mel said. "It was May or maybe it was June. Terri and I had just sat down to dinner when the hospital called. There'd been this thing out on the interstate. Drunk kid, teenager, plowed his dad's pickup into this camper with this old couple in it. They were up in their mid-seventies, that couple. The kid—eighteen, nineteen, something—he was DOA. Taken the steering wheel through his sternum. The old couple, they were alive, you understand. I mean, just barely. But they had everything. Multiple fractures, internal injuries, hemorrhaging, contusions, lacerations, the works, and they each of them had themselves concussions. They were in a bad way, believe me. And, of course, their age was two strikes against them. I'd say she was worse off than he was. Ruptured spleen along with everything else. Both kneecaps broken. But they'd been wearing their seat belts and, God knows, that's what saved them for the time being."

"Folks, this is an advertisement for the National Safety Council," Terri said. "This is your spokesman, Dr. Melvin R. McGinnis, talking." Terri laughed. "Mel," she said, "sometimes you're just too much. But I love you, hon," she said.

"Honey, I love you," Mel said.

He leaned across the table. Terri met him halfway. They kissed.

"Terri's right," Mel said as he settled himself again. "Get those seat belts on. But seriously, they were in some shape, those oldsters. By the time I got down there, the kid was dead, as I said. He was off in a corner, laid out on a gurney. I took one look at the old couple and told the ER nurse to get me a neurologist and an orthopedic man and a couple of surgeons down there right away."

He drank from his glass. "I'll try to keep this short," he said. "So we took the two of them up to the OR and worked like fuck on them most of the night. They had these incredible reserves, those two. You see that once in a while. So we did everything that could be done, and toward morning we're giving them a fifty-fifty chance, maybe less than that for her. So here they are, still alive the next morning. So, okay, we move them into the ICU, which is where they both kept plugging away at it for two weeks, hitting it better and better on all the scopes. So we transfer them out to their own room."

Mel stopped talking. "Here," he said, "let's drink this cheapo gin the hell up. Then we're going to dinner, right? Terri and I know a new place. That's where we'll go, to this new place we know about. But we're not going until we finish up this cut-rate, lousy gin."

Terri said, "We haven't actually eaten there yet. But it looks good. From the outside, you know."

"I like food," Mel said. "If I had it to do all over again, I'd be a chef, you know? Right, Terri?" Mel said.

He laughed. He fingered the ice in his glass.

"Terri knows," he said. "Terri can tell you. But let me say this.

If I could come back again in a different life, a different time and all, you know what? I'd like to come back as a knight. You were pretty safe wearing all that armor. It was all right being a knight until gunpowder and muskets and pistols came along."

"Mel would like to ride a horse and carry a lance," Terri said.

"Carry a woman's scarf with you everywhere," Laura said.

"Or just a woman," Mel said.

"Shame on you," Laura said.

Terri said, "Suppose you came back as a serf. The serfs didn't have it so good in those days," Terri said.

"The serfs never had it good," Mel said. "But I guess even the knights were vessels to someone. Isn't that the way it worked? But then everyone is always a vessel to someone. Isn't that right, Terri? But what I liked about knights, besides their ladies, was that they had that suit of armor, you know, and they couldn't get hurt very easy. No cars in those days, you know? No drunk teenagers to tear into your ass."

"Vassals," Terri said.

"What?" Mel said.

"Vassals," Terri said. "They were called vassals, not vessels."

"Vassals, vessels," Mel said, "what the fuck's the difference? You knew what I meant anyway. All right," Mel said. "So I'm not educated. I learned my stuff. I'm a heart surgeon, sure, but I'm just a mechanic. I go in and I fuck around and I fix things. Shit," Mel said.

"Modesty doesn't become you," Terri said.

"He's just a humble sawbones," I said. "But sometimes they suffocated in all that armor, Mel. They'd even have heart attacks if it got too hot and they were too tired and worn out. I read somewhere that they'd fall off their horses and not be able to get up because they were too tired to stand with all that armor on them. They got trampled by their own horses sometimes."

"That's terrible," Mel said. "That's a terrible thing, Nicky. I guess they'd just lay there and wait until somebody came along and made a shish kebab out of them."

"Some other vessel," Terri said.

"That's right," Mel said. "Some vassal would come along and

spear the bastard in the name of love. Or whatever the fuck it was they fought over in those days."

"Same things we fight over these days," Terri said.

Laura said, "Nothing's changed."

The color was still high in Laura's cheeks. Her eyes were bright. She brought her glass to her lips.

Mel poured himself another drink. He looked at the label closely as if studying a long row of numbers. Then he slowly put the bottle down on the table and slowly reached for the tonic water.

"What about the old couple?" Laura said. "You didn't finish that story you started."

Laura was having a hard time lighting her cigarette. Her matches kept going out.

The sunshine inside the room was different now, changing, getting thinner. But the leaves outside the window were still shimmering, and I stared at the pattern they made on the panes and on the Formica counter. They weren't the same patterns, of course.

"What about the old couple?" I said.

"Older but wiser," Terri said.

Mel stared at her.

Terri said, "Go on with your story, hon. I was only kidding. Then what happened?"

"Terri, sometimes," Mel said.

"Please, Mel," Terri said. "Don't always be so serious, sweetie. Can't you take a joke?"

"Where's the joke?" Mel said.

He held his glass and gazed steadily at his wife.

"What happened?" Laura said.

Mel fastened his eyes on Laura. He said, "Laura, if I didn't have Terri and if I didn't love her so much, and if Nick wasn't my best friend, I'd fall in love with you. I'd carry you off, honey," he said.

"Tell your story," Terri said. "Then we'll go to that new place, okay?"

"Okay," Mel said. "Where was I?" he said. He stared at the table and then he began again.

"I dropped in to see each of them every day, sometimes twice a day if I was up doing other calls anyway. Casts and bandages, head to foot, the both of them. You know, you've seen it in the movies. That's just the way they looked, just like in the movies. Little eye-holes and nose-holes and mouth-holes. And she had to have her legs slung up on top of it. Well, the husband was very depressed for the longest while. Even after he found out that his wife was going to pull through, he was still very depressed. Not about the accident, though. I mean, the accident was one thing, but it wasn't everything. I'd get up to his mouth-hole, you know, and he'd say no, it wasn't the accident exactly but it was because he couldn't see her through his eye-holes. He said that was what was making him feel so bad. Can you imagine? I'm telling you, the man's heart was breaking because he couldn't turn his goddamn head and *see* his goddamn wife."

Mel looked around the table and shook his head at what he was going to say.

"I mean, it was killing the old fart just because he couldn't *look* at the fucking woman."

We all looked at Mel.

"Do you see what I'm saying?" he said.

Maybe we were a little drunk by then. I know it was hard keeping things in focus. The light was draining out of the room, going back through the window where it had come from. Yet nobody made a move to get up from the table to turn on the overhead light.

"Listen," Mel said. "Let's finish this fucking gin. There's about enough left here for one shooter all around. Then let's go eat. Let's go to the new place."

"He's depressed," Terri said. "Mel, why don't you take a pill?"

Mel shook his head. "I've taken everything there is."

"We all need a pill now and then," I said.

"Some people are born needing them," Terri said.

She was using her finger to rub at something on the table. Then she stopped rubbing.

"I think I want to call my kids," Mel said. "Is that all right with everybody? I'll call my kids," he said.

Terri said, "What if Marjorie answers the phone? You guys, you've heard us on the subject of Marjorie? Honey, you know you don't want to talk to Marjorie. It'll make you feel even worse."

"I don't want to talk to Marjorie," Mel said. "But I want to talk to my kids."

"There isn't a day goes by that Mel doesn't say he wishes she'd get married again. Or else die," Terri said. "For one thing," Terri said, "she's bankrupting us. Mel says it's just to spite him that she won't get married again. She has a boyfriend who lives with her and the kids, so Mel is supporting the boyfriend too."

"She's allergic to bees," Mel said. "If I'm not praying she'll get married again, I'm praying she'll get herself stung to death by a swarm of fucking bees."

"Shame on you," Laura said.

"Bzzzzzzz," Mel said, turning his fingers into bees and buzzing them at Terri's throat. Then he let his hands drop all the way to his sides.

"She's vicious," Mel said. "Sometimes I think I'll go up there dressed like a beekeeper. You know, that hat that's like a helmet with the plate that comes down over your face, the big gloves, and the padded coat? I'll knock on the door and let loose a hive of bees in the house. But first I'd make sure the kids were out, of course."

He crossed one leg over the other. It seemed to take him a lot of time to do it. Then he put both feet on the floor and leaned forward, elbows on the table, his chin cupped in his hands.

"Maybe I won't call the kids, after all. Maybe it isn't such a hot idea. Maybe we'll just go eat. How does that sound?"

"Sounds fine to me," I said. "Eat or not eat. Or keep drinking. I could head right on out into the sunset."

"What does that mean, honey?" Laura said.

"It just means what I said," I said. "It means I could just keep going. That's all it means."

"I could eat something myself," Laura said. "I don't think I've ever been so hungry in my life. Is there something to nibble on?"

"I'll put out some cheese and crackers," Terri said.

But Terri just sat there. She did not get up to get anything.

Mel turned his glass over. He spilled it out on the table.

"Gin's gone," Mel said.

Terri said, "Now what?"

I could hear my heart beating. I could hear everyone's heart. I could hear the human noise we sat there making, not one of us moving, not even when the room went dark.

THE FOREVER BED

NOW THAT I AM NEVER ALONE

Tess Gallagher

In the bath I look up and see the brown moth
pressed like a pair of unpredictable lips
against the white wall. I heat up
the water, running as much hot in as I can stand.
These handfuls of water over my shoulder—how once
he pulled my head against his thigh and dipped
a rivulet down my neck of coldest water from the spring
we were drinking from. Beautiful mischief
that stills a moment so I can never look
back. Only now, brightest now, and the water
never hot enough to drive that shiver out.

But I do remember solitude—no other
presence and each thing what it was. Not this raw
fluttering I make of you as you have made of me
your watch-fire, your killing light.

LEGACY

Laurie Duesing

The new man sends 3 cans of tuna,
a brown bag of filberts and a letter.
When I am ready, he writes, we will hunt
chanterelles in Oregon. Fish in Alaska.

The label on the tuna says Bumble Bee
and large yellow insects nestle their bodies
in bright flowers. I am 40 years old.
The man I love died 9 weeks ago.

In every room of my house I can see
at least one photograph of him. In the one
I look at now he sits sidesaddle
on his motorcycle, smiling at me.

He was always in motion. But since he died,
I can't stop moving. I am looking
for his body, backlit by the sun. I walk
out to the yard filled with plants

he gave me. Gladiolas spray peach and magenta
into the air. See what you've done,
I say. Nothing can keep me from it.
Everything you gave me is in bloom.

A MIRACLE

After you'd been killed, you often walked up
behind me and rested your hands on my shoulders.
That was no miracle. Neither was the fact I'd catch
you in peripheral glance pacing the living room,
your right arm crooked over your head,
fingers raking your thick dark hair.
Nor the mornings I found the garage door open
your tools rearranged on the cement floor.
I knew you'd never leave me, something the physician
who would not let me hold your dead hand
failed to understand. He was trying to separate
the living woman from the dead man and did not know
the living and the dead never let go.
Simply because they don't have to.
So when I lift your green T-shirt from the drawer
to feel your body's smells or when you speak
to me in my dreams, never think I am ungrateful.
But even with the sweetness of nothing, flesh longs
for its kind. The next time your spirit walks
the house, if you'd stop, hold still
and let me come to you, hold your hand in mine,
that, my love, would be a miracle.

A WONDERFUL WOMAN

ALICE ADAMS

Feeling sixteen, although in fact just a few months short of sixty, Felicia Lord checks into the San Francisco hotel at which her lover is to meet her the following day. Felicia is tall and thin, with the intense, somewhat startled look of a survivor—a recent widow, mother of five, a ceramicist who prefers to call herself a potter. A stylish gray-blonde. Mr. Voort, she is told, will be given the room next to hers when he arrives. Smiling to herself, she then follows the ancient wizened bellboy into an antique elevator cage; once inside, as they creakingly ascend, he turns and smiles up at her, as though he knows what she is about. She herself is less sure.

The room to which he leads her is a suite, really: big, shabby-cozy living room, discreetly adjoining bedroom, large old-fashioned bath, on the top floor of this old San Francisco hotel, itself a survivor of the earthquake and fire, in an outlying neighborhood. All in all, she instantly decides, it is the perfect place for meeting Martin, for being with him, in the bright blue dazzling weather, this sudden May.

San Francisco itself, connected as it is with Felicia's own history, has seemed a possibly dangerous choice: the scene of her early, un-likely premarital "romance" with Charles, her now dead husband; then the scene of holiday visits from Connecticut with the children, treat zoo visits and cable-car rides, Chinese restaurants; scene of a passionate ill-advised love affair, and a subsequent abortion—all that also took place in San Francisco, but years ago, in other hotels, other neighborhoods.

Why then, having tipped the grinning bellboy and begun to un-pack, silk shirts on hangers, silk tissue-papered nightgowns and un-derthings in drawers, does she feel such a dizzying lurch of apprehension? It is too intense in its impact to be just a traveler's nerves, jet lag. Felicia is suddenly quite weak; she sits down in an easy chair next to the window to absorb the view, to think sensibly about her situation, or try to. She sees a crazy variety of rooftops: mansard, Victorian curls, old weathered shingles and bright new slate. Blue water, paler sky, green hills. No help.

It is being in love with Martin, she thinks, being "in love," and the newness of Martin Voort. I've never known a farming sailor before, and she smiles, because the words don't describe Martin, really, although he owns some cranberry bogs, near Cape Cod, and he builds boats. Charles was a painter, but he was rich (Martin is not rich) and most of his friends were business people. Martin is entirely new to her.

And at my age, thinks Felicia, and she smiles again, a smile which feels tremulous on her mouth.

"Wonderful" is the word that people generally have used about Felicia. She was wonderful with Charles, whose painting never came to much, although he owned a couple of galleries, who drank a lot. Wonderful to all those kids, who were a little wild, always breaking arms or heads.

Her lover—a Mexican Communist, and like Charles a painter, but a much better painter than Charles—Felipe thought she looked wonderful, with her high-boned face, strong hands and her long, strong voluptuous body. She was wonderful about the abortion, and wonderful too when he went back to his wife.

Felicia was wonderful when Charles died, perfectly controlled and kind to everyone.

Wonderful is not how Felicia sees herself at all; she feels that she has always acted out of simple—or sometimes less simple—necessity.

Once married to Charles, and having seen the lonely, hollow space behind his thin but brilliant surface of good looks, graceful manners, skill at games—it was then impossible to leave him; and he couldn't have stood it. And when the children had terrible coughs, or possible concussions, she took good care of them, sometimes staying up all night, simply because she wanted them well, and soon.

During the unanesthetized abortion, she figured out that you don't scream, because that would surely make the pain much worse, when it is already so bad that it must be happening to someone else, and also because the doctor, a Brazilian chiropractor in the Mission District, is hissing, "Don't make noise." And when your lover defects, saying that he is going back, after all, to his wife in Guadalajara, you don't scream about that either; what good would it do? You go back to your husband, and to the clay pots that you truly love, round and fat or delicately slender.

When your husband dies, as gracefully as he lived, after a too strenuous game of tennis, you take care of everything and everyone, and you behave well, for your own sake as well as for everyone else's.

Then you go to visit an old friend, in Duxbury, and you meet a large wild red-haired, blue-eyed man, a "sailor-farmer," and you fall madly in love, and you agree to meet him for a holiday, in May, in San Francisco, because he has some boats to see there.

She is scared. Sitting there, in the wide sunny window, Felicia trembles, thinking of Martin, the lovely city, themselves, for a long first time. But supposing she isn't "wonderful" anymore? Suppose it all fails, flesh fails, hearts fail, and everything comes crashing down upon their heads, like an avalanche, or an earthquake?

She thinks, I will have to go out for a walk.

Returned from a short tour of the neighborhood, which affords quick beautiful views of the shining bay, and an amazing variety of architecture, Felicia feels herself restored; she is almost her own person again, except for a curious weakness in her legs, and the faintest throb of blood behind one temple, both of which she ascribes to fatigue. She stands there for a moment on the sidewalk, in the sunlight, and then she re-enters the hotel. She is about to walk past the desk when the bellboy, still stationed there, waves something in her direction. A yellow envelope—a telegram.

She thanks him and takes it with her into the elevator, waiting to open it until she is back in her room. It will be from Martin, to welcome her there. Already she knows the character of his gestures: he hates the phone; in fact, so far they have never talked on the telephone, but she has received at least a dozen telegrams from Martin, whose instructions must always include: "Deliver, do not phone." After the party at which they met he wired, from Boston to Duxbury: HAVE DINNER WITH ME WILL PICK YOU UP AT SEVEN MARTIN VOORT. Later ones were either jokes or messages of love—or both: from the start they had laughed a lot.

This telegram says: DARLING CRAZY DELAY FEW DAYS LATE ALL LOVE.

The weakness that earlier Felicia had felt in her legs makes them now suddenly buckle; she falls across the bed, and all the blood in both temples pounds as she thinks: I can't stand it, I really can't. This is the one thing that is too much for me.

But what do you do if you can't stand something, and you don't scream, after all?

Maybe you just go to bed, as though you were sick?

She undresses, puts on a pretty nightgown and gets into bed, where, like a person with a dangerously high fever, she begins to shake. Her arms crossed over her breast, she clutches both elbows; she presses her ankles together. The tremors gradually subside, and finally, mercifully, she falls asleep, and into dreams. But her sleep is fitful, thin, and from time to time she half wakes from it, never at first sure where she is, nor what year of her life this is.

A long time ago, in the early forties, during Lieutenant (USN) Charles Lord's first leave, he and Felicia Thacher, whom he had invited out to see him, literally danced all night, at all the best hotels in town—as Felicia wondered: Why me? How come Charles picked me for this leave? She had known him since childhood; he was one of her brother's best friends. Had someone else turned him down? She had somewhat the same reactions when he asked her to marry him, over a breakfast glass of champagne, in the Garden Court of the Palace Hotel. Why me? she wondered, and she wondered too at why she was saying yes. She said yes, dreamily, to his urgent eyes, his debonair smile, light voice, in that room full of wartime glamour, uniforms and flowers, partings and poignant brief reunions. Yes, Charles, yes, let's do get married, all right, soon.

A dream of a courtship, and then a dream groom, handsome Charles. And tall, strong-boned, strong-willed Felicia Thacher Lord.

Ironically, since she had so many, Felicia was not especially fond of babies; a highly verbal person, she was nervous with human creatures who couldn't talk, who screamed out their ambiguous demands, who seemed to have no sense and who often smelled terrible. She did not see herself as at all a good mother, knowing how cross and frightened she felt with little children. Good luck (Charles's money) had provided her with helpful nurses all along to relieve her of the children, and the children of her, as she saw it. Further luck made them all turn out all right, on the whole. But thank God she was done with all that. Now she liked all the children very much; she regarded them with great fondness, and some distance.

Her husband, Charles, loved Felicia's pregnancies (well, obviously he did), and all those births, his progeny. He spoke admiringly of how Felicia accomplished all that, her quick deliveries, perfect babies. She began to suspect that Charles had known, in the way that one's unconscious mind knows everything, that this would be the case; he had married her to be the mother of his children.

"I have the perfect situation for a painter, absolutely perfect," Charles once somewhat drunkenly declared. "Big house, perfect studio, money for travel, money to keep the kids away at school. A wonderful kind strong wife. Christ, I even own two galleries. *Perfect.* I begin to see that the only thing lacking is talent," and he gave a terrible laugh.

How could you leave a man in such despair?

Waking slowly, her head still swollen with sleep, from the tone of the light Felicia guesses that it must be about midafternoon. Eventually she will have to order something to eat, tea or boiled eggs, something sustaining.

Then, with a flash of pain, Martin comes into her mind, and she begins to think.

She simply doesn't know him, that's half the problem, "know" in this instance meaning able to predict the behavior of, really, to trust. Maybe he went to another party and met another available lady, maybe someone rather young, young-fleshed and never sick or tired? (She knows that this could be true, but still it doesn't sound quite right, as little as she knows him.)

But what does FEW DAYS mean to Martin? To some people a week would be a few days. CRAZY DELAY is deliberately ambiguous. Either of those phrases could mean anything at all.

Sinkingly, despairingly, she tells herself that it is sick to have fantasies about the rest of your life that revolve around a man you have only known for a couple of months.

Perfectly possibly he won't come to San Francisco at all, she thinks, and then: I hate this city.

When the bellboy comes in with her supper tray, Felicia realizes for the first time that he is a dwarf; odd that she didn't see that before. His grin now looks malign, contemptuous, even, as though he recognizes her for what she now is: an abandoned woman, of more than a certain age.

As he leaves she shivers, wishing she had brought along a "sensible" robe, practical clothes, instead of all this mocking silk and lace. Looking quickly into the mirror, and then away, she thinks, I look like an old circus monkey.

She sleeps through the night. One day gone, out of whatever "few days" are.

When she calls to order breakfast the next morning, the manager (manageress: a woman with a strong, harsh Midwestern accent) suggests firmly that a doctor should be called. She knows of one.

Refusing that suggestion, as firmly, politely as she can, Felicia knows that she reacted to hostility rather than to concern. The manageress is afraid that Felicia will get really sick and die; what a mess to have on their hands, an unknown dead old woman.

But Felicia too is a little afraid.

Come to think of it, Felicia says to herself, half-waking at what must be the middle of the afternoon, I once spent some time in another San Francisco hotel, waiting for Felipe, in another part of town. After the abortion.

She and Felipe met when he had a show at one of Charles's galleries; they had, at first tipsily, fallen into bed, in Felipe's motel (Charles had "gone to sleep") after the reception; then soberly, both passionately serious, they fell in love. Felipe's paintings were touring the country, Felipe with them, and from time to time, in various cities, Felicia followed him. Her excuse to Charles was a survey of possible markets for her pots, and visits to other potters, which, conscientiously, she also accomplished.

Felipe was as macho as he was radical, and he loved her in his own macho way, violently, with all his dangerous strength. She must leave Charles, Charles must never touch her again, he said. (Well, Charles drank so much that that was hardly an issue.) She must come with him to Paris, to a new life. All her children were by then either grown or off in schools—why not?

When they learned that she was pregnant he desperately wanted their child, he said, but agreed that a child was not possible for them. And he remembered the Brazilian chiropractor that he had heard about, from relatives in San Francisco.

The doctor seemingly did a good job, for Felicia suffered no later ill effects. Felipe was kind and tender with her; he said that her courage had moved him terribly. Felicia felt that her courage, if you wanted to call it that, had somewhat unnerved him; he was a little afraid of her now.

However, they celebrated being together in San Francisco, where Felipe had not been before. He loved the beautiful city, and they toasted each other, and their mutual passion, with Mexican beer or red wine, in their Lombard Street motel. Then one afternoon Felipe went off alone to visit a family of his relatives, in San Jose, and Felicia waited for him. He returned to her very late, and in tears: a grown man, broad-backed, terrifically strong, with springing thick black hair and powerful arms, crying out to her, "I cannot—I cannot go on with you, with our life. They have told me of my wife, all day she cries, and at night she screams and wakes the children. I must go to her."

Well, of course you must, said Felicia, in effect. If she's screaming that's where you belong. And she thought, Well, so much for my Latin love affair.

And she went home.

And now she thinks, Martin at least will not come to me in tears.

Martin Voort. At the end of her week in Duxbury, her visit to the old school friend, Martin, whom in one way or another she had seen every day, asked her to marry him, as soon as possible. "Oh, I know we're both over the hill," he said, and then exploded in a laugh, as she did too. "But suppose we're freaks who live to be a hundred? We might as well have a little fun on the way. I like you a lot. I want to be with you."

Felicia laughed again. She was secretly pleased that he hadn't said she was wonderful, but she thought he was a little crazy.

He followed her home with telegrams: WHEN OH WHEN WILL YOU MARRY ME and ARRIVING IN YOUR TOWN THIS FRIDAY PREPARE.

And now, suppose she never sees him again? For the first time in many months (actually, since Charles died) Felicia begins to cry, at the possible loss of such a rare, eccentric and infinitely valuable man.

But in the midst of her sorrow at that terrible possibility, the permanent lack of Martin—who could be very sick, could have had

THE FOREVER BED

a stroke: at his age, their age, that is entirely possible—though grieving, Felicia realizes that she can stand it, after all, as she has stood other losses, other sorrows in her life. She can live without Martin.

She realizes too that she herself has just been genuinely ill, somewhat frighteningly so; what she had was a real fever, from whatever cause. Perhaps she should have seen a doctor.

However, the very thought of a doctor, a doctor's office, is enough to make her well, she dislikes them so; all those years of children, children's illnesses and accidents, made her terribly tired of medical treatment. Instead she will get dressed and go out for dinner, by herself.

And that is what she does. In her best clothes she takes a cab to what has always been her favorite San Francisco restaurant, Sam's. It is quite early, the place uncrowded. Felicia is given a pleasant side table, and the venerable waiters are kind to her. The seafood is marvelous. Felicia drinks a half-bottle of wine with her dinner and she thinks: Oh, so this is what it will be like. Well, it's really not so bad.

Returned to the hotel, however, once inside her room she experiences an acute pang of disappointment, and she understands that she had half-consciously expected Martin to be there; Martin was to be her reward for realizing that she could live without him, for being "sensible," for bravely going out to dinner by herself.

She goes quickly to bed, feeling weak and childish, and approving neither her weakness nor her childishness, not at all.

Sometime in the middle of the night she awakes from a sound sleep, and from a vivid dream; someone, a man, has knocked on the door of her room, this room. She answers, and he comes in and they embrace, and she is wildly glad to see him. But who is he? She can't tell: Is it her husband, Charles, or one of her sons? Felipe? Is it Martin? It could even be a man she doesn't know. But, fully awake, as she considers the dream she is saddened by it, and it is quite a while before she sleeps again.

The next morning, though, she is all right: refreshed, herself again. Even in the mirror, her face is all right. I look like what I am, she thinks: a strong healthy older woman. She dresses and goes downstairs to breakfast, beginning to plan her day. Both the bellboy and the manager smile in a relieved way as she passes the desk, and she smiles back, amiably.

She will see as much of San Francisco as possible today, and arrange to leave tomorrow. Why wait around? This morning she will take a cab to Union Square, and walk from there along Grant Avenue, Chinatown, to North Beach, where she will have lunch. Then back to the hotel for a nap, then a walk, and dinner out—maybe Sam's again.

She follows that plan, or most of it. On Union Square, she goes into a couple of stores, where she looks at some crazily overpriced clothes, and buys one beautiful gauzy Indian scarf, for a daughter's coming birthday. Then down to Grant Avenue, to walk among the smells of Chinese food, the incense, on to North Beach, to a small Italian counter restaurant, where she has linguine with clam sauce, and a glass of red wine.

In the cab, going back to the hotel, she knows that she is too tired, has "overdone," but it was worth it. She has enjoyed the city, after all.

An hour or so later, from a deep, deep sleep she is awakened by a knocking on her door, just as in her dream, the night before.

Groggily she calls out, "Who is it?" She is not even sure that the sound has been real; so easily this could be another dream.

A man's impatient, irritated voice answers, "It's *me*, of course."

Me? She is still half asleep; she doesn't know who he is. However, his tone has made her obedient, and she gets out of bed, pulling her robe about her, and goes to the door. And there is a tall, red-haired man, with bright blue eyes, whom of course she knows, was expecting—who embraces her violently. "Ah, Martin," she breathes, when she can.

It is Martin, and she is awake.

The only unfamiliar thing about his face, she notes, when she can see him, is that a tooth is missing from his smile; there is a small gap that he covers with his hand as soon as she has noticed. And he says, "It broke right off! Right off a bridge. And my dentist said I'd have to wait a week. How could I send you a telegram about a goddamn dentist? Anyway, I couldn't wait a week to see you."

They laugh (although there are tears somewhere near Felicia's eyes), and then they embrace again.

And at last they are sitting down on the easy chairs near the window, next to the view, and they are quietly talking together, making plans for the rest of that day and night.

SELVES

Madeline Tiger

Then when you came back, nervous,
stepping out of night,
I saw only the millefleurs walls,
the rose carpet darkening,
the white sheets sprayed with flowers,
the pillows softly propped.
I had drawn the shades,
hung my strewn clothes, closed
both closet doors, dimmed the lights
of the whole house, so when you came up
after all those weeks we saw
only ourselves, directly, so
when we opened the bed and turned
to each other we saw nothing but
our pale forms, our ideal
selves. And we took these wild
we took these dark,
these shadows—
gentle old buck, old doe, simple
and more human than the forest
of hidden mirrors allows.
We, entering, then, accepting
blindness, met each other
at the center of earth, and heaven
grew around us like the unknown
morning. In the morning
there were no reflections.
We moved away
from where we had touched
unspoken things

and I sealed the place
where my blood moves
into the shape of praise.
There is no marriage
in such a story,
and no end to this,
except a warning
about the beast in the courtyard,
about naming, holding
what is afraid, about no one
taming the other.

IN DREAM

David Ignatow

I died and called for you,
and you came from a distance,
hurrying but impassive. You
looked long and steadily
at my face, then left and strode
back into the distance, rapidly
growing smaller to the eye. You
vanished, but where I lay
I could hear your voice
low and quick, urging me
to awaken to the sunrise
at the window of the bedroom
where we slept together. I
rose up and followed you
into the distance, and there
heard the laughter and wit
with which we had spent
our days together. Then silence,
and I knew we both were dead,
for you had spoken to me
in death, as only the dead
could do, and so at last
we were together.

ON WAKING

Laura Chester

I reared up and saw my matching half, and laughed the laugh gods love, when human pain has passed, and the barn doors slide to a warmer state of mind, the kind you get when your Man comes home, when you find you're not alone anymore on this hard earth in white December—pipes that froze are running now with water—stationed in the desert, but now he's made it back, following the whinny of the one sweet call which is his name I say out loud. I rise to meet his face, his fur, receive his sure advances, and when he enters through my sleeping hair— We both entwine and laugh the laugh gods love to hear. When we awake, my long long arms will wind around him, warm *and* warm. A lovely morning on our dish will come. Just like the big doors kiss on barns.

THE IVY CROWN

William Carlos Williams

The whole process is a lie,
         unless,
                crowned by excess,
it break forcefully,
         one way or another,
                from its confinement—
or find a deeper well.
         Anthony and Cleopatra
            were right;
they have shown
         the way. I love you
            or I do not live
at all.
Daffodil time
         is past. This is
            summer, summer!
the heart says,
         and not even the full of it.
            no doubts
are permitted—
         though they will come
         and may
before our time
         overwhelm us.
            We are only mortal
but being mortal
         can defy our fate.
            We may
by an outside chance
         even win! We do not

                    look to see
jonquils and violets
                come again
                        but there are,
still,
                the roses!
Romance has no part in it.
                The business of love is
                        cruelty which,
by our wills,
                we transform
                        to live together.
It has its seasons.
                for and against,
                        whatever the heart
fumbles in the dark
                to assert
                        toward the end of May.
Just as the nature of briars
                is to tear flesh,
                        I have proceeded
through them.
                Keep
                        the briars out,
they say.
                You cannot live
                        and keep free of
briars.
Children pick flowers.
                Let them.
                        Though having them
in hand they have
                no further use for them
                        but leave them crumpled
at the curb's edge.
At our age the imagination
                across the sorry facts
                        lifts us

to make roses
            stand before thorns.
                        Sure
love is cruel
            and selfish
                        and totally obtuse—
at least, blinded by the light,
            young love is.
                        But we are older,
I to love
            and you to be loved,
                        we have,
no matter how,
            by our wills survived
                        to keep
the jeweled prize
            always
                        at our fingertips.
We will it so
            and so it is
                        past all accident.

Copyright Acknowledgments

annini. Originally published by Longhouse Press. Reprinted by permission of the author.

"Lying Under a Quilt" is taken from *A Son from Sleep* by Rachel Hadas. Copyright © 1987 by Rachel Hadas. Reprinted by permission of University of New England Press.

"The Song of Love" is taken from *Nostalgia of the Infinite* by Janet Hamill. Copyright © 1991 by Janet Hamill. Originally published by Ocean View Books. Reprinted by permission of the author.

"Love Too Long" is taken from *Airships* by Barry Hannah. Copyright © 1978 by Barry Hannah. Reprinted by permission of Alfred A. Knopf Inc.

"The Reception" by Deborah Harding. Copyright © 1992 by Deborah Harding. Used by permission of the author.

"Our First Summer" by Marie Harris. Copyright © 1992 by Marie Harris. Used by permission of the author.

Excerpts from *The Blood Oranges* by John Hawkes. Copyright © 1970, 1971 by John Hawkes. Reprinted by permission of New Directions Publishing Corporation.

"There's an Old . . ." is taken from *Almost Everything* by Bobbie Louise Hawkins. Copyright © 1982 by Bobbie Louise Hawkins. Originally published by Long River Books. Reprinted by permission of the author.

"Beaver Tales" by Elizabeth Hay. Copyright © 1992 by Elizabeth Hay. Used by permission of the author.

"The One" by Anselm Hollo first appeared in *The Coherences* published by Trigram Press. Copyright © 1968 by Anselm Hollo. Reprinted by permission of the author.

"In Dream" is taken from *New and Collected Stories 1970–1985* by David Ignatow. Copyright © 1986 by David Ignatow. Reprinted by permission of University Press of New England.

"The Marriage Made in Heaven," "Abraham Tells Ann He Loves Her," and "The Glass Is Broken" are taken from *The Unexamined Wife* by Sherril Jaffe. Copyright © 1983 by Sherril Jaffe. Originally published by Black Sparrow Press. Reprinted by permission of the author.

Selections from "In Bed" is taken from *Days and Nights* by Kenneth Koch. Copyright © 1982 by Kenneth Koch. Originally published by Random House, Inc. Reprinted by permission of the author.

Excerpt from "The Ache of Marriage" is taken from *Poems 1960–1967* by Denise Levertov. Copyright © 1964 by Denise Levertov Goodman. Used by permission of New Directions Publishing Corporation.

"North" is taken from *Leaving South* by Lyn Lifshin. Copyright © 1977 by Lyn Lifshin. Originally published by Red Dust. Reprinted by permission of the author.

"First Kiss" by Joan Logghe. Copyright © 1992 by Joan Logghe. Used by permission of the author.

Excerpt from *Chin Music* by James McManus. Copyright © 1985 by James McManus. Originally published by Grove Press. Reprinted by permission of the author.

"Sonnet" is taken from *Sonnet* by Bernadette Mayer. Copyright © 1990 by